EVERGREENS

LIAM BROWN

Legend Press Ltd, 51 Gower Street, London, WC1E 6HJ
info@legendpress.co.uk | www.legendpress.co.uk

Print ISBN 9781915643834
Ebook ISBN 9781915643841
Set in Times.

Cover design by Ditte Løkkegaard

Printed and bound in Great Britain by
TJ Books Limited, Padstow, Cornwall

Liam Brown is the author of four previous novels: *Real Monsters* (2015), *Wild Life* (2016), *Broadcast* (2017), and *Skin* (2019), which was shortlisted for the Guardian's Not the Booker Prize. His work has been optioned by a major Hollywood film studio and sold into multiple languages. *Evergreens* is his fifth novel. He lives in Birmingham, England.

Find Liam on Instagram and Twitter:
@LiamBrownWriter

This book is dedicated to May & Jim and Margaret & Frank. Thanks for all the stories.

2070

I

It's not always easy to spot the humans these days.

Take the nurses.

Sophie has been sitting in the intensive care unit for five hours and she's still struggling to distinguish between the real ones and the fakes. Several times she's been mid-conversation with a young man or woman in pale blue scrubs, only to discover her mistake, an unfamiliar combination of words triggering a glitch in their system, their expression freezing as they lock into a disconcerting mantra:

Please let me know how I can be of further assistance!

Please let me know how I can be of further assistance!

She feels like an old fool. But it's an easy mistake to make. The technology is so advanced that, other than a slight deadness in their eyes and a tendency to occasionally drift through the walls, it's almost impossible to tell these holographic Virtual Assistants from their flesh-and-blood counterparts. Not that there's many of those left. Almost everything from taking bloods to performing physical examinations has been automated for years now. Even the beds make themselves. The receptionists, pharmacists and bereavement counsellors have all gone, too. Outsourced to an army of beaming algorithms. Sophie gets it, of course. Holograms never get sick or tired or depressed. Never complain about unsociable hours or unsafe working conditions. There's no pension plan or holiday entitlement to worry about. They make perfect business sense.

Even so, she doesn't like them.

Maybe she's just old-fashioned, but she finds their presence unsettling. Offensive, even. Especially on a ward filled with people who are barely hanging on to life. There are more than enough ghosts around here without adding any more.

Besides, it's not like they're any good at answering her questions. Although perhaps that's not entirely their fault. And it's not as if the handful of human medics she's encountered have been any more helpful.

Why is this happening? Is he dying?

Human or hologram, all she ever gets is a glazed expression and a static smile.

Nobody knows what's wrong with Ben.

All they know is he won't wake up.

She turns her attention back to the handsome young man lying in the bed.

There's not a mark on his face. He looks so peaceful he could almost be sleeping – apart from the machines, of course. And the machines are difficult to ignore. They rasp and whir. Hiss and purr. And then there's the persistent chirrup of the heart monitor. A baby bird begging for a worm:

Feed me. Feed me. Feed me or I'll die.

Once again, she finds herself resisting the urge to tear him from the tangle of tubes that snake from under his bedsheets. To free him from the high-tech devices that are doing things so complex she can scarcely believe they are real. Hydrating, draining, pumping, sucking. Everything, in other words, that needs to happen in order for him to stay alive.

If you can call this a life.

Hanging from the gaping neck of the man's hospital robe is a small chain. A silver pine-cone pendant glistening in the antiseptic light. She reaches across and tucks it back under his gown, then finds his hand. It's reassuringly warm. She squeezes it. Stares at it. Aside from the plastic cannula taped to the back of it, it looks the same as it always has. Neatly trimmed nails. *The back of it smooth and hairless. Only the faintest of lines intersecting his palm.*

A boy's hand.

She slides her fingers between his. Interlacing. Interlocking. As if playing a game.

Here's the church and here's the steeple…

Compared to his hands, her own are a horror show. Smeared with age spots and snagged with bulbous blue veins. The skin sagging and bunched, seeming to slip away from her bones altogether in places, as if she's trying to escape herself. As if she's disappearing.

She squeezes again. This hand she's held so many times across the decades. And as she squeezes, she is gripped by a sudden anger. That it is him in the bed and her at his side, and not the other way around.

This is not how it was supposed to be.

She keeps squeezing. Her nails biting into his tender flesh until the capillaries burst and a thin seam of red trickles down his wrist.

Wake up, Ben. Wake up.

But still he doesn't respond.

She hears someone behind her. A woman in a white coat, a silver stethoscope wrung around her neck, a paper-thin tablet computer in her hand.

She's young. Pretty, too. Sophie has reached the age where she finds all young people pretty, their youth a prettiness in itself, but this doctor is disarmingly beautiful, her features free from the telltale signs of stem cell fillers or nanobot implants or anything else. She's all natural, this one.

Or is she?

Sophie stares into the doctor's dazzling green eyes, scanning for errant pixels.

'Are you real?' *she asks.*

The doctor looks amused. 'Sadly, very much so. I've got the blisters on my feet to prove it.'

Sophie nods. 'Well, that's something. Is there any news?'

The doctor glances down at her notes. Frowns. 'We're still waiting on some test results, Mrs Walker. But I promise, we're doing everything we can for your grandson.'

Sophie looks at her blankly, confused for a moment. And then she remembers. 'Oh. No. You've got it wrong. He's not my grandson. He's my husband.'

If the doctor is shocked by the difference in their physical appearance, she doesn't show it. There's a flicker of something. A slight fluttering of her lashes. But then her eyes are back on the screen. 'Well, as I say, we're waiting on some results from the lab. Once we get those back, we should hopefully have a clearer picture of what's going on. In the meantime, you should go home and get some rest. I assure you, Ben's in the best possible hands.'

And then she is heading off on her rounds, while Sophie once again takes up her lonely bedside vigil.

Wake up, Ben. Wake up.

After a while, she falls asleep in the chair. Recently, this has been happening more and more often. At home. At her family's house. At the theatre. She doesn't even feel it happening. One minute she's fully conscious, the next she's waking up with a stiff neck and drool on her chin. Just another indignity of old age to add to the list, she supposes.

When she opens her eyes again, she finds an entire hour has passed. She sits up sheepishly and wipes her face, for once glad of the dearth of human staff on the ward.

She glances at Ben and sees that he hasn't moved. She shakes her head. Maybe the doctor was right about her going home. She could freshen up. Grab a change of clothes. Feed the dog. She hauls herself to her feet and leans over him.

'I'll be back soon,' she promises.

As she stoops to place a kiss on his cheek, however, she stops. Something has caught her eye.

Buried in his thick mane of dark hair, there is something new. Something she's never seen before. At least, not on Ben.

A solitary silver hair stands out amongst all the others.

How curious, she thinks, as she peers closer to examine it. And then something even stranger happens.

As she watches, another hair begins to change colour. Starting at the tip and then moving to the root, it turns from brown to grey to white.

And then another. And another.

Sophie takes off her glasses and polishes them against her blouse, cursing her failing vision. But when she looks again, the effect is even more pronounced. Dozens of hairs have changed. Then hundreds.

As impossible as it seems, Ben's hair is turning white before her eyes.

2005

1

Inside the pub, the noise is punishing. Pummelling. A ceaseless squall of guitar and drums that fills every square centimetre of the venue. The Espy is an enormous white Victorian building, which in its heyday must have been one of the grandest hotels in town. Today, it's a sticky-floored dive bar with live music spread across three floors, making it impossible to escape the ear-splitting clatter of local bands. Usually, it's a fun night out.

But not tonight. At least, not for Sophie.

She is perched at the bar with her back to the band, the dregs of some exotic cocktail sitting in front of her. Beside her, her friends Samantha and Mags stare sullenly at their own drinks. Nobody is talking.

The three school friends have spent the last seven months travelling, a non-stop gap-year adventure to celebrate finishing sixth form. They've ridden rickshaws in Rajasthan and tuk-tuks in Thailand. They've visited the beaches of Boracay, the Killing Fields of Cambodia and the gleaming space-age towers of Kuala Lumpur. It has been, without a doubt, the best year of Sophie's life. Yet it is Australia she has enjoyed the most, particularly St Kilda, the beachside suburb of Melbourne they've called home for the last four weeks.

Or rather, she's enjoyed it up until now.

The trouble had begun earlier on the beach. Mags had bumped into a group of English boys and arranged for the three of them to meet up with them later that night. Sophie had been unenthusiastic, especially when Mags had pointed them out to her. Even from a distance, she could tell they were a dead loss. Two of them were Mags's usual type: hulking, muscle-bound poseurs, one with a shaved head, the other a bleached mohawk. The third, meanwhile, was even less promising; a tall, pale strip of a thing, his red board shorts hanging off his skinny body. Not her type at all.

Sophie had tried to wriggle out of it, feigning tiredness, but in the end, she'd allowed herself to be dragged along to the pub in order to keep the numbers even.

Only so far, the boys haven't shown.

As the hours have ticked by, the girls have grown impatient and snappy with each other, a situation that has not been helped by the copious amounts of alcohol they've all downed while waiting. Mags, in particular, appears to have decided to get as drunk as possible, ordering tequila shots to accompany each of the tooth-shredding cocktails.

Sophie is about to announce to the girls that she is calling it a night, when a boisterous yell from the other side of the room announces the boys' arrival. They amble up to them, full of apologies, excuses and, from the smell of them, beer.

After a swift round of introductions, it quickly becomes apparent that conversation isn't the boys' strong suit. Not that it's really possible to talk over the jagged screech and clatter blasting from the nearest stage. Paul, who Sophie quickly pegs as their ringleader, seems exclusively focused on getting everyone even drunker than they already are, ordering round after round of Jägerbombs for the table. Each time he orders, he makes an elaborate show of paying with a crumpled wad of dollars he pulls from his cargo shorts. When he speaks, it's only to fire cringeworthy one-liners in Samantha's direction, most of which are met with howls of laughter from Darren, a hyperactive man-child, whose sole contribution to the group is to leap up and flail around arrhythmically each time the band plays a song he half recognises while simultaneously trying to drag the girls up to join him on the dance floor. Their friend Ben

– the pale, slightly awkward one – seems a little better. He smiles brightly at her, attempting to make conversation. Where's she from? Where's she been? How long has she been travelling?

Before she can answer his questions, Darren crashes between them, spilling her red wine down the front of her top. He lets out a hyena-howl of a laugh then disappears again.

It's the last straw. She snatches up her bag and storms off. It's time to go home.

Halfway across the room, she realises just how drunk she is, the evening's excesses sloshing queasily around her empty stomach. She changes direction, deciding to pause for a cigarette to steady herself, and heads instead towards the set of double doors that lead out on to the balcony at the front of the pub. Once outside, she pushes her way through the crowd until, at last, she reaches the railing. The first rush of nicotine sets her head spinning. For a moment she feels like she might throw up. It passes though, and by the time she's halfway through the roll-up, she feels a little more together.

She turns away from the crowd and looks out over the edge of the balcony. Below her, a sea of people spills out of the beer garden and laps onto the streets. Most of them are around her age, a mix of locals and backpackers, everyone talking, laughing, shouting, drinking. Having a good time. Beyond them, the street lights pick out a row of palm trees that line the far side of the road. The sight of them immediately lifts her spirits. She remembers she's on the other side of the world. As far away from home as she can get without going back on herself. And sure, it might have been a rubbish night. But there will be other, better nights just around the corner. A million of them. There always are.

A tram shambles past, momentarily drowning out the revellers in the beer garden below. She takes another drag on her cigarette, sending a plume of smoke drifting into the night sky. Past the palm trees lies the ocean. Port Phillip Bay. And after that, the Bass Strait. Not that she can see any of that from here. It's a new moon tonight, and there is only a deep darkness where the land stops and the water begins. She keeps looking all the same, leaning further out over the balcony as she tries to catch a glimpse of the distant waves, when she suddenly senses someone standing close behind her.

She spins around to find Ben smiling at her.

He holds up a hand. Gives a shy wave. 'Hey.'

To her surprise, she realises that he's actually quite handsome. Huge green eyes. Thick brown hair. The faintest flicker of a moustache tracing his upper lip. There's a sweetness that radiates from him. Something soft and puppyish, which seems at odds with the oafish company he's keeping.

He points to the dark stain on the front of her dress. 'Sorry about Paul. He's just... I was going to say he's just had too much to drink. But on second thoughts, he's always like that, even sober. They both are.'

He laughs, and again Sophie is struck by how sweet he seems. 'So what are you doing with them if you don't like them?'

He wrinkles his nose. 'I mean, they're harmless, really. It's all just an act. You wouldn't know it by looking at him, but Paul's basically a millionaire. Or at least, his dad is. He runs some big wholesale business back at home. When he first came to school, he actually got bullied for his posh accent. He just puts on the tough guy thing because he thinks it impresses people. Or rather, he thinks it impresses girls.'

Sophie rolls her eyes. 'I'm obviously immune to his charms.'

'I suspect you're not the only one.'

They both laugh.

'Anyway, what about you?' Ben asks. 'What are you doing with those two?'

'Who? Mags and Samantha?' She crosses her arms. 'Why? What's wrong with them?'

'Oh, nothing. It's just you don't seem anything like them. You're so...'

Before he can finish, a scream rings out above the clamour of the crowd. The door to the balcony creaks opens and a snatch of argument reaches them. One of the voices is disturbingly familiar.

'…take your hands *off* me!'

It's Mags.

In a single movement, Sophie stubs out her cigarette and rushes away, leaving a confused Ben trailing in her wake.

Inside the pub, a scrum of onlookers has already formed. Sophie barges her way to the centre, where she finds Mags remonstrating with a pair of squat-necked bouncers.

'What's going on?' Sophie demands.

Mags spins around. As she does, it's painfully obvious just how drunk she is. Her lipstick smeared, her eyeliner running in inky streaks down her face. She's a mess.

'I can't find my bag,' she slurs. 'And when I told these *fuckers*,' she spits the word at the bouncers, 'they said I'm too drunk and that I have to leave. But the pair of them can—'

Before she can finish, she hunches forwards and vomits onto the floor, spraying Sophie in the process.

The bouncers explode into barks of purple-faced fury.

'Right, that's it. Get her out of here! Right now!'

Sophie steps forward to steady her friend, but by now Mags's knees have gone from under her, her eyes rolling in her head as she slips from consciousness.

But then, out of nowhere, Ben is there, skidding and slipping in the pool of sick as he scoops the drunk girl up into his arms and then half carries, half drags her towards the exit.

'Don't worry. We're going,' he says to the bouncers, before turning back to Sophie. 'Where are you staying?'

She looks at him in surprise. 'You're coming with us?'

'Well, you can't exactly carry her by yourself, can you?'

2

Ben's not sure how they make it back. It takes more than an hour, with Mags insisting on stopping every few minutes to hurl either insults or the contents of her stomach. Which, judging by the colour of it, contains at least two bottles of red wine alongside the countless Jägerbombs, cocktails and tequilas she'd downed earlier on in the night. Somehow, between them they eventually manage to steer, drag and cajole her back to her hostel. Once they arrive, Sophie tells Ben to wait for her outside while she attempts to wrestle her friend into bed.

'Just give me a minute, OK?'

'I can go if it's easier?'

'No, it's fine. I'll come back down and say goodbye properly once I've got her to sleep. It'll only take a minute.'

On cue, Mags gives an incoherent yell. They both turn to see her squaring up to the glass door at the entrance, apparently attempting to start a fight with her own reflection.

Sophie rolls her eyes. 'On second thoughts, you'd better make that two minutes...'

Once they've gone, Ben shuffles around uncertainly. Although it's late, the streets churn with late-night drinkers. Some are finishing up for the night, while others are just getting started. A scream echoes in the distance, followed by the percussive fizz of a bottle smashing against brick. Someone begins to sing, loud and out of tune.

You'll ne-ve-er walk al-one.

Ben's not quite sure what he's doing here. He worries it might seem a little presumptuous, hanging around like this. That Sophie might think he's hitting on her. But then again, hadn't she been the one to ask him to wait? Or was he misreading the whole situation? He wishes he hadn't had so much to drink earlier.

In his back pocket, his mobile phone begins to rumble, interrupting his thoughts. He tenses. He's only recently started carrying a phone, and even now, he's still caught off guard every time it rings. He hates the idea of being reachable no matter where he is, or what he's doing. Who wants that? Besides, he'd always felt they were faintly ridiculous things, strictly the preserve of stockbrokers and drug dealers and poseurs. And yet now the devices have gradually become so ubiquitous that he's finally been forced to relent, joining the hordes of hunched-neck sheep who sat on the bus playing *Snake* each morning, or blasting moronic polyphonic ringtones at full volume.

Taking out his phone, he sees the name *Nan* illuminated on the screen of his little grey Nokia. He shakes his head. Though he's been gone for less than a week, she's called him every single day, despite his countless attempts to explain the astronomical roaming charges he faces whenever he picks up the phone to her. Nor can she seem to figure out the time difference between the UK and Australia, forever ringing at the most inopportune moment, usually during the early hours, when he's *way* too drunk to speak to her.

He's used to these misunderstandings, of course. They're just one of the many hazards of being raised by an older relative.

He hadn't known either of his parents. His father had disappeared before he was born, and his mother, a troubled teenager with addictions to both hard drugs and horrible men, not long after that. While he loved his nan to bits, and was forever grateful that she had taken him in and brought him up, he still envied his friends' parents, many of whom seemed to be practically the same generation as them. Whereas his nan has always struggled to grasp the simplest things. Like when she bought him the latest PlayStation game for his birthday – great, only he didn't have a PlayStation. Or the time she booked them a weekend break at Butlins, only for them to arrive not only on the wrong day, but also at the wrong Butlins. Still, as infuriating as she could be, he knew everything she did came from a place of love. More importantly, she'd always been there for him. Which is more than he could say for his real parents.

His thumb hovers over the answer button.

'You're still here.'

Ben looks up to find Sophie standing in the doorway. He takes one last glance at the screen, then declines the call. *Sorry, Nan.* He'll speak to her another time.

'I'm still here.' He smiles. She's changed outfits, swapping her sick-stained dress for a pair of denim shorts and a red top. 'You look nice.'

Sophie flushes, tugging her shorts a little lower. 'I look terrible, but it's all I've got. Backpacker's wardrobe, I'm afraid. It's either this or an elephant-print sarong.'

'Well, you're definitely beating me on the not-being-splattered-with-sick front.'

She grimaces. 'Sorry again about my terrible friend.'

'Don't be. I'm sorry for my terrible friends, too. I guess that's something we have in common.'

She raises an imaginary drink. 'To terrible friends.'

'To terrible friends.'

'So who was that?' she asks, nodding to the Nokia. 'Hang on, don't tell me. It's your wife, right? You were due home hours ago and she's sending out a search party?'

'Wives,' he corrects her. 'Didn't I mention I'm a polygamist? My hostel's basically a harem.'

As if on cue, his phone lets out another frantic rattle. He kills the call again.

'Are you sure you don't need to take that?'

He shakes his head. 'It's fine. Anyway, how's the patient?'

'Mags? Oh, you know. One minute she's trying to headbutt me, the next she's snoring. So more or less back to normal, I'd say.'

They both laugh again, before an awkward silence settles over them. Ben's about to suggest they swap numbers, when Sophie speaks up instead.

'Look, do you want to go somewhere? I'd invite you in, but they're mega strict about guests here.'

'Sure,' he says, a little too eagerly, before remembering his ruined clothes. 'I mean, I'm not sure I'll get in anywhere? I don't know if you've noticed, but I stink of vomit.'

'Oh, shut up. It's Friday night – everyone stinks of vomit. It's an Australian tradition. Practically *de rigueur*. Anyway, we don't have to go anywhere. We can just walk. I'm not tired. And I can't face going back into that room again just yet.'

Ben's phone buzzes one last time. He kills the call again, before stuffing the infernal device back into his pocket.

Not now, Nan.

'OK, sure.' He smiles. 'Let's walk.'

3

Is it her idea to head to the beach or his? Or perhaps it isn't a conscious decision at all, and the two of them are simply drawn by the same invisible force that steers every trickle towards a tributary, every river to the sea. Either way, an hour or so later they wash up opposite The Espy, having more or less walked in a huge circle, stopping only for a slice of pizza along the way. They take a seat beside each other on a small stone wall next to the pier, their feet dangling over the water. Behind them, the old hotel is closing up for the night, the bands having finally fallen silent, the last few stragglers finishing up their beers and staggering off towards the dying embers of Fitzroy Street.

Since leaving the hostel, they have talked in fits and starts, cautiously mapping out common ground between them. Along the meandering course of their conversation, it's transpired that they're both due to start university in London in September, Sophie to study drama and theatre arts at Goldsmiths, while Ben is taking law at Greenwich.

'I can't believe we're both going to be living south of the river. We're practically going to be neighbours. We can hang out all the time. Have parties. It's going to be epic.'

Ben laughs. 'Hey, slow down. We don't even know each other yet. You might turn out to hate me.'

'Or you might turn out to be a serial killer.'

'Exactly.'

'Which would explain why you want to study law. So,

you know, you don't get caught. Or if you do, so that you can defend yourself with legal loopholes.'

'Bah! I can't believe you've seen through my evil master plan.'

'Consider yourself foiled.'

They both laugh.

'But seriously, I think it's cool you're studying law. I can totally picture you as a hotshot lawyer.'

'Maybe. Although if I'm honest, sometimes I don't know why I'm even taking it. I've got no real idea what I want to do once I finish. I've always been insanely jealous of those people who seem to have their whole lives planned from the age of five. How about you? I bet you've always wanted to be an actress, haven't you?'

Sophie shrugs. 'Well, I'm an excellent liar. Which is basically the same as acting, right? Besides, I figure drama's easier than a *proper* course. Like maths or particle physics. Or law, for that matter.'

'So you're looking for an easy ride?'

'Always.'

They laugh again.

Sophie rolls another cigarette and changes the subject, pointing out at the ocean. 'I was in Halong Bay in Vietnam a few months ago, and I saw the most amazing thing. They have these plankton there that glow when they're disturbed. Bioluminescence, it's called. Our guide turned the lights off on the boat and then sailed through a patch. It looked like the sea was on fire or something. It was mind-blowing.'

'That sounds incredible,' he says. 'I'd love to see it.'

'Well, what's stopping you? You can fly from here.'

Ben shakes his head. 'I don't think I've got time. I'm on a pretty tight schedule.'

'How long are you here for?'

'Four weeks. It was supposed to be a gap year at first. Then that became a gap month when I realised how little my local supermarket paid.'

'The checkouts?'

'Shelf stacker. Kwik Save. Four twenty-five an hour.'

'Nice.'

'Worth it for this holiday though. I've never been abroad before, never even been on a plane until last week. I've never been anywhere, unless you count Weston-super-Mare.'

'Where?'

'Exactly. That's why I was so determined to make the most of it here. I might only have a month, but I planned it all out. Bungee jumping and jet-skiing. Champagne sunsets at Uluru and boat trips at the Great Barrier Reef. But the only thing we've done so far is...'

'Drink?'

Ben shrugs. 'I guess I'm just scared I'm going to run out of time.'

Neither of them says anything for a moment. Only the sound of Ben's phone vibrating in his pocket breaks the silence. He waits for it to stop.

Take a hint, Nan.

Out on the water, a faint yellow light flashes intermittently. Sophie thinks about the night fishing trip they went on in the Philippines, clinging to a wooden catamaran while their guide attempted to lure sardines with a kerosene torch.

'You know I don't think it matters how long you've got here,' she says. 'I mean, it's quality, not quantity, right? If it was a choice of either having ten mediocre years or a single life-changing, mind-blowing evening, I know which one I'd choose.'

'Ten years?'

'Funny.'

'OK, fine. So if we wanted to transform this night from sick-splashed mediocrity into something truly mind-blowing, what would you suggest?'

She thinks for a moment. 'I mean, we could go and see the penguins?'

He stares at her, perplexed. 'Penguins?'

'Are you kidding me? How do you *not* know about them? They're practically world famous. There's, like, a thousand miniature penguins nesting on the rocks by the pier. Come on, I'll show you. They're just over here.'

With that, she hops off the wall and begins to jog away towards the sea.

'Hey! Where are you going?' he calls after her. 'You want to look for penguins now? It's three in the morning.'

But Sophie has already disappeared into the darkness.

4

As he follows her down the pier, Ben feels as if he is stepping off the edge of the world. Overhead, a row of lights illuminates the wooden slats beneath him, leaving an impenetrable blackness either side. Only the steady hiss and smack of the waves indicate there's anything out there at all. He keeps walking, passing a small wooden kiosk as he steps further and further out to sea. After a while, he pauses to look back at the city. From here, it looks like a string of fairy lights, glinting in the distance.

When he turns again, he finds Sophie waiting for him up ahead. 'So where are these penguins then?' he asks.

'They normally nest here. But you have to look really hard. They're tiny.'

She leads him to the side of the pier, where he squints to see a rocky breakwater sloping away from them. They stand for a while, scanning the shadows, the steady murmur of the sea the only sound. Minutes pass. Then more minutes.

Ben turns to her. 'There aren't any penguins, are there?'

'Shut up! There are. I swear.'

'Uh-huh? Because if I didn't know better, I'd say this was all an elaborate ploy to get me out here so you could murder me.'

'Wait, what? I thought you were the serial killer?'

'Call it a plot twist. What if you're the deranged killer instead? Way more interesting, trust me.'

'And trust *me* when I say there are penguins here.

Thousands of them, usually. I saw them a few days ago. There was a huge crowd of people watching them.'

Ben looks up and down the empty pier. 'A huge crowd?'

'Yes! Actually, thinking about it… I was here a bit earlier last time. Just after sunset. Maybe they've all gone to… roost? Do penguins roost?'

'No idea. You're the expert on the lesser-spotted Australian penguin.'

She laughs, then climbs up onto the railing, retrieving her tobacco and papers from her bag. He takes a seat beside her while she rolls up, her lighter sparking briefly in the darkness. They sit in silence again, smoke drifting out across the black nothingness beyond the rocks.

After a while, Ben becomes conscious of the proximity of her legs to his, her bare thigh brushing gently against his leg each time she repositions herself on the railing. He realises he'd quite like to kiss her. He pictures himself leaning closer. Pretending to brush a strand of hair from her eye or a stray eyelash from her cheek, just like in the movies. He's fairly confident she'd kiss him back. Wasn't that, after all, the real subtext of this daft penguin expedition? Or was he getting everything wrong? He curses his lack of experience. The last thing he wants to do is come across as some kind of sex-crazed sleaze. He's seen the way Darren, and particularly Paul, act around women, and it turns his stomach. And so he slides a little further away from Sophie, attempting to give her some space and make conversation instead.

'So what's out there then?' He points out vaguely into the darkness. 'New Zealand?'

'No, silly. New Zealand's over there. Practically behind you. There's not much out there at all, really. A couple of islands. The New Year Group, I think. And then Tasmania beyond that. But assuming you miss those, well… I guess there's nothing for about three thousand miles, until you slam straight into Antarctica.'

'So too far to swim?'

'Unless you're a *really* good swimmer.'

More silence, during which he becomes aware of the heat radiating from her body. Again the urge to kiss her is almost overwhelming. He swallows hard. Bites his lip. Digs his nails into the palms of his hands. *Keep talking*, he tells himself. *Just keep talking.*

'You know. I've got to tell you something. Something I haven't told anyone before.'

She turns to him then, wide-eyed. A trail of smoke ghosting from the corner of her mouth. 'Well?'

'I... I actually hate the sea.'

She chuckles. 'Who the hell hates the sea?'

'I mean, it's just so... huge. Like, overwhelmingly vast.'

'So are mountains. And sunsets. And the night sky. Do you hate all those, too? Or do you reserve your hatred strictly for bodies of water? How do you feel about lakes? Paddling pools? Puddles?'

'Shut up. I've not got anything against water, *per se*. Give me a proper, safe, chlorinated swimming pool and I'll stay in there all day. It's just the sea's got... things in it.'

'Like...?'

'Like insane murderous stuff. Before I came on holiday, I was reading about all the deadly creatures over here. Which it turns out is most of them. But the sea is particularly bad. Did you know there's a jellyfish that's less than an inch long that's a hundred times deadlier than a cobra? An *inch*! And then, at the other end of the scale, there's one whose tentacles are over a hundred feet long. What's that, three buses? And let's not even talk about sharks...'

Sophie is crying with laughter now. 'I'm amazed you made it over here at all. You know, you didn't strike me as the panicky type.'

'Have you even been listening to me? I think panic is a perfectly reasonable response to a swarm of gelatinous death machines.'

'OK, fair point. But you don't need to worry about that stuff here. All the killer jellyfish are up north, in Darwin. Which is about two thousand miles from here. That's like being in Manchester and worrying about something in Moscow trying to kill you.'

'Like nuclear missiles?'

'You know what I mean. You're more likely to be killed in a car accident than by something out there.'

'Hmmm. I'm not convinced.'

'Well, let's find out, shall we?'

Sophie finishes her cigarette, stubbing the butt in a shower of orange sparks, then abruptly hops down off the railing. Ben watches as she walks over to the opposite side of the pier.

'What are you doing?'

She doesn't answer. Instead, she peels off her top, kicks off her sandals and climbs up over the railing. She stands there on the edge for a moment in her shorts and bra, looking out over the black water.

Ben's heart is in his chest. 'Don't do anything stupid.'

'Like what?'

'I mean it, Sophie.'

'I've told you, it's perfectly safe. Look.'

With one hand holding on to the bar, she leans out backwards over the water.

'Seriously, don't. You don't know how deep it is. There could be rocks. Anything…'

But Sophie winks at him.

And then she lets go.

5

She hits the water awkwardly, a sharp slap sucking the air from her chest as she tumbles down into the darkness. For a moment she's disorientated, a violent roar in her ears as she sinks deeper, too stunned to swim. And then, quite abruptly, she breaks the surface, choking and spluttering. She treads water, catching her breath, while somewhere high above her a worried voice rings out.

'Jesus! Are you OK? For a second I didn't think you were going to come back up.'

She forces a laugh. 'I'm fine. You should come in. Honestly, the water's beautiful.'

'Yeah. Thanks, but no thanks. I've seen *Jaws* enough times to know what happens right after somebody says that.'

'Oh, come on. I swear, there's nothing to worry about.'

Yet even as she says it, she feels something slide past her toes. Seaweed? Or something else? Suddenly, she desperately wants to get out. What the hell is she even doing here? She'd been so desperate to impress this boy with her fearlessness that she'd forgotten that she's not fearless at all. She's sensible. Cautious. Careful. And yet here she is, half-drunk and shivering in the middle of the ocean.

Overhead, Ben calls to her again. 'How are you going to get out?'

'Oh, stop worrying, will you?'

But she doesn't know how she's going to get out. From here, the shore is a distant twinkle. Meanwhile, the walkway looms above her, high and unreachable. Eventually, she spots a stagger of steel steps jutting out from the pier, a hundred metres or so away. She sets off towards them. Yet almost at once, she finds herself struggling. The current is stronger than she's expected, and for every stroke she takes, she is knocked back two by the swell of the waves. She finds herself thinking about stories she's heard of dangerous riptides, violent currents that can drag a person out to sea in a matter of seconds. She takes a deep breath. Forces herself to keep calm.

For a moment, she considers shouting for Ben to throw her down one of the lifebuoys attached to the side of the pier. Of course, she'd *die* of embarrassment. But it's better than drowning. When she squints up at the pier again, however, there's no sign of him. He's gone. She's on her own. Moments later another big wave rolls into her, knocking her under again.

She gasps.

Chokes.

When she comes up, the steps are further away than ever. Another wave smacks into her, spinning her around. She can't see the steps any more. She's not even sure which direction she's facing.

Panic takes over.

She thrashes, splashes, swallows salt water as she tries to hurl herself forwards, her energy sapping with every futile kick. By now her head is spinning. She tries to call out for help – *help!* – to hell with the shame of it, but her voice is nothing but a hoarse rasp as wave after wave slams into her.

And then she is slipping under.

Sinking.

Until suddenly, she slams into something cold and hard.

Somehow, she's not been washed out to sea, but into the platform. She grapples around, trying to find a way to pull herself out. And then Ben is there, reaching down to take her hand and haul her up and out of the water.

'Are you OK?'

She nods. 'I'm sorry. I just… It was rougher than I thought.'

'You scared the life out of me.'

'I know. I scared myself.' She pauses. 'Still, it almost worked, didn't it?'

'What almost worked?'

'I almost got you in the sea. I reckon one more minute and you'd have been diving in to rescue me.'

He shakes his head, laughing. 'You're insane.'

She follows him back up the stairs to the pier. As they reach the top, she begins to feel self-conscious, acutely aware of her near-nakedness. She scrambles for her clothes. As she does, he reaches out for her, catching her lightly by her arm and spinning her around.

'Is this yours?'

He holds out one of her sandals. She reaches for it, her hand brushing against his as she does.

And maybe it's the adrenaline from her near-death experience, or maybe it's the last of the cocktails working their way through her system, but somehow the distance between them shrinks to almost nothing, their noses almost touching, their breath becoming one.

She smiles. Tilts her head. Closes her eyes.

And then, somewhere nearby, she hears a buzzing sound. His phone, ringing again.

The moment is gone.

He steps back, cursing.

'Impeccable timing as ever,' he says as he fumbles to stop it.

Almost immediately, the phone starts ringing again. With a sigh he brings it up to his ear.

'Hey, Nan. Now isn't...'

He stops. Listens.

She watches as his face freezes. Immediately, she knows that something is very, very wrong. She stands there shivering as snatches of dislocated conversation drift across to her.

'How long...? Who said...? Why didn't...?'

Until eventually he hangs up.

He stands there for a moment. The phone hangs limp in his hand.

'Is everything OK?'

He looks stunned. The blood drained from his face.

'Is your nan alright?'

He stares at her, his mouth opening and closing. His eyes shimmering. 'It wasn't Nan. It was my uncle. She's had a… I don't know. A funny turn, he called it. He found her collapsed.'

'Oh, fuck. That's horrible. Is she going to be OK?'

He looks at her then. Really looks at her. And when he does, she sees the terror in his eyes. 'Um… No. Not really. She's… She's…'

He can't finish.

He doesn't need to.

2070

II

It's Sophie's second visit to the hospital. An entire nine hours have passed since she was last here, during which time she went home and then comprehensively failed to shower, eat or sleep. Instead, all she did was sit there, counting the minutes until she could return to Ben's side, frantic with worry that something would happen to him in her absence.

As she makes her way to the intensive care unit now, she bumps into the pretty young doctor with the striking green eyes, who explains that none of the tests have revealed anything useful. 'Brain activity. Heart function. Bloods. Everything looks normal. Although, the change in hair colour is odd. Anecdotally, a rapid loss of pigmentation is sometimes associated with chronic stress, although it's not something I've personally come across before. Especially so quickly. If I had to take a stab, I'd assume it was some kind of autoimmune response. A rare virus, maybe? Or exposure to chemicals or strong medication? Do you know if Ben was undergoing any kind of treatment before he collapsed?'

'Treatment?' Sophie hesitates, unsure of how much she should say.

'I'm sorry to put you on the spot, Mrs Walker. We seem to be having trouble porting Ben's records over from his healthcare provider, so we're working somewhat in the dark.' She glances at her screen. 'All we have is his name, address and date of birth.' She frowns. 'And actually, looking at that…'

Before she can finish, an alarm sounds elsewhere on the ward. The doctor garbles an apology, promises to be in touch with an update soon, and then scrambles away to help some other poor, ailing patient.

Sophie breathes a sigh of relief. She knows that sooner or later she will need to share what she knows with the doctors. Although where she will begin, she has no idea. Let alone whether they will believe her once she does.

For now, she is content just to sit with Ben, willing him to wake up.

As she enters the room, it seems that nothing has changed other than his hair. He still wears the same peaceful expression on his face. Still looks more asleep than sick. She's relieved, almost daring to believe that the doctor is right. That all of this could be the result of some exotic pathogen, rather than any of the other stuff.

The stuff she's not supposed to talk about.

But as she takes a seat next to the bed, she sees that something is different, after all. Ben's complexion is a little duller than usual. The skin a little looser. A handful of fine lines branching out from the corners of his eyes.

It's not dramatic like the hair. Most people probably wouldn't even notice.

But Sophie notices.

She's known this face most of her life. And she knows that it's changing. Ageing. Right in front of her. If this is what Ben looks like after a few days, where will he be a week from now? A month?

Before she can examine this thought any further, she realises someone is standing outside the room. At first, she assumes it's another fake nurse. A stupid Virtual Assistant, ready to provide her with not-so-helpful advice and reassurance.

But then there is a knock and two people enter. One male, one female, both young enough to be her grandchildren. Both of them real. They're dressed in the standard all-white uniforms that all police wear these days. It's supposed to make *them look less threatening, but somehow it has the opposite effect. They look clinical. Like surgeons ready to slice her open. Not that Sophie is particularly worried about these two. They're about as menacing as a pair of puppy dogs.*

'Mrs Walker?'

They look nervous. As if embarrassed to be intruding.

'We were hoping you could spare a couple of minutes to talk to us?' says the male officer. 'There are a couple of things we'd like to clear up.'

Sophie's heart sinks. She knows what this is about. Still, she decides to play along until she finds out how much they know.

'Of course,' she says, allowing herself to be led away from Ben's room, the police slowing to match her pace as she drags her creaking body down the hall.

'Arthritis,' she says by way of apology. 'I was hoping they might have cured it by the time it caught up with me. They say a spine replacement would help, but it hardly seems worth the trouble. Not at my age.'

They arrive at a boxy office, where she takes a seat at a small desk. A few minutes pass while the young officers fuss around with their various devices, struggling to connect to the building's Li-Fi network.

Sophie chuckles. 'Some things never change. You know I'm still old enough to remember Wi-Fi,' she says. 'Dial-up, even.'

They nod politely in a way that tells Sophie they have no idea what she's talking about, before turning back to their machines.

There is something about the way they interact with each other, a hushed bickering, that makes Sophie wonder if there might be something beyond a professional relationship between them. But then, she always thinks that about young people. That they are incapable of interacting without jumping into bed with each other – something her granddaughter assures her most definitely isn't the case any more. Actually, most of the young people she meets these days seem depressingly sensible. Everyone's too health-conscious. Too career-focused. Sophie wants to shake them. Tell them to take some risks. Make some mistakes. Don't they know they haven't got forever?

Well, apart from the ones who do.

At last they get their devices working and are ready to begin the interview.

'Thanks for agreeing to speak to us, Mrs Walker. I understand that this is a difficult time for you.'

'It is,' Sophie agrees. 'But before we go any further, I wonder if there's something you could clear up for me. I guess I'm just a little confused as to why you're here? I didn't call the police. And, unless I'm mistaken, there hasn't been any crime committed? This is just a case of bad luck, isn't it?'

The two officers glance at each other briefly. Something private passing between them.

'You see, the thing is, Mrs Walker, we're not so sure it is bad luck. Detective Constable O'Rafferty and I are part of a special investigation into a number of cases that all bear a striking resemblance to your husband's.'

'I don't understand?'

'You see, this isn't the first time we've had reports of somebody fitting your husband's... profile... being taken into hospital under almost identical circumstances. In fact, in the last twelve months, there have been three other cases we're aware of. All of them suffering from the same symptoms. Unexplained coma. Rapid cellular degradation.'

Sophie feels as if the floor has dropped out from underneath her. She focuses on her breathing, struggling to maintain her composure. When she speaks again, her voice is a fractured rasp.

'And these people. These other cases. How long did it take for them to recover?'

Again, the detectives share their secret glance, before the woman clears her throat. Her expression is soft. Sympathetic.

And yet something cold and vaguely accusatory in her eyes reminds Sophie of the holographic nurses who haunt the wards.

'Oh no, Mrs Walker. I'm afraid they didn't recover. Within a week of collapsing, all three of them were dead.'

2006

6

London rushes. London rumbles. London roars with the grinding clamour of almost eight million lives. Everyone doing their own thing. Everyone focused on the square foot of space immediately in front of them as they hop from train to Tube to pavement and back again. Eyes down, headphones jammed in their ears as they weave in and out of each other's paths. Everyone scrambling after whatever it is that gets them out of bed in the morning. Money or sex or power or desperation or duty. Everyone trapped in their own invisible bubble.

Together, alone.

And yet, seen from just a couple of steps back, the space between each person becomes almost indistinguishable, their faces and features blurring into one, so that it appears the streets are flooded with a single stream that courses through them. Everyone moving in the same direction. Everyone stopping and starting as one. An endless human tide that ebbs and flows depending on the time of day but never disappears completely.

Alone, together.

Staring out of the window of The Mitre pub in Greenwich, Sophie feels both part of the city and totally separate from it. It's three o'clock on a Tuesday afternoon, and behind her the early evening rush is already in full flow, a steady throng of drinkers yelling their orders at the bar. Students, OAPs, professional drinkers. A few office drones dotted around, their late liquid lunches seamlessly morphing into post-work cocktails. It sounds fun back there. People talking, laughing, swearing, flirting, the buzz of voices shot through with the clang and zap of fruit machines and the low burble of muzak. But Sophie isn't drinking. Instead, she has her coursebooks spread out over the sticky table. Her handwritten lecture notes. Her photocopied worksheets. She has coloured pens and Post-it notes. A rubber-band ball. Her laptop is open, a long-cold herbal tea standing beside it. In other words, she has everything she could conceivably need to write her assignment.

And yet, she is not writing.

She has not written a single word in the two hours she has been sitting here. Rather, she has stared blankly at the world outside the window and desperately fought the urge to put her head on the table and go to sleep.

Sophie is hungover from a heavy session last night. Which followed on from a heavy session the night before. Which in turn followed even heavier sessions on Friday and Saturday night. In fact, she can hardly remember the last time there hasn't been a heavy session. At this point, she's been chasing a hangover more or less permanently for the fourteen months she's been at university. Going to bed as the sun comes up then waking up shaking a few hours later. Vomiting into a wastepaper bin. Showering and sprinting to make a lecture, where she sits slumped at the back of the hall, terrified she'll be called on to speak, before heading back to the pub with her friends for a quick lunchtime hair of the dog, where a glass inevitably becomes a bottle as more people join the group, the day sliding towards evening towards night, at which point her consciousness generally begins to fray at the edges and the next thing she knows she's opening her eyes to find herself face down on some random bedroom floor, a mysterious bruise on her backside or a graze on her knee, missing a shoe or a handbag or a coat, ready to start the whole booze-sodden cycle all over again.

But not today.

This morning, as she opened one bloodshot eye to find the ceiling violently spinning above her, she decided to change her life. This random, drizzle-drenched mid-November Tuesday would mark a line in the sand. From here on in, there would be no more benders. No more missed deadlines. No more slept-through lectures. She would exercise. Eat healthily. Take up a hobby. Find some balance and moderation in her life. This time, she was determined to make a fresh start of things. It was a new day.

A new Sophie.

Sitting here now, however, the bleary optimism of a few hours earlier already seems like a distant memory. She was clearly still drunk when she'd woken up. There is no other explanation for why she would voluntarily decide to drag herself away from the warm comfort of her room and attempt to endure her first day of sobriety in a *pub*, of all places. It was nothing short of suicidal. Especially now that her hangover has well and truly announced itself. Her head pounding. Her stomach churning. A trickle of sticky sweat sliding down her back.

Behind her, the clink of glasses threatens to push her over the edge. Perhaps she should just admit defeat? She knows a single drink would be enough to stave off the nausea and ease her jitters. It might even help her focus and get some work done. She pictures a cool gin and tonic with a wedge of lime jammed down the side. Ice cubes rattling. The glass beaded with condensation. Would it really be such a disaster if she gave in and ordered one? It's not like she has a problem. And this is what university's all about, right? Falling out of bars. Making lifelong friends and terrible sexual decisions. It was an extension of backpacking, really. Everyone here for a good time. Building up a bank of outrageous stories they can look back on wistfully when they're middle-aged and terminally dull.

Besides, it's not like drinking has done her any harm. If anything, the opposite is true. Her initial few months in

London had proved excruciatingly lonely, as she struggled to settle into her new surroundings without Mags or Samantha for company. Yet as soon as she'd established herself with the party crowd, things had improved exponentially. By proving that she could drink the hardest, dance the wildest, stay up the latest, she'd made no end of new friends. For the first time in her life, Sophie was actually, properly popular. To the point where she'd almost found herself feeling sorry for her old friends when she'd gone home for the summer. Samantha, who was studying medicine at Liverpool, was quite clearly taking her studies far too seriously, her only topic of conversation the stress she was under and the amount of revision she was doing. Mags, on the other hand, had taken a job in a local phone shop and had started dating her line manager. The last Sophie had heard, they were saving up for a mortgage and talking about having a baby together. Sophie couldn't believe it. Mags had always been destined for greatness. At school she was top of every class. First picked for every team. Lead in every school play. Sophie would have put money on her becoming a film star. Or prime minister. Or first woman on the moon. And yet there she was, preparing to settle for a life in the suburbs. It was a bloody *tragedy*.

Well, that might be enough for Mags, but not for her. Sophie still has plenty more adventures to cram in before she swaps her own dreams for a life of soiled nappies and Sudocrem. She wants to travel again. She wants a career. She wants fame, fortune, glory…

But before she can do any of that, she really, *really* needs to finish this assignment.

She stares at the cursor blinking on the blank page. Her eyeballs throbbing in her skull. Her mouth dry. Her stomach churning. She picks up her phone and checks it, just in case a friend has messaged to invite her to a party. Or the supermarket. Or anywhere. There's nothing. She turns back to the computer screen. Grits her teeth. Grinds her jaw. Massages her temples with her fingertips. Behind her, the noise of the bar seems to grow louder by the second. Drinks pouring, glasses slamming, people screaming.

It's too much to bear. She reaches for her purse.

But then she pauses.

Because something outside the window has caught her eye. Someone walking past the pub, on the opposite side of the road. A boy she half recognises, though from where she has no idea. She casts her mind back across a hundred hazy nights. Could they have met in a pub or a nightclub somewhere?

And then the boy turns his head slightly, and suddenly she is back on St Kilda Pier, soaking and shivering under a moonless sky.

Without even pausing to pack away her laptop, she dives for the door of the pub and chases after him.

7

Is it late or early?

Ben can't tell any more. He's sitting in the back room of The Gipsy Moth with half a dozen empty glasses strewn across the table in front of him. Meanwhile, Sophie has gone to the bar again, having insisted on ordering yet another round of drinks.

This is not how he'd planned to spend his evening. He's not much of a drinker these days. Certainly, he doesn't drink like Sophie drinks. As if the bar is in danger of running dry. As if swallowing wine is a competitive sport. He tries not to think about everything he's supposed to do tomorrow. The coursework that needs finishing. The deadlines he has to meet. Or the fact he's down for an early morning shift at the pub.

For the last twelve months he's been supplementing his student loan by toiling away as a kitchen assistant at a gastropub in London Bridge, staying in halls over the summer and working throughout his holidays rather than going back to Birmingham. Not that he's mentioned this to Sophie. He's not sure why. Perhaps he's embarrassed that instead of living off the bank-of-Mum-and-Dad like most of the students in his class, he's forced to work almost full-time, trying to fit university around his shifts in the kitchen, rather than the other way around. He doesn't have a mum or a dad. All he had was his nan. And now she's gone. Not that she'd have been able to help him out financially, even if she was still alive.

Once the funeral was out the way, he'd found himself in

the unenviable position of executor of her estate. Although as it turned out, 'her estate' consisted of little more than a stack of maxed-out credit cards and outstanding catalogue debt. It was all such a mess. A knotty tangle of paperwork, half of it covered in Nan's indecipherable scrawl, a meaningless tally of numbers and dates. He ended up binning it all. He had bigger things to worry about than paying Littlewoods back. The most pressing of which was finding somewhere new to live. As an eighteen-year-old, he found he was liable for both the rent and bills, an impossible amount to cover with his minimum-wage supermarket job his only source of income. And while he could technically apply for social housing, the waiting list was ridiculous, leaving him with a choice of either moving into a homeless shelter or taking up residence on his uncle Mal's couch while he waited to move into halls the following September. It was no choice. As difficult as his uncle could be, he was family. And it was only for six months.

To his disappointment, however, relocating to London hasn't made life much easier. While his student loan covers his rent and fees, almost nothing is left over for food, let alone socialising. For the first couple of months, he'd debated waving the white flag and jacking it all in. But then what was the alternative? Go back to Birmingham and Uncle Mal's lumpy couch? Stack shelves in his local supermarket for the rest of his life? And so, he looked for a job, finding one at The Great Fryer of London. Five nights a week, with double shifts at the weekend. Chopping garlic and onions and parsley until his wrist spasmed. Triple dipping baskets of chips until his clothes and hair were permanently permeated with the stink of stale oil. Yet in spite of these hardships, he found he enjoyed the work. The sense of camaraderie with the other chefs. The siege mentality during the evening rush. The celebratory air when they finally flicked off the heat lamps at the end of the night. He liked the way it made his body feel. The aching legs. The spasming back. The extra muscles he'd gained from hauling twenty-kilo bags of potatoes from the delivery van to the stockroom every morning. Even the little burns and nicks and welts that covered his hands felt like a trophy. Battle scars that marked him out as different from the other students in his class, most of whom seemed content to squander their parents' savings on what was, for them, essentially a three-year party.

But as much as he likes the job, the thought of the brunch rush tomorrow morning brings him out in a cold sweat now. Four hours of chopping mushrooms and frying eggs and bacon. He's stayed out far too late for the shift to be anything other than an agonising ordeal. How long has he been drinking now? Five hours? Six? And the cost of drinks here is extortionate. A round costs almost double what he makes in an hour. He'll be working for free at this rate. All to sit talking to a girl he hardly knows? It's ridiculous.

Only, it doesn't feel ridiculous. It feels like the most natural thing in the world. Despite the fact that almost two years have passed since they last spoke, they've picked up pretty much precisely where they'd left off. Seeing her again, Ben feels woozy with nostalgia for a more innocent time. A time before he picked up his phone and his world blew apart.

Besides, Sophie is fun to be around. She is everything he isn't any more. Carefree. Optimistic about the future. Not to mention totally crazy. The kind of girl who'd dive off a pier into the darkness without stopping to check for rocks below.

Who wouldn't want to be around her?

'It was cheaper to get a bottle…'

He looks up to see her grinning, a bottle of house red and two glasses clamped to her chest.

'Jesus, are you trying to kill me? I'm going to feel horrible in the morning. I'm a total lightweight.'

'Yeah, me too.' She grins, sloshing wine into the glasses. 'But tonight's an exception. This is a reunion, remember?'

Remember? How could he forget.

The phone call, back on the pier. How many times has he replayed that call over and over in his mind? Every word perfectly preserved. Every stutter. Every swallow. How surreal it was to hear his uncle Mal sobbing. Mal. A huge slab of a man, whose knuckle tattoos and freshly skinned head still provokes nervous glances in the street to this day, despite the fact he's pushing sixty. Mal, who'd never talked to Ben about anything beyond football. Who'd only ever shown the slightest flicker of emotion once, when Villa lost the FA Cup Final to Chelsea five years earlier. Mal, strangely broken, his voice cracking down the line.

She's gone, son. She's gone.

He remembers trying to play it down to Sophie after he'd hung up. Telling her he was fine. Everything was *totally fine*. All the while apologising constantly. He couldn't stop saying sorry to her. He had this weird sense of guilt, like he was putting a massive downer on everything. Ruining a perfectly good night with his dead-nan shit.

'What are you going to do?' she'd asked as they stumbled back down the pier together.

He had no idea. For a brief, stupid moment he wondered if he could just carry on the holiday. He'd worked so hard to be there. All the months of planning. All the money he'd saved. Maybe he could just swallow it down for the next three weeks and then go home and deal with everything then? But, of course, he knew that he wouldn't. He couldn't.

'I guess I'd better go to the airport.'

He'd offered to walk her back to the hostel, and when she refused he put her in a taxi. She hugged him then, hard and long, pressing her face into his chest before making him promise he'd stay in touch. He was so dazed that it wasn't until her car disappeared and he sank to the pavement that it occurred to him that they'd never actually got around to exchanging numbers.

'So what is it you're studying again?'

He grins. 'I told you already.'

'I know you did. But that was almost two years ago, and I was a teeny-weeny bit tipsy that night. Come to think of it, I'm a teeny-weeny bit tipsy now, too.'

'Law. I'm studying law. Second year.'

'That's right! I remember now. So you can commit the perfect murder, right?'

'Exactly.'

'And how's it going? The course, I mean. Not the murdering.'

'Actually, the murdering is easy. It's the course that's hard. The reading is really heavy going. There's just so much of it. And most of it's utterly impenetrable. All these arcane terms and Latin phrases. But then, I suppose it's designed that way.'

'What do you mean?'

'Have you ever been to a courtroom? I visited one on a school trip years ago. Even then, I remember thinking how crazy it all was. The barristers dressed up in their gowns and badly fitting wigs, like they're in some terrible BBC period drama. And then there's all the weird traditions. Like bowing to the royal coat of arms when you enter the court and swearing the judicial oath before giving evidence. It's like stepping into some secret members-only club. Which is exactly what it is, really. They don't *want* people to understand what they're doing. They definitely don't want the likes of you and me to understand.'

Sophie frowns. 'But why not?'

'Well, because then they can control us, can't they? Wrap us up in contracts we don't understand. Hit us with fines. Take away our freedom.'

'You know for a student of law, you don't seem to be much of a fan of the legal system.'

He laughs. 'It's not that. It's fascinating, actually. Once you get your head round it. It's just the more I study it, the more inaccessible I realise it is. Who knows, maybe once I qualify I can get a job where I can help reform it or something.'

'So you want to change the world?'

'Is that so crazy?'

She smiles. 'No, actually. I don't think it is crazy. In fact, I think it's pretty cool.'

They look at each other across the table. A loaded look. Ben swallows hard, his cheeks flushing pink, his mouth dry.

'Wait, there's something I need to do,' Sophie says, breaking the silence. 'Before I forget.' She reaches towards him and plucks his phone from the table.

'What are you doing?'

'I'm giving you my number,' she says. 'So you don't get away a second time.'

Eventually, the night begins to wrap itself up. A bell rings. Last orders are called. The bottle is finished. And then they are outside, rubbing their hands in the cold night air.

'So what now?' Sophie asks.

The way she says it, the look in her eyes, tells him he should invite her back to his. It would be so easy. Yet he can't seem to find the words. Instead, he stumbles away from the pub, over to the river. Sophie follows, a few steps behind him. When they reach the railing, they stop, both of them staring out at the brown churn of the Thames.

'You know they've spotted dolphins in there?' she says. 'Seals, too. And seahorses.'

'No penguins?'

'Funny.'

She leans forward over the bar, her feet tipping up slightly.

'Careful.'

'Oh right, I forgot. You're the boy who's scared of water, aren't you?'

'Not water. The sea.'

'And how are you with rivers? Would you jump in to save me this time?'

'I'd rather not find out.'

They both fall silent again. In the distance, he can make out the geometric skyline of Canary Wharf, a red light blinking on the tip of the tallest tower. Without looking, he realises Sophie has moved closer to him. Or maybe he's moved closer to her. Either way, their arms are touching. He pictures white sparks jumping between two exposed wires. His hands are shaking slightly. He jams them into his pockets, hoping she hasn't noticed. Though he's received plenty of romantic interest since moving to London – a couple of the waitresses at work, a boy in his criminology class – he's pushed them all away. Since his nan died, he feels ugly. As if grief has disfigured him somehow. His sense of humour has withered completely. He's morose. Brooding. Miserable.

But not tonight. Not with Sophie. With her, he feels more like his old self.

Beside him, he senses her shift to face him. He's feeling really drunk now. The wine giving the world a soft-edged sheen. And then suddenly he isn't thinking any more. Instead, he lets go, his body turning to meet her. She smells amazing. Her perfume sweet and peppery.

And all at once they are back on the pier again, almost two years earlier. Her eyes closed. Chin tilted up.

But then he pauses. Something pulls him back.

What happens after this moment? he thinks. After they kiss. Because even if tonight goes well, how long will he be able to shield her from his sad little life?

Throughout the evening, she's dropped little details about herself into the conversation. Her family's holiday home in France. Her older brother, Christopher, who lives in Manhattan. The fact that she fucking *skis*. He knows she's not bragging. She's just oblivious to the fact these things are utterly alien concepts to someone like him. It would take him a hundred years just to catch up to the place where she started. Not that he holds it against her. But what can he realistically offer her? A spot on his uncle's couch? A share of the debt he'd inherited from his nan? A portion of his measly gastropub earnings? As these thoughts tumble through his mind, he feels his chest tighten. His throat closing up.

Sophie opens her eyes, her face twisting in confusion. 'What is it?'

He struggles to answer, shaking his head.

'Oh God,' she says, her eyes filling with tears. 'It's me, isn't it? I'm such an idiot.'

She breaks away, but he pulls her back. 'No! Don't be ridiculous. It's not you. It's just...' He fumbles for a way out without hurting her feelings. 'It's just... I'm seeing someone else.'

The lie lands with a dull thud. Like something dead dropped between them. Ben looks at the floor. The river. The sky. Anywhere but her. 'I mean, it's not serious,' he rambles on. 'I don't know. I should have said earlier. I'm... I'm really sorry.'

She steps back then, her cheeks burning. 'No! Don't be silly! I'm the one who should be sorry. I misread things. I thought... I don't know what I thought. I should go. I need to go home.'

And then they are back on the main drag of the High Road. People. Cars. Lights. And she is flagging down a taxi and they hug. And it's weird. And it's awful.

'So... Do you want me to call you?' he says.

'Do you *want* to call me? I don't want to make any trouble with your girlfriend.'

He senses a snap in her tone, but he lets it go. 'Yes. I want to call you. Tonight was fun. It's just... But yes, I'll call. I promise.'

'OK. Well. You have my number.'

'I do.'

And then, just like before, she is gone, and he is alone.

He sinks to the kerb.

Appalled.

Aghast.

Astounded by his seemingly endless capacity to take something great.

Something wonderful.

And turn it to absolute shit.

8

They visit museums. Art galleries. One night, Ben gets them discounted tickets to a very confusing play at the Royal Court where all the actors get naked, paint themselves orange, speak Russian and simulate incredibly realistic-looking sex. He doesn't understand any of it, of course, but he knows Sophie enjoys this kind of thing, and so he enjoys it, too. They go to concerts. They eat dinner together. They go to stand-up comedy gigs and student nights at local bars.

In other words, they do everything a newly courting couple might do.

Only they are not a couple.

Ben and his ridiculous lie have taken care of that.

Each time before they meet up, Ben tells himself that he will admit the truth. He will tell her that he was simply drunk and that he'd concocted the story about a girlfriend because he felt insecure. And that now he sees it was stupid and he's sorry and that he'd very much like to kiss her.

Please?

Yet, how can he? If he can't even bring himself to tell her about his kitchen job, so wary is he of attracting her pity, how can he possibly tell her that he lied about something as big and stupid as this?

And so, as the weeks go by, the lie about his 'girlfriend' grows unchecked, becoming more elaborate by the day. Despite his attempts to keep things vague, he finds himself furnishing his imaginary partner with not only a name (Nina), but also an entire backstory (she's a Dutch biomedical student with a sickly father, necessitating frequent trips back home). Already it's reached the point where it's difficult to see how he could possibly explain the situation without coming across as anything other than deeply, and very possibly criminally, disturbed.

He tells himself that might be for the best. As much as he likes Sophie, the same doubts about his suitability as a boyfriend remain. Or grow, even. The more he discovers about her world, the less he is able to reconcile it with his own. The friends she's introduced him to so far have all been, without exception, obnoxious. Faux-bohemians, like Rupert and Jeremy, who spend their weekends blitzed on coke and ketamine, quoting Kerouac or Bukowski to anyone in earshot whilst still receiving weekly pocket money from their wealthy parents. Or dull, horse-faced girls like Belinda and Stephanie, who have their own Central London apartments and talk a hybrid language dotted with references to obscure European festivals he's never been to and arthouse films he's never watched.

All of these so-called friends wear the same curious expression on their faces whenever Sophie introduces him, as if they are encountering a fascinating but slightly disgusting insect for the first time. His accent is a constant source of amusement, with each of them taking turns to do an impression while he grins moronically, wishing the ground would open up and devour him. Stephanie in particular seems completely baffled by him, struggling to decipher a single word he says and asking, in all seriousness, which part of Scotland he's from (she later admits to never having been further north than Islington).

Yet as awful as they are, he can see how much they have in common with Sophie. And, conversely, how different they are to him. It isn't simply a case of money. The fact that he didn't go to private school or won't be jetting off to the Swiss Alps or Sorrento for his holidays this year. And it's not just that they dress differently to him. Although, of course, they do. Whereas he's always made an effort to keep his ancient tracksuit and Nike trainers spotless, Sophie and her friends have a strict uniform of expensive vintage clothing, everything artfully faded and self-consciously crumpled. But it's more than any of that. Ultimately, it comes down to confidence. The way they carry themselves through the world. They don't shrink away or try to make themselves invisible. They want to be seen. They aren't afraid for their voice to be the loudest in every room. Unlike Ben, who learnt at school that it was best to keep his head down and his mouth shut if he wanted to stay out of trouble, these lot love attention. If anything, they demand it.

More than anything, they each seem to share the same unshakeable conviction that their lives will turn out alright in the end. Sure, they might flunk their course and develop a drug habit and have a nervous breakdown and rack up tens of thousands of pounds worth of debt along the way. But things will come good for them, eventually. Someone will always be there to bail them out. It's this invisible safety net that really sets them apart from Ben. Whereas they have the freedom to mess around and mess up as much as they like without fear of any serious, long-term consequences, the same is not true for him. He knows there's nobody waiting in the wings, ready to catch him if he slips. If he falls, he's on his own. And there's no guarantee he'll ever get back up again.

In spite of her horrible friends, however, Ben finds himself liking Sophie more than ever. While she's self-assured, she's never arrogant or brash like the others. She's kind, generous, self-deprecating. She's *fun* to be around. Most of all, he likes himself more when he's in her company. All of Sophie's best qualities seem to be contagious. When he's with her all of his angst and anxiety seems to melt away, leaving someone better in its place. Someone who, like Sophie, is bright, funny and relaxed.

Everything, in other words, he's not when he's alone.

So he tries not to be alone.

He suggests more nights out, more dates-that-aren't-dates, as he makes evermore unbelievable excuses for Nina's continued absence. Anything for a few more minutes with her.

And that is why, when she texts him one evening in early December and asks if he wants to come along to a free lecture at her university, he doesn't even bother to ask what it's about. He simply says:

Yes.

Of course.

Count me in.

9

Ben stands in the carpeted foyer of a sparsely filled lecture theatre. Sophie is late, and while he waits, he glances again at the glossy flyer for tonight's event:

Who Wants to Live Forever? The Ethics of Eternal Life

Below the title, three speakers are listed: a cultural sociologist, a professor of philosophy and, most mysteriously of all, somebody called Dr V. Andersson, who is described as a *biogerontologist*. Ben shakes his head, wondering if it isn't too late to suggest going somewhere a little lighter. Like a funeral. Or a public execution.

'Sorry I'm late.'

Ben looks up to find Sophie swaddled in a faux-fur coat, her cheeks flushed, hair sequined with rain.

'Mum called while I was getting ready,' she continues. 'And then I managed to lose my keys and then… Well, hey, at least I made it, right? Have you been waiting long?'

At the sight of her, any thoughts of leaving evaporate. He fights the urge to throw his arms around her, and instead holds up the flyer. 'I can't believe you've invited me to a cult meeting. This is how it starts, isn't it? First a lecture in Lewisham, next a one-way ticket to Guyana.'

She grimaces. 'Oh dear, does it look rubbish? They put one of these free lectures on every month, but I've never actually been. I think the last one was about aliens or something. My friend Lucinda says there's complimentary wine at the end, so that alone makes it worth it, right?'

'You're sure it's not Kool-Aid?'

She laughs. 'Look, why don't we stay for the first half? If it's unbearable, we can always sneak out at the interval.'

'I'm happy if you're happy.'

'It's a deal. Now let's go in, or we'll never get a seat.'

As they enter the theatre, Ben sees that finding somewhere to sit will not be an issue. There are half a dozen people dotted around the room, most at least ten years older than them.

He grits his teeth. It's going to be a long night.

The first talk, delivered by a tall Scottish woman in a nasal monotone, is a crushingly boring PowerPoint presentation that skips through Buddhist, Christian, Jewish and Taoist views of immortality, before somehow segueing into a random montage of clips from Eighties and Nineties movies: *Indiana Jones*, *Highlander*, *Death Becomes Her*. She finishes to an indifferent smattering of applause, before being replaced by an ancient male professor. He is dressed in a dusty-looking tweed jacket, with an oversized pair of glasses propped on the end of his nose, which magnify his eyes to disconcerting proportions. For some reason, he reminds Sophie of a giant turtle. Unlike the previous speaker, he eschews any sort of visual aid, preferring to mumble random passages of philosophical discourse, mostly from his own textbook, which he constantly reminds the audience is available to purchase in the foyer after the talk.

Throughout this torture, Sophie is acutely aware of Ben's discomfort beside her. He sighs, tuts, wriggles around in his chair, crossing and uncrossing his legs continuously. A couple of times he takes out his phone, shielding the light with his hand while he taps out messages on his lap. Talking to Nina, probably. Telling her what a terrible night he's having with his weird friend. How much he'd rather be out with her.

Nina.

Though she's never seen a picture of her, and Ben is only willing to share the vaguest of details, Sophie can already guess what she's like. Beautiful. Charming. Intelligent. *Thin*. It's only natural that Ben would end up with a girl like that. While he might be oblivious to the attention he receives, she's seen the way people in the street look at him. The shop girls who take a little too long ringing him up at the till. The barmen who linger longingly while fixing his drink. Of *course* he's dating some exotic high-flyer.

Not that she's jealous exactly. She's long since given up on the hope of any kind of romantic relationship developing between them. But she is starting to worry that once Nina is back in the country more regularly, it might put an end to their friendship altogether. He certainly won't be able to see her as often. And what will she do with herself then?

As the Philosophy Turtle makes one last desperate pitch for the audience to buy his book before leaving the stage, she turns to Ben.

'We can probably creep out if you want?' she whispers.

'Are you not enjoying it?'

'No, it's not that… Wait, are *you* enjoying it?'

'Sure. I mean, the last guy was a bit full of himself, but he still made a few interesting points. Anyway, didn't you want to stay for the free wine?'

Before Sophie can answer, the chair of the event introduces the final speaker of the evening. 'And now we'd like to welcome to the stage Dr Victor Andersson. Researcher, biomedical gerontologist, and chief science officer and founder of the Evergreens Programme.'

There's a light ripple of applause as a tall, dark-haired man steps up to the lectern. He is dressed sharply in a sleek navy jacket and pale chinos, his white shirt open at the collar to reveal a flash of tan flesh. Polished brogues, no socks. A chunky silver watch on his wrist. Though they are sitting ten rows back, Sophie can imagine the woody musk of his aftershave. Expensive. Liberally applied. He looks at first glance not so much like an academic, but a middle-aged film star. Or at least somebody who reads glossy magazines about middle-aged film stars and has enough money to shop in the same places as them. Yet the longer she stares at him, the more she realises there is something not quite right about his appearance. His thick dark hair is a little *too* thick and dark, his hairline geometrically precise. His face, too, has the unnerving quality of the surgically altered, the skin pulled taut, his complexion slightly waxy, making it difficult to tell his age. Sophie realises he could be either significantly older or significantly younger than she'd originally assumed. She's about to lean over and make a joke about him to Ben, when the doctor clears his throat and begins to speak.

'Good evening. I'd like to start by thanking the previous presenters for their *exhaustive* analysis. It's great to get an historical and cultural context for this stuff. I don't know about you guys, but I took two key ideas from their talks. The first is that we, as a species, have been obsessed with the idea of immortality ever since our ancestors crawled out of the swamp and started worshipping the sun. The second is that almost everyone agrees that immortality is a fundamentally shitty idea.'

Dr Andersson looks around the half-empty hall, his eyes twinkling with mischief. A few giggles break out amongst the audience. The man is a strong public speaker. He reminds her of a game show host. His pauses are timed for maximum impact. As with his age, Sophie finds his accent hard to place. Neither British nor American but stranded somewhere in the middle of the Atlantic.

'Now as it happens, I tend to agree with that assessment,'

he continues. 'It *is* a shitty idea. And an impossible one, too. After all, the world isn't going to last forever. Nor even the universe. I'm afraid that every good thing must eventually come to an end.'

Another self-assured smile.

'But the how and the when of it? Now *that's* worth discussing. Why is it that we're prepared to settle for eighty, ninety, one-hundred-at-a-push years? The last twenty of which you'll likely spend in sickness and decrepitude. Why not two hundred years? Or five hundred? Or five thousand?'

Again, he glances around the room, daring someone to speak up.

'Now this really isn't such a radical proposal. We already collectively spend over one hundred billion dollars every year trying to beat cancer. Think about that for a minute. One hundred billion dollars. Heart disease isn't far behind. And then there's dementia. Diabetes. We pour an obscene amount of money into treating these *symptoms*, without showing the faintest interest in curing the actual *disease*. By which I mean, ageing itself. Unlike death, ageing is not some natural process that should be accepted and respected. Far from it. Ageing is a plague. A pandemic that needs to be stopped once and for all. Ageing needs to be cured.

'Look at it this way. After so many miles on the road, your car starts to wear out. You replace the tyres, the exhaust, the clutch, discs, alternator, pump. And over the years, you keep spending. Spending, spending, spending. You spend more than the damn thing was worth in the first place, just trying to keep it limping along the road. Until one day – *kaput!* – it craps out on you anyway. And that's it. Off to the big scrapheap in the sky and back to the showroom you go. But why spend all that time and money and energy fiddling with brake pads and brushes and not just design a better car? One that keeps going? One that doesn't break down in the first place?

'Why is that such a crazy idea? After all, that's precisely what I've done. For the past fifteen years, my team and I have dedicated ourselves to building a better person. Actually, we began by building a better type of yeast. Then better worms. Then mice. And now, finally, we are beginning our first human trials. And let me tell you, the results are unbelievable. *Unbelievable*. In fact, we might just be about to change the world forever.'

By now, a few little whispers have begun to hiss around the hall. The odd snort. A scoff. Sophie knows how the dissenters feel. The whole thing reminds her of an infomercial, rather than a lecture. Some snake-oil salesman promising miracles for nine easy payments of nine ninety-nine.

'What a fraud,' Sophie whispers.

Ben nods, though whether he is agreeing with her or simply acknowledging the fact she's spoken, she's not sure.

'Now I know there have been numerous false dawns over the decades. A while back, there was a lot of noise and excitement over cellular reprogramming. This idea that we could simply rejuvenate old tissue. Make the old young again. Sadly, that really does look like science fiction. But all is not lost. You see, after years of research, my team and I have found the answer is far simpler than we had originally anticipated. In fact, it's just three syllables long: *telomeres*.

'For those of you who haven't heard of telomeres before, the best way to think of them is as a sort of protective cap that sits on the end of each strand of our DNA. As we get older, these caps gradually wear away. Until eventually, when they get too short, our cells can no longer reproduce and our DNA begins to fray at the ends. Things begin to unravel. Break. Eventually we die.

'But what if we were to take these caps and then add a protective layer to them, so that our cells were free to replicate indefinitely? Then, there'd be no degradation. No destruction. In other words, no more ageing.

'And what then, I hear you ask. What happens if every single one of us simply stopped getting older? If we no longer had to worry about how long we had left on the clock? Well, that's where things gets really interesting. And perhaps, as a scientist rather than a philosopher, I'm not best placed to answer. But if it's OK with Professor Grindthorpe,' he nods at the tweed-clad academic who is sitting in the front row, 'I'd like to throw my hat in the ring and hazard a guess. And I have to say, I'm rather optimistic about what that world would look like. You see, rather than the nightmarish dystopia that pop culture would have us believe in, I think society would actually become both happier *and* fairer if we stopped ageing. Happier, because almost overnight, regret would become a thing of the past. There'd be no more soul-searching decisions. Should I go here or go here? Study this or study that? Do both, I say. Do more. Do it all. It's not like you don't have the time.

'As for fairer, that's a no-brainer. After all, isn't one of society's biggest problems that we all start the race from a different place? This guy over here happens to be privately educated and descended from seven generations of landed gentry, while this one is the first person in her family to learn how to write her own name. But with unlimited time at our disposal, we could change all that. We'd have a chance to catch each other up, so that eventually, over the course of, say, a few hundred years, we'd reach a truly level playing field. I'm not saying we'd be completely equal. We're still competitive animals at heart. But with time on our side, we'd have a shot at creating a true meritocracy, wouldn't we?'

As the doctor continues to talk, Sophie finds herself feeling not just incredulous but furious at this nonsense. How on earth is this lunatic allowed a public platform? Yet when she turns to sneak another look at Ben, she's surprised to find an expression of deep concentration on his face. She follows his gaze back to the stage, where Dr Andersson is by now glistening under the lights, further adding to the impression of a slightly melted waxwork figure. She gives an involuntary shudder.

Surely, there's no way Ben is buying into this rubbish.

Is there?

10

When the talk is finally over, Sophie drags Ben from the hall and makes a dash for the complimentary wine in the lobby. She needs a drink after that ordeal. She needs several.

As she makes a beeline for a bottle of Merlot, however, she becomes aware that Ben is no longer with her. She turns to see that the evening's speakers have emerged from backstage and are now congregating around the lobby. Boring Cultural Studies Lady stands awkwardly in the corner chewing her nails, while Philosophy Turtle hunches hopefully over a mountain of unsold textbooks, his pen poised and ready to sign, despite the fact that no one in the room appears to be paying him the slightest bit of attention. Instead, the few people that are here are focused exclusively on Dr Andersson, who stands in the centre of the room like some Z-list celebrity, meeting and greeting his adoring public.

Which, to Sophie's horror, includes Ben.

She turns back to the table and fills a plastic cup to the brim with plum-coloured wine, knocking it back in one gulp. She is midway through pouring another, when a roar of laughter interrupts her, Andersson's laugh ringing out longer and louder than anyone else's. Sophie scowls, swallows another huge swig of wine, then grabs the rest of the bottle and reluctantly sidles up to the small circle that has formed in the centre of the room. She intends to convince Ben to leave, but when she gets there, she's irritated to find him talking directly to the doctor, their heads bowed together, engaged in deep conversation. She hovers at a distance, too far to follow what they're saying, but too close to retreat without looking weird. She stands awkwardly, sipping her wine, until at last Dr Andersson notices her. 'Can I help you, young lady?' He flashes a set of glacier-white teeth in her direction, although the muscles in his face hardly move.

Before she can answer, Ben turns around. He's smiling, too: a strange, slightly punch-drunk grin she's never seen before. She thinks back to the joke he made at the start of the evening. About this being a cult meeting.

'Oh, right. Doctor, this is my friend, Sophie. Sophie, this is Dr Andersson.'

'I know. I was at the talk, remember?'

Ben's smile falters a little, but Dr Andersson's artificially white grin only grows wider. 'An absolute pleasure to meet you, Sophie. I was just telling your friend Benjamin here about the latest round of human trials for our Evergreens Programme. We're looking for volunteers at the moment. We like to think of them as our very own pioneers, heading for the promised land, bravely paving the way for future generations.'

'Nice. And are your pioneers planning on slaughtering a whole continent of indigenous people when they get there?'

She'd meant it as a joke, but Ben looks horrified. Dr Andersson only laughs though. 'I sense that you have some reservations about my work?'

Sophie shrugs. It's not the doctor's *work* that's annoyed her so much. It's more Ben's reaction to it. That he's being taken in by this charlatan. 'I guess I'm just a little sceptical.'

'About the science? Well, that's understandable. Before antibiotics were discovered, people accepted dying from childbirth or tonsillitis as just a fact of life. God's will, or what have you. But now it's almost unimaginable. It's a tragedy if it happens. I suspect that someday soon, we will look at ageing in the same way.'

'And I suppose you'll be first in the queue for treatment?'

'Alas, I fear it will all come too late for me. At the moment, we're only accepting volunteers who are in peak physical condition. A club I'm afraid I no longer qualify for.' He pats his abdomen and chuckles. 'One day, however, I envisage everyone having access to this treatment. Old, young, rich, poor. One day, I envisage anti-ageing as a fundamental human right.'

Sophie's eyes widen in disbelief. 'But you can't really want *everyone* in the world to stop ageing? That's insane. I don't know if you've noticed, but the population is already out of control. The air, the sea, the soil. The earth can't cope with all of us as it is. It's straining at the seams. And you want everyone to suddenly stop dying?'

The doctor's smile tightens a little. 'Well, that's not *quite* what I'm suggesting. As I said earlier, the end of ageing doesn't automatically equal immortality. It's not only growing old that kills us. No matter how good the technology is, cars will still crash. Viruses will still break out. People will still choke on chicken bones and slip getting out of the shower. Natural disasters. Murders. Suicides. Anti-ageing won't fix any of that. And while it's true our Evergreens will live for longer, centuries longer in some cases, none will keep going indefinitely.'

'But that's still a pretty major problem, isn't it? Even if people only live an extra fifty years, the pressure that would put on the environment would be unbelievable. And then there's society to think about. It would stagnate. What about jobs? Houses? My generation has already been screwed over by the one above us hoarding everything for themselves. And you want to give them another century or two to vacuum up what few crumbs have been left on the table? Cheers, doc. Sounds like a hell of a future you're cooking up.'

'Sophie, come on—' Ben begins, but Dr Andersson waves a hand.

'No, no. She makes some good points. In truth, ones I don't necessarily have all the answers to at the moment. Although, in my defence, I'd argue that it's not my *job* to provide those answers. Remember, society has always bristled at the dawn of any technological revolution. When Gutenberg introduced his printing press, people thought the mass availability of Bibles would lead to our moral ruin. When telephones were invented, people feared that civilisation would unravel now that we no longer needed to meet face to face to talk. Trains, television, the internet? All were met with suspicion, scepticism and fear. Yet each time, society has found a way to adapt. More than adapt. It's thrived.'

Sophie snorts. 'I'm sorry, but that sounds awfully like a cop-out to me. Did society thrive after the invention of the machine gun? Or crack cocaine? Are you honestly telling me that you're happy to take no responsibility for your so-called invention whatsoever? That you're happy to wave your magic wand and then walk away, letting someone else figure out how we live with it?'

'That's not what I'm saying to you at all. I'm simply stating that I can't speak for the future. When it comes to the present, however, I can assure you I take my ethical responsibilities incredibly seriously. For instance, your point about overpopulation is something we've discussed in great detail. Which is why we've taken the decision to sterilise anyone that takes part in our initial trial.'

Sophie stares back, speechless. She's not sure if he's joking or not. The whole concept is simultaneously ridiculous and disturbing. She shakes her head vigorously, ready to argue her point. As she does, however, she somehow loses her footing. She stumbles backwards and launches the entire contents of her plastic tumbler down the front of her white dress.

Chaos erupts. Ben dives to grab a fistful of napkins from the nearest table, while Sophie apologies to the doctor, her cheeks burning with embarrassment.

'Not at all,' he says, his flashbulb smile back with a renewed vigour. 'We'll have to continue our conversation another time. It was most... illuminating.'

It takes her fifteen minutes in the bathroom to dry off, but it's clear her dress is ruined. She needs to go home and change. The night is as good as over.

When she gets back to the foyer, the crowd of students have mostly dispersed. Boring Cultural Studies Lady is slumped over the remains of the free bar, while Philosophy Turtle stands forlornly in the corner, piling his unsigned books into boxes. Dr Andersson, meanwhile, has disappeared altogether. For a horrible moment Sophie worries that he's taken Ben with him. But then suddenly he's beside her again, an outstretched arm ready to console her.

'Are you OK?'

'You mean apart from making a complete idiot of myself?'

'Don't be silly. It could have happened to anyone.'

'Yeah, but it happened to me. I'm so clumsy sometimes. I hate it.'

'Really, it's fine. Besides, it's probably for the best.'

'What do you mean?'

'Just that things were getting pretty heated between you and Victor back there. I guess he's lucky he didn't end up with a bottle of wine over *his* head, huh?'

'Hey, it's not my fault he was such a creep. I mean, talk about deluded, right?'

Ben shrugs.

'What? So you agree with what he was saying? You think to hell with the planet, we should all just castrate everyone and live forever?'

He holds up his hands. 'I'm going to invoke my legal right to remain silent on this one.'

'Chicken.'

'I just know when I can't win. Anyway, if you want to carry on the fight, why don't you drop him a line?' Ben reaches into his tracksuit and holds up a business card.

Sophie catches a flash of a logo, a silver pine cone, before he slips it back into his pocket.

'You took his card?'

'No comment.'

'So what? Are you two, like, best friends now? Drinking buddies?'

'No comment.'

'Ugh, you're infuriating.'

'And you're the one who decided to hang out with a law student.' He laughs, steering her towards the exit. 'Now come on. Let's get you home before you throw any more wine around.'

2070

III

The policeman presses a button on his deck – a portable holographic projector about the size of a pack of playing cards – and a 3D image snaps into the air.

Sophie flinches, braced for another Virtual Assistant.

But the image that hovers in the air isn't a person. It's a document. Something ancient. An antique. From back when they still used paper. Yellow and frayed at the edges, with a coat of arms printed in red ink at the top. A lion and a unicorn. And underneath that, three words:

CERTIFICATE OF BIRTH

'We drew a blank on the Digital Citizens Index,' the policewoman says. 'We had to dig back through the archive until we found him. A lot further back, as it happens.'

Sophie squints to read the smear of handwriting. Black slashes of old-fashioned biro, the kind they'd used back when she was at school. Still, the name is unmistakeable:

BENJAMIN ANTHONY WALKER

'Obviously, we assumed it was a mistake. I mean, if Mr Walker really was born in 1987, that would make him... Well. He'd be your age.'

She stares hard at Sophie. By now, she has dropped the sweet, nervous act. Her voice is hard. Cold. Her eyes are wild with accusations.

'But then we started digging, didn't we, Detective Gilligan?'

'We did. We dug.'

She swipes the deck and the image fans out to reveal three additional documents. Three more birth certificates. A different name and date on each.

NADIA HOWLEY, born 1988

MARTIN HARDRIDGE, born 1989

ADAKU OLUWA, born 1988

'These were the other three cases we mentioned earlier. The ones that resembled your husband's. And do you know what? We found something funny.'

'Funny as in strange,' Detective Gilligan clarifies. 'Funny as in most peculiar.'

'You see, like Mr Walker, all of the three victims – Miss Howley, Mr Hardridge and Ms Oluwa – were born at the end of the twentieth century. Yet each of them initially appeared to be much, much younger than they really were. And, like Ben, all three also lived in London. And finally, like Ben, all three arrived in hospital at some point in the last five years having collapsed into a coma with no obvious cause. After which, they each underwent some sort of rapid cellular degeneration which led them to age prematurely. Or rather, if their birth certificates are to be believed, belatedly.'

Sophie sits motionless. Conscious of the detectives watching her, she does her best to give nothing away. Now is the time to speak, she realises. To tell them everything she knows. Yet, something about their demeanour makes her wary. They seem less intent on helping Ben than of accusing him of a crime. Perhaps in that case, it would better to say nothing? A phrase drifts back to her across the decades:

No comment.

She smiles inwardly. Ben would like that. She makes up her mind to keep quiet. To listen carefully. To wait and find out how much they already know.

Although, as it turns out, it doesn't take long for them to put their cards on the table.

The policewoman is the first to break the deadlock. She

pushes a button on the deck and the images collapse into thin air.

'Now I'm going to ask you a question, Mrs Walker. And I'd like you to think very carefully before you answer it. What do you know about the Evergreens Programme?'

2007

11

'Are you sure this is OK? I don't want Nina to get the wrong idea.'

Ben swallows hard.

It's late March, a few weeks before the end of term, and he and Sophie are squeezed onto the hot, cramped carriage of the 17.42 Chiltern Railways from Marylebone to Moor Street. When he'd first suggested they attend his uncle Mal's sixtieth birthday party in Birmingham, it had seemed like a great idea. A whole weekend with his favourite person in the world. What could be better than that? Yet so far, the journey has been unbearably tense, on account of the fact that Sophie keeps bringing up his fictitious girlfriend.

Not that it's surprising really. By now, Ben's backstory about Nina has taken on novelistic proportions. There's an almost impossible tangle of details to try and keep track of, most of which have been cooked up to explain away her enduring absence, and provide a tangible reason for why Sophie has yet to actually meet her. This time he'd spun some nonsense about her Shih Tzu puppy, Bruno, having a seizure and requiring emergency medical treatment (remembering this now, he realises how insane the situation has got, having invented an imaginary illness for his imaginary girlfriend's imaginary dog).

'It's fine,' he replies. 'I already told you; she's totally cool with us. She knows we're just friends.'

Just friends.

The words feel like a physical blow. Yet somehow, he keeps smiling.

He swallows down his self-hatred and once again tries to change the subject.

After what seems like an eternity, the train finally shudders to a stop, spewing its passengers into the chilly early evening. As Sophie follows Ben down the platform and out of the station, she's struck by the silver sci-fi bubble of Selfridges department store, which injects a sense of futuristic excitement into the otherwise drab landscape. From there, however, the city quickly becomes less interesting, the same bland corporate loop of chain stores that are familiar to cities all over the world. She could be in Sydney or New York or Toronto. Still, her initial impression is that it is neither as ugly nor depressing as its reputation, or Ben for that matter, has led her to believe.

A small, morally deficient part of Sophie had initially dared hope that this trip might prove an opportunity for her and Ben to get drunk and no-so-accidentally fall into bed with each other. To her disappointment, however, he'd booked her a room at a local Holiday Inn, explaining there was no space for her at his uncle's flat.

'Great,' she said, forcing a cheery smile.

So much for a dirty weekend.

Once they've dropped off her bags at the hotel, they hop on a bus and begin a long, stop-start journey into the suburbs. Peeking through the windows, she sees a far less welcoming landscape beginning to unfurl. Crumbling council flats, graffiti-smeared hoardings, bookies, off-licences, takeaways, payday loan lenders. She turns back to Ben.

'So what's your uncle like?'

'Mal? Oh, he's great. I mean, he's a bit rough around the edges. But he's a teddy bear at heart. And he'll *love* you.'

Sophie laughs. 'Are you sure? He'll probably think I'm some snotty southerner, here to laugh at his primitive ways.'

'He won't. I promise, he'll adore you,' Ben says, before adding more quietly: 'Everybody does.'

When they eventually arrive at the social club, Sophie's heart sinks. While she wasn't expecting anything fancy, she's still not prepared for the brutal concrete building that sits on the corner of a dimly lit residential road. With its faded sign and coils of barbed wire strung around the perimeter fence, it looks more like a halfway house than a party venue. Inside, the décor is like something from the 1970s. Brown carpet and wood-panel walls, the ceiling a stomach-churning shade of nicotine yellow – hardly surprising considering the haze of cigarette smoke that hangs in the air.

As she follows Ben deeper into the dingy club, she can't help herself from making mental comparisons to her own family gatherings. It had been her father's fiftieth the previous year, and her mum had gone all out, getting a team of interior decorators to splash the village hall with bunting and flowers and balloons and fairy lights, everything carefully coordinated in either silver or white. She'd hired caterers for the event, uniformed waiters and waitresses sauntering around with trays of hors d'oeuvres and fizzing glasses of Veuve Clicquot, while a local string quartet had been booked to play classical covers of Dad's favourite pop songs. Sophie remembers rolling her eyes at the time. It was so cringy. But it was also sort of sweet. Mum had put so much hard work into researching and overseeing everything that even Sophie had to admit it looked pretty magical in the end.

Magical is not a word she would use to describe Mal's birthday party. The only decoration is a limp plastic banner that has been sellotaped to the back wall that reads: *Happy Birth*, the 'day' presumably having gone missing at some point in the previous four decades. The entertainment consists of an ancient stereo system in the corner playing two-tone ska at tinnitus-inducing volume, while the buffet is an unappetising beige spread, which mostly consists of sausage rolls, crisps and stale ham sandwiches.

As soon as Ben's uncle spots them, he rushes across the room, engulfing them both in an enormous bear hug. For a moment, Sophie is terrified. Uncle Mal, or *Call-me-Malcolm*, as he introduces himself, is a colossus of a man, with the unmistakeable aura of an English football hooligan. His freshly shaved head bears all manner of bumps and scars, one of his ears is a misshapen flap of a thing, and his arms and hands are smeared with a sleeve of green tattoos. Thankfully, it quickly transpires that he is also kinder and gentler than almost anyone else she has ever met, his eyes sparkling when he speaks to her.

'Sophie, is it? Yeah, Benny-boy told me all about you.'

She shoots a glance over at Ben, surprised. Was it really possible Ben had mentioned her to his uncle?

'*Mal*,' Ben hisses. 'You're embarrassing me.'

'Ben's told me all about you, too.' Sophie beams. 'So, are you having a good birthday party?'

'It's got a lot better since you two arrived.' He grins, before turning to Ben. 'Have you seen your mates yet?'

'Huh?'

'Didn't I tell you? I invited a few of the lads from your school. I figured you'd get sick of hanging out with us old codgers all night. I think they're over at the bar.'

Sophie watches the blood drain from Ben's face as she follows his gaze across the room, where she is surprised to see some people she recognises. Two boys, one with a shaved head, the other with a blonde mohawk. Before she can say anything, Darren spots them and waves. Forcing smiles, they head to the bar, where Ben greets the boys with a slightly uncomfortable series of handshakes and fist bumps and high fives, before he steps back to introduce Sophie. 'And this is—'

'I know who this is.' Darren laughs. 'We met before,

right? Back in Melbourne. With those other chicks. Do you remember, Paul?'

Paul nods enthusiastically. 'Good to see you again.'

'Jesus, I have so many questions,' Darren continues. 'Starting with, what the hell are you doing in Birmingham?'

Sophie laughs. 'Now *that* is a long story. But first, who do I have to dismember to get a drink around here?'

As the evening progresses, the awkward foursome gradually warm to each other's company, helped along by a steady supply of alcohol, which Sophie notes is astonishingly cheap. She learns that Ben has only seen the other two boys a handful of times since returning from Australia, and only once since he'd left for university. Both of them have stayed local, Darren taking up an apprenticeship as a mechanic, while Paul is now an executive at his dad's wholesale company. To her immense relief, she finds that both of them have matured significantly since she'd seen them last, particularly Paul. Gone is the boorish banter, replaced instead by a quiet confidence and a surprisingly sharp sense of humour.

It's refreshing to be out somewhere like this, she decides. While the cultural stuff Ben drags her to is great, the art galleries and films and plays and all the rest of it, it's nice to be back in her natural habitat, joking around with a glass in one hand and cigarette in the other. Even Ben seems to have finally loosened up a bit, drinking more than usual, talking and laughing with his friends.

As the hours roll on, she begins to feel pleasantly tipsy. They chat to Uncle Mal's terrifying friends. They even dance, jumping around to the distorted buzz of The Specials and Bad Manners that blasts from the stereo, until she suddenly notices that Ben is no longer by her side. She scans the room, but there's no sign of him.

Leaving Darren and Paul on the dance floor, she wanders over to the bar to look for him. Then she checks the toilets, calling his name through the door. When she receives no reply, she decides to look outside, just in case.

Even before she reaches the front door, she hears shouting. A man's voice, loud and angry. She freezes, reminding herself that she's in a strange city. The last thing she needs is to stumble into a brawl. But then another shout rings out. This time she recognises the voice. With a growing sense of dread, she pushes open the door to find Ben and Mal squaring up to one another, Ben gripping onto the scruff of his uncle's collar, Mal's fist hovering mid-air.

At the sight of her, they break apart. Mal brushes himself down and marches off, muttering obscenities as he stalks away.

'Hey,' she says, moving towards Ben. 'What's going on? Are you OK?'

He looks at her, and for the first time she notices that his eyes are red, his cheeks streaked with tears. 'It's nothing.'

'Well, it's obviously not nothing. You don't have to hide it from me. I can see you're upset. Did he—'

'Jesus fucking Christ, Sophie. I said it was nothing, didn't I?'

For a horrible second, she thinks he's going to lash out at her. Instead he turns and storms away in the same direction as his uncle, leaving Sophie standing outside the club.

A moment later, the door swings open again. It's Paul, a bleary grin on his face, a shot glass in each hand. 'There you are. I thought you'd left or something. What the hell are you doing out here? It's bloody freezing.'

She shakes her head. 'I was… I was looking for Ben…'

'That's weird. Mal was looking for him earlier, too. Said he had something to tell him. You know what these family dos are like. They'll be spilling their guts to each other in the bogs or something. Now are you coming back in or what?'

Sophie takes a final look down the road. But Ben has already disappeared.

'Here, do you want this?' Paul asks, holding out a shot glass for her to take, the familiar aniseed sting of Jägermeister wafting towards her.

She thinks about Ben's furious face. His snarled words. Her shock already hardening into anger. It's not her fault he's had a fight with his uncle, is it? There's no need to take it out on her. She was only trying to be nice.

'Sure,' she says, snatching the glass. 'What the hell. You only live once, right?'

12

When Ben awakes the next morning, for a brief, beautiful moment, he remembers nothing of the night before. There is only a vast black void where his memory should be. He has no idea where he is. He doesn't even know *who* he is.

But then he opens his eyes, and reality lurches in.

He is sprawled across his uncle Mal's sofa, fully dressed except for one shoe. On the coffee table, the dregs of a whisky bottle, two glasses still standing beside it. He sits up. Nearly throws up. Breathes deeply through his nose. Stays very still, while at the same time trying to piece together the gaping holes in the night before.

How had everything gone so wrong? Especially when things had begun so brightly. Despite the crummy surroundings, Sophie had seemed to enjoy herself. That's one of the million things he loves about her. She has a way of finding the fun in even the dreariest situations. Last night, it was infectious. Dancing with the boys. Joking with Mal. She was like a fairy, sprinkling magic dust wherever she went.

Which makes everything else that happened afterwards even worse.

It started at the bar. He'd left Sophie on the dance floor to get a drink, when he'd bumped into Mal.

'Can I buy you a beer, Uncle?'

Mal shook his head. His face dour, eyes serious. 'I need to talk to you, son.'

Ben stifled a sigh. It had clearly reached the point in

the evening where Mal was drunk enough to start getting sentimental. Any minute now he'd throw an arm round his shoulder and tell him how proud he was of him. How proud his *nan* would have been. He might even try and bring up his mum. There had been more than enough nights like this when he had lived with him. Before he could make his excuses and wriggle away though, he found himself being steered outside, clamped in his uncle's cast-iron grip.

Outside, the evening had grown cold. Ben's skin broke into goosebumps. Back inside the club, he could still make out the throb of a bassline. Chatter and cheers. People having fun. Sophie having fun. He desperately wanted to be with her.

'Lovely girl you've got there, Benny-boy,' Mal began.

'Oh, no. We're not together.'

'Really? You could have fooled me. Well, if you're not, you should be. She's a keeper, that one. Don't let her get away.'

For an awful second, Ben envisaged Mal giving him a sex talk. That he'd dragged him out there to outline the perils of STIs and explain the importance of contraception. Instead, he said something else entirely.

'I'm dying, son.'

Ben blinked. The way he'd said it, so flatly, so matter-of-fact, Ben assumed he'd misheard. Or else this was the set-up for a bad joke about getting old. That any moment Mal would burst out laughing and slap his back and get him in a headlock or a bear hug, the way he always had, ever since he was a kid. But Mal just kept talking.

'Cancer of the pancreas. Not that I could point to my pancreas. Somewhere here maybe?' He tapped his stomach. 'I thought I'd pulled a muscle in my back at first. Turned out it was a bit more serious than that. A lot more serious.'

Ben felt like he was falling. As if a trapdoor had opened up in the chewing-gum-flecked pavement and he was tumbling down a long, dark shaft towards the centre of the earth.

Not Mal. He couldn't lose Mal as well.

'But they can treat it, right?' he heard himself say. 'An

operation? Chemotherapy? Radiotherapy? They must be able to do something.'

Mal shrugged. 'I don't think so.'

'You don't *think* so?'

'I mean, the doc laid out some options, but from what I can see, there isn't much point.'

'From what you can see?'

Already, Ben could feel his bewilderment giving way to rage. He'd seen this side of Mal before when he was dealing with his nan's funeral arrangements. His uncle's failure to engage with paperwork. His tendency to put his head in the sand when faced with difficult decisions.

'Well, you know what the quacks are like,' Mal continued. 'A lot of fancy ways to say the same thing. I'm done, basically. Sure, they could try and prolong the inevitable. But I've had mates who've gone down that road. And from what I've seen, the cure is as bad as the disease. Worse, even. Puking into a bucket for weeks on end. Sweats. Cramps. Losing your hair. Not that I've got any to lose. And for what? Another year at most. No, the best thing to do, as far as I'm concerned, is to get my head down and crack on.'

'Head down? Crack on?' Ben was shouting now. 'This isn't a fucking football match we're talking about. This is your life.'

'Exactly. It's *my* life,' Mal yelled back. 'And I'm not going to let some little runt who knows next to nothing about the world tell me how to live what's left of it.'

The next part is a blur. He'd lunged at Mal. Or had Mal lunged at him? It hardly matters. All he remembers is a white-hot fury coursing through him. He couldn't believe this stupid, stubborn old man was refusing to put up a fight. If not for himself, then for Ben. Couldn't he see he needed him? That, without Mal, he had no one else he could call family? He *owed* it to Ben not to lie down and die. He had to fight. He simply had to.

And then, in the middle of all that madness, Sophie had walked in. Sophie. Who has only ever wanted the best for him.

Who has only shown him kindness and concern. And what had he done? Bitten her head off and then abandoned her while he chased Mal back to his flat. When he got here, the argument had continued for hours, the whisky that Mal presented as a peace offering like adding petrol to a bonfire, both of them shouting and crying, until eventually, with nothing resolved, the fight had drained from them, and Ben had collapsed into a drunken, miserable heap.

Now he sits here, his head between his knees, a toxic sheen of sweat coating his skin as his body attempts to purge itself of last night's excesses. He listens for the telltale rumble of Mal's snores from down the hall. Nothing. He's probably up and out already. He's always been an early riser. He'll be picking up a paper. Grabbing a fry-up at the local café. Acting like everything is totally normal. He could go out and look for him. Talk to him about his options. Try to convince him again. But what would be the point? He sees clearly now that he'll never change Mal's mind. And maybe he has no right to? For as painful as it is for him to concede, it is his uncle's life. It's his decision.

Right now, he needs to focus on his own life. That means finding Sophie and apologising. Not just for the way he acted last night, but for everything. He needs to be honest with her. About Nina. About the way he feels for her. Because he can't put it off any longer. The excuses. The endless deception. It's too much.

It's time to tell her the truth.

The bus journey to the city centre is murder. Several times along the way, he is convinced he won't make it. That he is so hungover he will simply collapse and expire. Somehow though, he hangs on, staggering through the city until he reaches the Holiday Inn where Sophie is staying.

He stands in the lobby and tries to call her.

Hi! It's me! Please leave a message after...

He hangs up. Decides to go back to Mal's and wait for her to call. Then he changes his mind. He needs to see her now. He'll go to her room instead. He hits the button for the lift, but it takes forever. He takes the stairs instead, running now, terrified, that she's gone to the train station without him. That he's too late.

By the time he reaches her room, he's out of breath. He has no idea what he's going to say to her. Where does he even begin? He wants to turn and run. Instead he knocks.

No answer.

He knocks again.

It takes her forever to open the door.

So long that he starts to worry that he really has missed her. But then there's a stumble of footsteps, and suddenly Sophie is standing in the doorway. Her eyes scrunched against the light. Her hair morning-wild. Her breath spiked with stale alcohol. She looks surprised to see him. And sad, too. Like whatever he's about to say is coming twelve hours too late.

'Hey,' she says.

'Hey.'

There's an uncomfortable silence, in which Ben struggles for the right way to begin. 'Listen, about last night...'

'It's fine.'

'No. It's not fine. I treated you like shit. Shouting at you. Running off. I acted horribly. I'm so sorry, Sophie. You deserve better.'

'Ben, really. You clearly had some family stuff going on. And we'd all had too much to drink. *Way* too much. My head feels like someone used it as a punchbag. I hardly even remember last night. Seriously. It's fine.'

'Stop saying that. It's not fine.' He takes another deep,

shuddering breath. 'It's not just about last night, either. I've been such an idiot, Sophie. For weeks now. Months. And it's because... Because...'

He stutters, words failing him. To his surprise he realises he's crying. His eyes and nose streaming. He can't remember the last time he cried. Not for years now. Not since the funeral. Even then, it wasn't like this. Uncontrollable. Like some defence deep inside him has been breached.

'Oh, Ben.'

She steps towards him, but he ducks away, determined to finish. 'It's because I love you, OK? It's because I'm fucking in love with you. I always have been.'

She stares at him in shock. Eyes wide. Mouth twisted in confusion. Now she's the one struggling to speak. 'But I don't understand? What about Nina?'

He shakes his head, tears streaking across his cheeks. 'Don't you see? There is no Nina. I made her up. I wanted to... I don't know what I wanted. I guess I was scared and...'

He stops abruptly. Drags his sleeve across his face. Because while he's been talking, the door has gaped open a little wider behind her, allowing him to see into the room for the first time.

To see the bed.

And on that bed, lying there amidst the tossed pillows and crumpled sheets, is a man.

A naked man.

A naked man with a bleached mohawk.

'Paul? You slept with fucking *Paul*?'

Sophie moves quickly to close the door behind her.

It's too late though. He's seen everything he needs to see.

'Ben, wait. Stop. I can explain.'

But Ben doesn't wait. He is already staggering away from her, her words echoing off the walls, distant and meaningless.

He heads back along the corridor and down the stairs. Out through the lobby and into the street.

Where he finally stops, gasping.

He doubles over, clutching his stomach as if he's been stabbed.

And sprays vomit into the gutter.

13

Months pass. Flowers bloom and die.

July arrives. With her second year finished, Sophie is back home for the summer. While friends decamp to festivals and foreign holidays, and her parents disappear to their cottage in France, Sophie opts to spend the full eight weeks at home. Mostly in her bedroom. Mostly listening to sad songs and staring at her phone. Waiting for a text or a call from Ben. A text or a call that even now, months after the party, has still not arrived.

She's tried calling him. She tried almost hourly after he stormed out of the Holiday Inn. Or rather, once she'd managed to get rid of Paul. God, that whole encounter is still excruciating to remember. Not that she remembers a whole lot of it. After Ben had left the party, she'd stayed at the bar, growing angrier with each drink she downed. How could Ben abandon her like that? Eventually, the lights came on and the music stopped, but she wasn't ready to stop drinking yet. There was talk of going to a nightclub, a place called Snobs. But then Darren disappeared and suddenly it was just her and Paul. And then he'd kissed her, or maybe she'd kissed him. And then?

And then it was the morning and Ben was banging at the door and she'd never wanted to die more in her entire life.

She kept trying to call him for weeks. Even when it became obvious he wasn't going to answer. She left long, rambling voicemails begging him to pick up, to hell with dignity. She even thought about going to his digs. She'd never been there before, having never been invited, but she knew roughly where he lived. Maybe she could ask around? Press random buzzers until someone let her in. Or else lie in wait in the bushes, ready to pounce and force him to talk when he walked by?

It was crazy, she knew. But then, she felt crazy. She'd lost her mind. It was the uncertainty that was killing her. The not-knowing of it all. During that godawful garbled conversation in the doorway of her hotel room, Ben had said all kinds of wild things. That he loved her? That Nina didn't exist? None of it made any sense. Ben was her friend. Her best friend. Never mind that she'd been in love with him since virtually the first time they'd met. She'd swallowed down those feelings, determined not to let them wreck their friendship.

He *owed* her a proper explanation.

But that explanation never arrived.

Now that she's back home, she has mostly stopped trying to call him. Rather, she has retreated into herself. She imagines herself as the survivor of a bad accident. Laid up in hospital, drowsy and numb, waiting to recover while the world rolls on without her. She broods. Mopes. Stays in bed for days at a time. She watches films and then forgets them the second the credits roll. Reads books without taking in a single word. She stays away from alcohol altogether, sick of the damage and misery it has wrought on her life. Instead, she takes to comfort eating. She grazes constantly. Chocolate bars. Takeaways. She moves up a dress size. Despises herself. Keeps eating anyway.

And then, just like that, summer is over and it's time to go back to university, where she moves in with a couple of girls she hardly knows in a house in Sidcup, Kent.

For a while it seems as if the summer slump will spill over into autumn. She barricades herself in her room. Sleeps through lectures. Sees no one. But then, one morning, she wakes up early, and it's as if a switch has flipped in her brain. She's still sad. But the sadness feels smaller somehow. It doesn't eclipse everything else. And instead of crawling back under the sheets, she gets up and rummages through her still unpacked suitcase until she finds a pair of jogging bottoms and trainers.

And then, she goes out for a run.

Twenty minutes later, she is back home again, slick with sweat, her face crimson, her heart threatening to hammer its way out of her chest. She hasn't run in years. Not since the gruelling cross-country jogs they made her do at school. But she feels good. Well, not good exactly. Physically, she feels the opposite of good. She feels as if she's going to throw up, pass out and very possibly die. But mentally, she's better then she has been in months. She washes. Gets dressed. Eats a proper breakfast. She even makes conversation with her startled housemates.

And then she takes herself off to class.

From here, things take a turn for the better. Every morning, no matter how bleak the weather is outside or how tired she feels, she forces herself to get up and out. She stays off alcohol, and quits smoking, too, growing tired of hacking up her lungs when she gets back from her morning turn around the local park. And she keeps going to class. More than at any other time in the previous couple of years, she throws herself into her studies. She reads more. Takes better notes. In early October, she auditions for a role in a play, a strange and hallucinatory piece called *4.48 Psychosis* by one of her favourite writers, Sarah Kane. Though the script is unbelievably dark, Sophie finds something strangely cathartic about the poetic fragments, and sets about channelling the preceding months of misery into a startlingly strong performance, one that wins her praise from her tutors and fellow students alike.

She realises she's getting better.

More time flitters by, the days growing shorter, colder, darker, until one day it occurs to her that, for the first time in as long as she can remember, she's not thinking about Ben. Even when she does, it no longer brings with it the tsunami of sadness it once did. December arrives. Party season. Not that she's much of a party animal any more. Her old friends, the dropouts and the drunks and the drifters, have all faded from her life now. These days she socialises almost exclusively with her housemates. Melissa, an English literature undergraduate, and Farida, who is studying something called Anthropology and Visual Practice and who has recently converted their downstairs bathroom into a makeshift darkroom. Both girls are smart and interesting and diligent in their studies, and have introduced Sophie to hitherto unknown pleasures, such as going out for sushi and skipping the sake, or forgoing the pub in favour of the local Moroccan coffee house, where they sit and drink sweet mint tea and talk politics, discussing whether they think Gordon Brown is doing any better than that crazed warmonger Blair, or whether this new guy in America, Barack-something-or-other, really stands a chance at becoming president.

A week before they are due to break up for the Christmas holidays, Farida arranges a house night out. Sophie is initially sceptical. Not only does she have a final piece of coursework to hand in before she breaks up, but she has another play coming up in January, having recently won the role of Lulu in a production of Mark Ravenhill's *Shopping & Fucking*, and she needs to start learning her lines. Farida is persistent though, promising it will not be a wild night out, but a simple pub meal where, thanks to a family connection, she has a fifty per cent discount.

And so, a few days later, the three of them catch the Overground train to London Bridge, where Farida leads them to a not-terribly-promising-looking place called The Great Fryer of London.

Farida shrugs when Sophie raises an eyebrow. 'What can I say? My aunty works for the Tourist Information Centre. It was either this or half-price tickets to *We Will Rock You*.'

As it turns out, the pub is far better than any of them

are expecting. The food is simple but tasty and the staff are lovely, especially the Portuguese waiter, Tomas, who brings over Sophie's mocktail and spends way longer than necessary explaining the ingredients to her.

'He was flirting so hard.' Melissa laughs once he's out of earshot. 'You should give him your number.'

Sophie looks at the table. It's still too soon for anything like that.

After the meal is finished, they stay and talk. Once again Sophie finds herself marvelling at how little she misses drinking. She'd always thought of alcohol as being central to her self-confidence. A vital component to keep the conversation flowing. Yet sober, she finds herself talking more than ever, only she never slips into the slurred, slightly unhinged rants that used to characterise her late-night conversations. As impossible as it seems, life is actually more fun like this.

By the time they're finished, they are pretty much the last customers left in the place, the staff already wiping down the tables and stacking the chairs for the night. They pay the bill, Sophie blushing as Tomas thanks her a little too enthusiastically, and then they head for the door.

But then she stops.

Because sitting at the bar, dressed in a chef's whites, is a member of kitchen staff. And though he has his back to her, she recognises him instantly. The slope of his shoulders. The curve of his spine. She'd know him anywhere.

As if sensing her, he turns in slow motion. And there he is. The face she hasn't seen in eight months. In a second, the world around her dims to nothing. The restaurant. Her friends. It's as if she is back on the barren set of *4.48 Psychosis*, a stark white spotlight suspended above each of them. The only two people in the world.

For a moment she forgets everything. The fight. The abandonment. The pain. There is only a rush of relief at seeing him again. A pulse of pure joy that begins in her stomach and radiates outwards. Her instinct is to run to him. To throw her

arms around him. She sees the same thing in his face. She's
certain of it. He's happy to see her.

But then his expression falters. The lights come back up.
And suddenly, they are just two people who kind of sort of
used to know each other a bit.

Or at least thought they knew each other.

Ben stands. Starts to walk towards her. Then stops
awkwardly, stranded halfway between her and the bar. He
raises a hand.

'Hey.'

'Hey.'

Behind her someone says her name. Farida or Melissa. She
doesn't know. She hardly hears them. She mumbles something
about bumping into an old friend. About meeting them back
at home. And then they are gone, and Ben is leading her to a
quiet corner, away from the other staff. He unstacks a pair of
chairs and they take a seat. For the first time in months, she
has a powerful urge to drink. Who has she been kidding all
this time? Sobriety is horrible. If she'd had a few glasses of
wine, she could take control of things. Speak her mind. As it
is, they both sit nervously, until finally she breaks the silence.

'So how long have you worked here?'

He looks at his lap. Coughs. 'A year and a half.'

'A year and a half?' she says, struggling to keep her
composure. 'And you never thought to mention...' She trails
off, shaking her head. It's unbelievable. But then again, it's
not like it's the first lie he's told her. She wonders how many
things he's concealed from her.

Another uncomfortable silence settles over them. Sophie
wonders if she should get up and leave. But then Ben speaks
again.

'Mal's dead.'

For a second, she thinks she's misheard him. But then he
looks up, and she sees at once it's true.

'Oh, Jesus. I'm so sorry, Ben. When? How?'

'A few months back. Cancer. The stubborn bastard

wouldn't get treated. He wouldn't even tell anyone about it. No one except…'

Sophie thinks back to the night at the social club. Ben and Mal fighting in the street.

'He told you, didn't he? At his birthday party. That's when you found out?'

He shrugs. 'I'm sorry I was so awful to you that night.'

'No. I mean, you had every right to be. You had all that going on. I'm the one who should be sorry. If I'd known, I never would have… Fuck.'

They lapse into silence again. The unwelcome spectre of Paul falls between them. Ben looks down at the table again. Sophie begins to panic. She has so much to say. So many questions to ask. But she doesn't want to scare him off or make him angry. If they part on bad terms tonight, who knows if she'll ever see him again? Yet if this really is the last time they speak, she can't leave things like this. She has to find out if the things he'd told her were true.

She takes a deep breath.

Before she can say a word though, he looks up. 'Listen. They'll be closing up here in a minute. I need to get changed and grab my stuff from upstairs.'

Sophie's heart stops. 'Oh. I thought… Never mind…'

'No. We need to talk. Just wait for me, will you? Outside. I'll be five minutes.'

Sophie waits so long that she begins to fear he isn't coming at all. That he has simply sneaked away via a back exit. Skipped through a fire escape. Jumped out of a window. *Just one more minute*, she tells herself. *If he doesn't show in the next minute, I'll walk away and never look back.*

But then, suddenly, here he is, bundled up in the same blue

parka he's worn since she first met him at The Gipsy Moth over a year ago.

They begin to walk, aimlessly at first, chatting rather than talking. Little meaningless morsels of nothingness, like two old friends catching up. The weather. The news. Ben tells her a bit about his work in the kitchen, and as he does she is taken aback by his passion. Again she finds herself swallowing down her anger that he'd never mentioned it in all the time they'd spent together. She considers how strange it is that you can know someone so well, yet there can still be whole areas of their life you have no access to. Like finding a locked door – or rather, a whole hidden floor – in the house you call home.

Somehow, they find themselves at the train station. They head to the platform, as they have a hundred times before. And while neither of them says anything directly about Nina or Paul or any of the rest of it, it's OK. It's almost normal.

Once they've boarded the train, their small talk is quickly drowned out by the rattle of the carriage and the screech of the rails. And so they just sit here. Side by side. Their shoulders and thighs pressed up against each other. And maybe this is language enough? At the very least, there seems to be an unspoken understanding between them when, ten minutes later, the train shudders to a stop and Ben reaches out a hand and, still without a word, guides her lightly towards the door. Through the winter streets. Their hands pressed firmly together now, fingers interlocking, eyes straight ahead as they walk in silence to a place she's never been before.

To a block of dingy student digs.

And then Sophie realises they don't need words.

Not right now.

Not as they tumble through the door of his flat and into his room, their bodies already intertwined, everything a blur of hand and hair and skin and teeth and lips and tongues.

Not as she tears hopelessly at his coat, trying to find a way in. Failing miserably and laughing as she steps back so that he can wrestle with the zip himself.

Not until she stops for a moment and looks around his room.

Because it is now that she realises they might need words, after all.

A lot of words.

'Ben, what's going on? What is all this stuff?'

Even in the dim light, she can see that there is something very odd about the room. Whenever she's tried to picture it in the past, lost in her obsessive, forbidden fantasies, she has always imagined a small, austere space. Film and band posters Blu-Tacked to the walls. A guitar propped in one corner. The air heavy with a heady mix of aftershave and boy-musk.

What she never imagined, not even once, was that it would resemble a cross between a science lab and a pharmacy, his desk piled with various pill bottles and syringes, an IV bag and drip by his bed, along with a host of other complicated medical contraptions she doesn't recognise.

She turns back to him to see Ben's eyes are wide and deadly serious.

'There's something I need to tell you,' he says. 'And I need you to promise you won't be angry.'

2070

IV

Sophie plays dumb. Her face gives nothing away.

'Evergreens?' she repeats when Detective Gilligan presses her. 'I've never heard of it. And you're saying all three of them were members of this… club?'

'Programme, Mrs Walker. The Evergreens Programme.'

'We believe it was some sort of research project or…'

'Medical trial, or…'

The police officers look at each other.

'We're not entirely sure,' Detective O'Rafferty admits. 'But all three victims, four including your husband, were wearing one of these.'

She swipes her deck, and a new image appears in the air. A silver chain with a small silver pine-cone pendant.

'We weren't sure what to make of it at first. But then we found this.'

Another image materialises. An ancient business card, again with the silver logo of a pine cone embossed on the front, along with a phone number, a website and a name:

Dr V Andersson, CEO, The Evergreen Programme

'This card was found amongst your husband's paperwork,' Detective Gilligan explains.

He stares at her, waiting for a reply. They both do.

'Well, have you tried calling the number?' Sophie asks.

'Yes,' he says. 'It's disconnected.'

'And the website?'

'Yes.' His tone is clipped. Irritated now. 'It doesn't work.'

'Oh,' Sophie says. 'Well, that is a shame. In that case, I'm afraid it sounds like you have a bit of a mystery on your hands. Maybe you can ask Ben about it? Once he wakes up, that is...'

The detectives share a glance. 'Mrs Walker, if there's something you know but aren't telling us or are scared to talk about...?'

'There isn't,' Sophie says firmly. 'But if I do think of something, I promise you'll be the first to know. Now, if you don't have any other questions, I think I'll be getting back to Ben.'

The detectives stare at her, their indignation smouldering. They look like they definitely have more questions to ask. Lots more questions. But they let her go all the same.

As Sophie reaches the door, however, Detective O'Rafferty calls out to her.

'Don't forget, you can always call us, Mrs Walker. If you remember anything...'

'Anything at all...' her partner adds.

'Anything that might be useful. No matter how small or inconsequential it might seem, please do get in touch. We just want what's best for Ben.'

Sophie nods. And lets the door swing shut.

Once she is outside the room, she allows herself a deep breath. She feels hot. Nauseous. The police know she's lying. But what does it matter? They don't have anything. Not really. And even if they eventually figure it out, what good will it do?

By then, it will be too late to save Ben.

She heaves herself down the hall. Her knees aching. Back spasming. Everything falling apart. When she reaches Ben's room, she pauses. Peers in through the little window at the unchanged tableau:

The boy with a shock of bright white hair. The bed. The machines.

He's still unconscious. Unresponsive.

Only now his face seems even older. The lines more pronounced. The skin starting to sag.

She thinks back to the records the detectives had shown her.

Nadia Howley.

Martin Hardridge.

Adaku Oluwa.

All of them Evergreens. All of them dead within a week.

How long has it been now? Forty-eight hours? So that leaves...

Five days.

She turns from the door. There's no time to lose. Because there is only one person in the world who can help Ben right now. And it's not a doctor or a detective.

No.

The only one who can help him is the person whose name was on that business card.

And Sophie might just know where to find him.

2018

14

Ben hunches under the spluttering, low-pressure shower, alternately scalding and freezing himself as he attempts to feel a little more human. He curses. Nothing works in this house. Heating, plumbing, electrics. Everything is broken. Faulty. Neglected for years. Every now and then he tells himself he should do something about it. Fix it. Call the landlord. Or just move out and start again. Yet somehow, he never quite gets around to it. And so, the problems continue to pile up, proliferating like the spores of mildew which speckle the ceiling above his head, or the stack of unpaid bills on the dining room table downstairs. Just another issue that needs to be sorted out – another time.

The shower gives another spasm, spraying him with a jet of boiling water. He lets out a yelp and then curses. This isn't working. He still feels horrible. Why the hell did he drink so much last night? Still, he doesn't beat himself up too much. Hangovers are practically an occupational hazard in his line of work.

After failing to finish his law degree, he has spent the last decade working full-time in kitchens, most recently at Steel & Stone, an upmarket pizza restaurant where, for the last four months, he has worked as a line chef. Tonight, he is scheduled for an eight-hour shift there, which will mean getting home just after midnight. Assuming there isn't another post-work celebration.

Before that, he must drag his aching body from Slough to London for his monthly appointment at the Evergreens clinic. The thought makes him curse again. In the eleven years that have passed since he first joined the programme, much of the treatment has been streamlined. The complex round of intravenous and intramuscular injections he was initially required to self-administer has thankfully been whittled down to a single tablet, taken once a day. Yet his regular check-up at the clinic, where Dr Andersson personally assesses his health and adjusts his medication accordingly, remains a contractual obligation. Something Victor never fails to remind him of when he shambles in half an hour late each month.

The shower lets out one last burning blast and then cuts out altogether. There's nothing for it. It's time to go.

Two hours later, he arrives at the clinic, his hangover having finally subsided. That's something to be grateful for, at least. Unlike some of his friends, who have begun to lament the crippling side effects of a heavy night out since turning thirty, he finds he can still operate reasonably well on only a couple of hours' sleep, no matter the excesses of the night before. Nor has he had to contend with any of the other physical issues his peers have started to face: their burgeoning beer bellies or retreating hairlines or persistent black bags under their eyes. According to Dr Andersson, he still has the body of a twenty-one-year-old.

Quite literally, in fact.

As he climbs the white stone steps of the anonymous Georgian town house on Harley Street, he remembers his first appointment here. He'd felt nauseous with nerves, unsure he was even at the right address. There was no sign above the door, no building number. The only thing to mark it out from any of the other private health clinics that lined the street – the colonic irrigators and cosmetic surgeons and laser eye correctors and all the rest of them – was a small silver plaque next to the buzzer, which was engraved with the outline of a pine cone. The same logo that had been on Dr Andersson's business card.

This was in the aftermath of his great falling-out with Sophie. Those lost few months he had spent alone in his room. Drunk, mostly. And seething. He was so angry. At Paul. At his nan. At Mal. At Sophie. But mostly, he was angry with himself. University had unravelled by then. He couldn't concentrate. He missed assignments. Skipped class. None of it seemed to matter any more. Somehow, he managed to hang on to his job at the pub. He didn't have a choice about that. It was his sole source of income. Without it, he wouldn't eat. Not that he ate much anyway, his calories coming almost exclusively from the litre bottles of Smirnoff he bought from the corner shop on his way home from work, before locking himself in his room, where he spent the nights drinking and brooding.

Of all the people in the world she could have gone with, it had to be Paul. With his posh job and his daddy's money and his prospects for the future. How could he ever compete with that?

It was confirmation of the same terrible truth he'd always known.

He had nothing to offer her.

It was midway through one of these fevered, furious drinking sessions, while desperately searching through his desk drawers for stray coins so that he could return to the off-licence, that he came across the ivory rectangle of Dr Andersson's business card. He hadn't thought about it since the night of the lecture. A half-memory flickered. He opened up his laptop and typed in the address.

Like the business card, the website was a stark affair. White space punctuated with a few stock photos of glamorous young people. There was no real detail about the project, other than a single slogan in bold black text at the top of every page:

Ageing is a choice.

Reading those words, something in him jolted. Ever since the night on the pier, he'd thought of himself as cursed. His parents had abandoned him. Nan dead. Mal was sick. And now, even Sophie was gone. He saw a bleak future stretching out ahead of him. Hardship. Loneliness. Until eventually something awful came and snuffed him out for good.

Yet staring at the screen, he saw a chink of light in the darkness.

Ageing is a choice.

It didn't have to be like that. He didn't have to end up like his nan. Old and broken, dying alone on the floor of a dingy little flat. Or like Mal. Fading away, strapped to a hospital bed as he gasped his last.

None of it was inevitable.

It could be a choice.

His choice.

He kept flicking through the pages, the screen sparkling with images of beaming twenty-somethings. A project like this – assuming it was real – would change everything for him. Not only would it keep him healthy, but it would buy him time. He'd no longer have to worry about trying to catch up with the likes of Paul. He'd be running a different race altogether. One he'd actually stand a chance of winning.

And so, before he had a chance to talk himself out of it, he fired off an email expressing his interest in the programme, before finally collapsing face down in a drunken stupor.

He awoke the next morning to find a reply already waiting in his inbox. An invitation from Dr Andersson's secretary, inviting him to drop into their offices that very afternoon. That first bewildering, hungover meeting with Dr Andersson had been the beginning of what turned out to be a long, gruelling application process. Months of interviews. Physical tests. Blood work. Written exams. Psychological evaluation. It was like applying to join the Royal Marines. He didn't have a chance. But slowly, the number of applicants dropped away. One hundred became fifty. Then thirty. Until finally, only twelve remained. The chosen few, each of whom were rewarded with a small silver chain with a pine-cone pendant to welcome them onto the Evergreens Programme. He's been wearing it, and coming back to this office, ever since.

He hits the buzzer and a crackly female voice replies.

'Hello?'

'It's Ben.'

A pause. 'Ben? Sorry, we're not expecting any Bens. At least, not at this time of day. The only Ben on my list was due hours ago.'

'Very funny. Come on, Becks. Let me in.'

A longer pause. An audible sigh. And then a click.

Inside, he's greeted by the familiar surroundings of the foyer. White walls. White lights. A few potted bonsai trees the only nod towards decoration. Everything is calm and clean and crisp in here. It reminds him of a private dental surgery. At the desk, he finds the receptionist, Becky, waiting for him. She looks annoyed.

'Don't tell me. Car wouldn't start?'

'Train,' he mumbles. 'Running late.'

'Again?'

'Again.'

As she disappears to print his security pass, he again thinks back to his first time here. There was so much bureaucracy to get through. Endless forms to fill. Disclaimers and waivers. Indemnity statements and limitations of liability. Clause after sub-clause of small print and legal jargon, far beyond anything he'd studied at university. He closed his eyes and scrawled his initials. Ticked the boxes. Hoped for the best.

He'd had to hand over his bank details, too. Not that this was costing him anything. The opposite, in fact. As impossible as it seemed, they were actually paying him to take part in the trial. Good money, too. A lump sum, followed by monthly instalments for as long as he took part in the project. Not enough so that he'd never have to work again. But for someone who still felt a reflexive surge of panic every time he got to the supermarket checkout, it was more than enough confirmation that he was making the right decision.

At last, his pass is ready. He slips the lanyard round his neck and thanks Becky, before making his way through the frosted-glass doors that lie beyond the reception desk. Almost as soon as he's seated in the sterile waiting room, he hears Dr Andersson's door groan open. The doctor's assistant, Mia, sticks her head out and frowns.

'Traffic?'

'Trains.'

She rolls her eyes. 'You'd better come in.'

An hour later and he is back on Harley Street, having completed the usual barrage of tests. Height and weight. Blood pressure, heart rate, oxygen levels. Blood samples. Hair samples. Urine and sputum. As ever, he was given a clean bill of health. Although this was tempered with the usual lecture about the importance of looking after himself. A warning to cut back on his drinking. To eat a healthy and balanced diet. To sleep eight hours a night. 'And your medication?' Dr Andersson asked. 'You're taking it every day?'

Ben nodded. Flapped a dismissive hand. 'Sure, sure.'

'I can't stress the importance of this. Missing even one dose could have catastrophic implications for the trial.'

'Relax, doc. I've managed so far, haven't I? I'm on it. You don't have to worry about me.'

Ben takes a right, heading in the direction of Euston Square. If he times it right, he'll have just enough time to pop home for a shower before his shift at Steel & Stone begins.

Just then, he hears a sound. A flamboyant rapping of knuckles on glass. He looks around to see two young men standing in the window of The Lucky Pig cocktail bar. Michael O'Donohue and Pete Meadows, fellow Evergreens and frequent drinking partners. Ever since the early years of the project, the three of them have met up regularly to enjoy day-long benders, often following their monthly check-ups.

Having successfully got Ben's attention, Michael gestures for him to come and join them, pointing at his beer and miming drinking. Of the two of them, Michael is the wildest. Fresh-faced, with a mane of untameable blonde hair, the man seems to have spent the last ten years perpetually partying. God knows how he supports himself, as he never seems to work.

Michael raps the window again. More imaginary pints are downed. Several of them. Followed by a couple of imaginary tequila shots.

Ben hesitates. He has work in a few hours, and he can't afford to be late.

On the other hand, what's the point of being perpetually

young if you can't have a little bit of spontaneous fun now and then?

And it is just one drink.

He waves at Michael and heads towards the door.

15

Sophie beams.

Dressed in a smart blazer and sensible blouse, she sits at an ordinary dining table in an ordinary kitchen, surrounded by her family. Two beautiful, blonde-haired, blemish-free pre-teens.

Child A and Child B.

Unlike Sophie, however, the children aren't smiling. Rather, they each stare down forlornly at their dinner plates, which are piled with a rather depressing combination of chips, sausages and egg. A faint whiff of chemicals rises up from the plates, on account of the brown paint used to colour the sausages.

Sitting opposite her is a handsome, grey-haired man with a spray of salt-and-pepper stubble. Her husband. She can't remember his name. Like the children, he is also depressed about his dinner. Or at least, Sophie assumes he is depressed. The lights are so bright it is hard to make out the precise expression on his face.

Sophie's family are frozen. Nobody moves a muscle. Nobody breathes. They are like a mannequin family. Shop dummies, heads bent over plates of fake food.

Until someone in the distance calls out an instruction and Child A jerks into life.

'Ugh. Chips again?'

A frown. A scowl.

'Why is dinner always so boring, Mum?' Child B adds.

Her husband attempts to be a little gentler than the children. 'Don't worry, love. Maybe we should get a takeaway instead?'

Despite this barrage of criticism, Sophie's smile doesn't falter. Oh no. She is confident. Calm. In control. After all, she is *Super Mum*. Career woman by day, domestic goddess by early evening. She is the ladder-climbing, glass-ceiling-shattering embodiment of the hopes and dreams of second-wave feminism. Breadwinner, cleaner, cook and carer, all rolled into one.

At least, that's what her notes say.

And so, when confronted by this culinary catastrophe, she doesn't fold. Not Super Mum. Instead, she simply reaches under the table and retrieves a brightly coloured bottle of sauce. Some dreadful, industrially produced, E-number-spiked, corn-syrup-saturated, savoury-flavoured concoction, and slams it down on the table. A spotlight clicks into life, framing the neon-pink bottle, so it seems to glow with an almost radioactive vibrancy. Which is quite appropriate, given the carcinogenic nature of its ingredients.

There's a beat, while the whole family stare in silent wonder at the sauce bottle. And then, with a carefully rehearsed flourish, Sophie stands up and whips off her sensible blazer to reveal a sparkling, not to mention fairly revealing, negligee underneath.

And then she turns.

She turns away from the table. Away from her family. Until she is staring squarely out at the blinding wall of lights. Staring at all of us, obliterating the fourth wall.

There's another beat. And then she winks. Licks her lips. Arches a lone eyebrow. And then she opens her mouth to say four simple words.

And, while they may be the only four words she is permitted to say all afternoon, they are four words more than she normally gets to say, and so she relishes each of them:

'I'm a saucy mummy.'

She freezes again. Her heart rattling. Mouth dry. Her blood humming in her ears.

Until someone, somewhere, shouts out:

'Cut.'

And then:

'OK, let's reset and take it from the top.'

Despite the entire sequence being less than a minute long, it takes the rest of the day to finish filming, the afternoon splintering into countless close-ups and reshoots, not to mention the lengthy break they are all forced to take when Child B has a panic attack and has to be cajoled by her mother to return to the set.

Hours later, once she has finally wrapped for the day, Sophie sits in a trendy West London bar, a gin and slimline tonic in one hand, her phone in the other. Sitting opposite her, sipping at a steaming peppermint tea and also staring at her phone, is her friend Sinead. Like Sophie, Sinead is also an actress. Although unlike Sophie, she gets to appear in actual dramas, rather than adverts for toxic condiments that she takes in order to pay her rent.

That's unfair.

Sophie does still do some real acting. It's just that while Sinead has managed to sustain a reasonably successful TV career for several years now, including a recent walk-on role in *Game of Thrones*, no more than a handful of people ever watch the independently produced plays that Sophie spends her evenings rehearsing and performing.

She's known Sinead for eight years now. Long enough to remember when they were both struggling, agent-less nobodies, turning up at open casting calls and padding out their résumés with days of thankless extra work while dreaming of the big time. Unlike most of her contemporaries from university, who have long since abandoned the arts for the relative stability of teaching, or else retrained and made a fortune in the private sector, Sophie has kept plugging away, taking part-time agency jobs whenever finances necessitate, but never allowing her dream to be snuffed out entirely. And all that work has paid off. Sort of. When someone asks her what she does for a living, she can hold her head up and truthfully answer 'actress'. Even if she does then struggle with the inevitable follow-up:

'Will I have seen you in anything?'

Well, that depends if you watch adverts for poisonous sauces or not.

Still, most days she is proud of what she's achieved. And most days she's certain that, just like Sinead, her big break is only a single successful audition away.

Most days.

Sometimes, however, particularly after shoots like the one today, she begins to feel the familiar doubts gnawing at the edges, and wonders if her chance might have passed her by? If she might have peaked already? If this, whatever *this* is, could be as good as it gets?

'You know, this is the third mum I've played this year,' Sophie says, looking up from the mindless scroll of her Instagram feed. 'I'm thirty-two, for crying out loud. One of the kids today was about thirteen. Do I really look that old?'

'*Of course* you don't look that old,' Sinead says, still staring at her phone. 'But this is showbiz, *dahling*. You know the rules. Twenty-five is middle-aged these days. You're lucky they didn't cast you as a *grand*mother.'

'It's so depressing.'

'What do you expect from an industry that's spent half a century holding up hairless, anorexic pre-teen bodies as the pinnacle of desirability? It's hardly surprising that we're thrown on the scrapheap for a couple of crow's feet.'

'You did *not* just call out my crow's feet.' Sophie grabs hold of her face and pulls back her skin. 'Do you have any idea how much I spend on moisturiser each year?'

'Oh, come off it.' Sinead laughs as she finally looks up. 'You haven't got a wrinkle on you. Besides, being cast as a mum at thirty-two isn't that outrageous really, is it? I mean, is it really so unthinkable we could be mothers at our age?'

Sophie sighs. For the last few years, her social media feeds have been utterly cluttered with puke-inducing pictures of her friends' perfect families. Wild nights out and professional triumphs muscled out in favour of artfully filtered snaps of babies and husbands and dogs and home improvement projects. Melissa and Farida both have toddlers now, while Mags is on to her third. Three kids by thirty? It's insane. Sophie feels like she's still figuring out what she wants from her own life, let alone being custodian for someone else's. Even worse than the barrage of crappy finger paintings on Instagram have been the glances of pity she's started to attract from former friends and strangers alike. Just the other day, she'd made the mistake of making eye contact with a frazzled-looking woman in the park. She had a child in a pushchair, and another strapped to her back, like she was some kind of human climbing frame. The woman smiled back manically, no doubt excited by the possibility of an adult interaction.

'They're lovely,' Sophie said automatically.

'Thank you so much,' the woman gushed. 'They're hard work, but *totally* worthy it.'

An awkward pause. And then the dreaded question:

'Do you have little people of your own?'

Little people?

Resisting the urge to vomit, Sophie shook her head. 'No. I don't.'

The woman had scrunched up her face then. Tilted her head sympathetically. Stuck out her bottom lip. 'Don't worry,' she said. 'There's still time.'

How she managed to escape the park without pushing the lot of them in the pond, she'll never know. Even her own mother has started dropping not-too-subtle hints about making her a grandma, despite the fact her brother Christopher is still living like some eternal bachelor in New York.

'I just don't want you to leave it too late, love,' she says whenever Sophie protests. 'After all, the clock's ticking.'

She could scream. Sometimes it feels like she's walking around with an expiry date stamped on her forehead. A best-before, after which she's useless. Chuck her away, along with all the other barren old maids who have failed to undertake their sole biological purpose on earth. Never mind that she has *chosen* this life for herself. That she has *chosen* to focus on her career rather than changing nappies. And isn't that equally valid? Isn't that why women hurled themselves under horses and chained themselves to railings all those years ago? For the right to choose? And so what if she sometimes wants to die when she sees a cute baby in the street? Or if it feels like a physical blow to her womb when a child hugs a mother on TV? She can swallow it down. Suck it up. Get over it.

Because it's her fucking *choice* to do so.

'Come on, Soph, don't look so depressed,' Sinead says. 'It might be terrible for your career, but there are plenty of upsides to getting older.'

'Such as?'

Sinead thinks for a moment. 'How about no more periods? That's got to be a good thing, right?'

'So, let me get this straight. I get to swap a week of cramps and mood swings each month for years of hot flushes, headaches and low libido? Where do I sign up?'

'Well, at least there's senility to look forward to after that. And then, well, death.'

Sophie lets out a groan and knocks back the last of her gin. 'You know what? This Saucy Mummy feels like getting trashed. Why do you have to be so sensible?'

'Because I'm not nineteen any more and it takes me about three months to recover after a single night out,' Sinead says. 'Besides, I'm due on location at six tomorrow morning. Which means I should probably be getting to bed.' She glances at the clock on her phone. 'Oh, shit, about an hour ago.'

Sophie pouts. 'Fine. Abandon me. See if I care. But I'm warning you, it'll be on your head if you open your news app tomorrow morning to find a slew of male casting directors have been mysteriously massacred overnight.'

Once they've finally said their goodbyes, Sinead resolutely refusing to have her arm twisted into ordering an alcoholic beverage, Sophie begins the long, uncomfortable journey home. It takes forever.

Bus.

Tube.

Train.

Bus.

As she rattles her way west, heading ever further from the capital, she tries not to think about the fact Sinead will already be back home by now, having recently moved to a new apartment in Kensington. It's small, obviously, the way that everything in London is small unless you're a Russian billionaire, but beautifully furnished and perfectly appointed, a stone's throw from all the action London has to offer. Sophie, on the other hand, made the heart-breaking decision to move out of the city about five years ago, having finally admitted to herself that she simply couldn't afford the exorbitant rent. These days, she lives in a drab commuter town, enduring the three-hour round trip between home and the city whenever she has a job. Not that she ever moans openly about the journey. Just a few hours earlier, she was boasting to Sinead about how nice it is to be away from the hustle and bustle of London life. How she has access to the countryside right on her doorstep. How she can be at Heathrow in fifteen minutes.

How, for the first time in her adult life, she has a garden...
While conveniently leaving out the fact that, in the five years
she's lived there, she's never once visited the countryside.
Or been on holiday. And as for the shady patch of concrete
she calls a garden, it's as run-down and miserable as the rest
of the house.

At last she makes it to her front door. She is already
picturing the hot bath she is going to run herself. Plenty of
bubbles. Flickering candles. Maybe even a glass of wine.

As she gets into the hallway, however, she's greeted by
the sound of the television blaring from the living room. A
computerised football match in full swing. She eases open the
door to find Ben on the sofa, a controller clamped between
his fingers.

Ben.

Still as handsome as he was the day she first set eyes on
him back on that beach in Australia. Although that all seems
a lifetime ago now.

As she enters, he doesn't acknowledge her. Doesn't look
up from the screen.

'You're home from work already?' she says. 'I thought
you had a late shift?'

He turns to her. As he does, she's hit by a wave of alcohol
fumes. His eyes are glassy, his face fixed in a familiar goofy
grin.

'Yeah. About that... I was a little bit late for my shift. Just an
hour or so. But then when I got there, it turned out I'd got mixed
up. I was actually scheduled for a double. So technically... I
was eight hours late.' He laughs. 'Crazy, right?'

Sophie silently counts to five before she speaks. 'So they
sent you home?'

'I mean, that's one way of putting it. They sent me home.
Only, permanently.'

There's a burst of noise from the television. Someone
has scored a goal. As Ben turns his attention back to the
screen, Sophie takes the opportunity to leave the room.

There's no point in trying to have a sensible conversation with him tonight.

As she reaches the door, however, he calls out to her, his voice sloppy, his eyes still on the game. 'You know this isn't necessarily such a bad thing. Losing the job. It could actually turn out to be a blessing in disguise. It might give me the time and space I need to figure out, you know… stuff…' He trails off, the thought apparently complete.

'Yeah,' Sophie says. 'Sure. OK. Right.'

She leaves the room. She's too tired to go through this all now.

She's heard it all before, the last time he lost his job. And the time before that.

And the time before that.

16

'Happy anniversary!'

Ben opens his eyes to find Sophie standing over him, a handmade card in her hand, the number *10* written on the front in a shimmer of glitter. A burst of panic roars through his mind.

Shit.

Ever since he lost his job six weeks earlier, he's had trouble keeping track of the days, everything blurring into one endless, bleary, beer-sodden weekend. Although, if he is honest, he's not sure he can pin the blame entirely on unemployment. After all, he's forgotten their anniversary for the last five years running. Not that it's a real anniversary. Their 'getting together' anniversary, Sophie calls it. Although how she can be so sure exactly when that date was, he has no idea. Things hadn't exactly gone smoothly for them. Following their first fumbling kiss in his room, and the hours of explanations and arguments that followed, they had flip-flopped endlessly, coming together and breaking it off for months on end before Sophie finally decided she could live with his decision to continue his treatment and they officially became an item.

He sits up. Coughs. Rubs his eyes. Prepares to put on a show. 'Oh, wow. Thank you *so* much.'

His voice is a sandblasted scrape. He needs coffee. He needs another five hours' sleep. But he's conscious of Sophie watching him. Studying his reaction. He rubs his face again.

Forces himself to look excited. Opens the card. Inside there's a blotchy felt-tip drawing of a duck, a speech bubble coming from its mouth:

Happy Anniversary!

Underneath, a promise of undying love, her name and ten 'x's. One for each year they've been together.

'Thank you so much,' he repeats, relieved to hear himself sounding at least partially alive this time. 'This is lovely. What time is it? It's still dark.'

'Seven thirty,' she says, pointing to the card. 'Look, it's a penguin.'

'I *know* it's a penguin. I can see that. Just like the time... we saw those penguins...'

'St Kilda. And we didn't see them. Remember?'

'Exactly. That's what I meant. St Kilda. Crazy. So long ago now. But *great* memories. Thanks, Soph. It's a lovely card.'

Still, she doesn't leave. She hovers. An expectant expression on her face, despite his miserable track record.

Shit. Shit. Shit.

'Actually, if it's OK with you, I want to wait until tonight to give you your card. I thought we could...' He stumbles. Stalls. Desperately racks his brain. 'I thought we could have a meal together? Make a night of it?'

She smiles then. A flat, slightly disappointed smile. But a smile all the same. 'That sounds perfect.'

'Great. It's a date then. And hey, go easy at lunch. I'm going to make us a feast you'll never forget.'

'Can't wait. Now, why don't you go back to sleep for a few hours, huh?'

He shakes his head. 'I'm awake now. I might as well get up. Apply for a few jobs. Bit of DIY around the house. The early bird catches the worm, right? Something like that?'

She stoops and presses a weary kiss into his forehead. 'Something like that. I'll see you tonight.'

And then she's gone.

When Ben opens his eyes again, it's the afternoon. He sits up with a start. As he does, a crumpled wad of card unsticks itself from his skin and lands on the bed. It takes him a moment to recognise it as the anniversary card Sophie gave him this morning. He sits stunned for a moment, racking his sleep-fogged brain as he tries to remember the details of their exchange.

Card.

Penguins.

Meal – he'd agreed to cook her a meal.

Well, that doesn't sound too bad. He is, after all, a chef. Just then, his attention is snagged by an electronic rasp, coming from somewhere nearby. Heaving himself over the side of the bed, he eventually spots the battered form of his smartphone, half-camouflaged beneath a discarded pair of boxer shorts. He scans the cracked screen. There are around a dozen messages and missed calls. Before he can read them, however, the device begins to vibrate again and Pete Meadows's name flashes across the screen.

'Pete?'

'Where the hell are you?'

'What do you mean, where am I? I'm at home.'

'Home? You didn't get the message?'

'Message? I've literally just woken up.'

'Jesus, Ben. I'm at the clinic. We all are. Victor emailed everyone last night. You're supposed to be here.'

'I don't understand. My check-up isn't for another fortnight.'

'It's not a check-up. He's called an emergency meeting. There's some issue he wants to discuss.'

'What kind of issue?'

'I'm not sure. He wants to talk to us all together. Listen,

I've got to go. Just come here right now, OK? Grab a cab or something.'

'A cab? Do you know how much that will cost?'

But Pete has already gone.

An hour later, his wallet sixty-five pounds lighter, Ben once again finds himself walking into the reception of the Harley Street clinic. As the door swings shut behind him, Becky glares up from her desk.

'I don't even want to know. Just go straight through. They're all upstairs.'

'What's this all about?'

'Not now, Ben,' she says, swatting him away. 'He'll explain everything. Just hurry, will you? Everyone's waiting.'

As Ben makes his way to the conference room, it occurs to him that he hasn't been up here for years. Not since the endless rounds of interviews he'd attended before joining. He remembers one particularly excruciating afternoon, when he'd been asked to deliver a ten-minute presentation to a panel of doctors and psychologists:

What would I do with a thousand years?

It was a goofy task. For one thing, Victor had emphasised countless times that he was only intending to extend lives by a few decades at most – at least at this stage of the programme. The focus for now was squarely on keeping this first batch of participants young and healthy. Any additional longevity was purely a happy side effect. For another, it was practically impossible to imagine what the world would look like that far into the future. A thousand years ago, we were busy fighting Vikings and dying of typhoid. Who knew what the next millennium would look like? Or if there would even still be humans around to see it?

Still, Ben played along. Initially, he'd dedicate himself to study, he told the panel. Law, history, literature, philosophy, economics. He'd learn it all. Immerse himself in knowledge. And then he would set about making a real difference to society. He wanted to change things. To help people. To make the world a better place.

Did he really believe all that stuff? It's hard to say. He liked to *believe* he believed it. Never mind that right then he was struggling to finish his current degree course, let alone sign up for a dozen more. But then that was the whole point, wasn't it? The Evergreens Programme bought him time. Enough time to fix himself *and* fulfil his potential. Enough that he'd have a fair chance at competing with everyone else and become the person he knew he was supposed to be.

And so, he spun his story to the panel.

Educate himself.

Help people.

Save the world.

He sounded ridiculous, but they lapped it up. Nodding. Smiling. Scribbling notes. Once he'd finished, there was a short Q & A session. He batted every question away with an empty answer and an earnest smile. He knew exactly what he was doing. He was level-headed. Pragmatic. Mature. They could rely on him to be an ambassador for the programme.

More nods, more scribbled notes. As the talk came to an end, the room thrummed with positive energy. He thanked them all. Shook their hands. Told them he looked forward to seeing them again soon.

Before he could walk away, however, a middle-aged psychiatrist called Dr Slater put her hand up. Up until then, she hadn't said a word all afternoon, simply nodding and taking notes as he spoke. But suddenly, right at the finish line, it seemed she'd found her voice.

'Actually, if it's OK with you, I wanted to ask how you feel your participation in the project is likely to affect your romantic relationships?'

Ben's smile froze, visions of Sophie swimming through his mind. 'Yes. Well. I'm not in a relationship. I'm single.'

'But will that always be the case? Surely you're not planning on being single forever?'

Ben shook his head, unsure where she was going.

'And assuming you do meet someone,' she continued. 'How do you think your partner will feel about all this? I'm thinking chiefly about sterilisation. That's a big decision to make at your age. One that could affect not just you, but a future partner, too.'

She paused and glanced over at Dr Andersson, who by now was watching her closely, his fingertips pressed together, as if in prayer.

Ben nodded thoughtfully. He'd already answered several questions like this over the course of the selection process. He was on comfortable ground. 'Actually, I agree with you, Dr Slater. It is a big decision. But it's something I'd thought about long before I heard about this project. I've never wanted children. That's not something that's going to change.'

For the most part, this was true. Ben's own childhood had been so troubled and dysfunctional he'd long ago made up his mind not to inflict that on anyone else. Perhaps for a brief while, he'd allowed himself a little fantasy of starting a family with Sophie. But all that was over now.

Dr Slater nodded, seemingly satisfied with his answer. But she still wasn't finished yet. 'Fair enough. But taking children out of the equation, there's no denying that participation in the programme will inevitably impact the dynamic of any future relationships. For example, while I'm sure my husband would be quite happy with me staying young and glamorous forever – not that I'm either young or glamorous – I'm not sure I'd honestly feel the same way about watching him grow old. Assuming we stayed together, I'd be potentially committing myself to becoming his carer. To watching him die.'

Ben's smile wavered a little. 'But isn't that the same with every couple? One will almost always outlive the other. And there are hundreds of examples of successful relationships with large age discrepancies. Charlie Chaplin was married to someone almost forty years younger than him. Which, OK, is kind of weird. But even if a couple are the same age, there are plenty of healthy people who end up caring for a partner who has become disabled through sickness or an accident. It's not exactly without precedent.'

'That's true. But I wonder how many of them go *into* a relationship knowing for certain that that is how it will end up? And then of course there is the possibility of doing it more than once. Dozens of times possibly over the course of an extended lifetime. The same cycle of meeting someone and watching them falter and fade. Assuming that you still have the stomach for love after all that...'

At that moment, Dr Andersson finally intervened.

'I think we may have gotten ourselves a little off-topic here, Carolyn. After all, it's important to remember that this trial is just the first step in what promises to be a far longer journey. If things go the way I think they will, your sad little scenario will become largely irrelevant. Eventually, everyone will have access to treatment, so it won't be a case of one partner ageing and the other staying young. In the future, no one will be left behind.'

Dr Slater frowned. She looked like she had more questions, but Dr Andersson held up his hand. 'Now if everyone's in agreement, I think poor Benjamin here has had more than enough of a grilling for one day...'

Ben stumbled away, certain he'd blown the interview. Dr Slater's questions had genuinely rattled him. Over the course of the last few months, he'd been so wrapped up in his pain at losing Sophie that he'd never once stopped to consider he might meet somebody else. While right then, the idea was unthinkable, he was reluctant to rule it out completely. But Dr Slater had painted a deeply depressing picture. Was that really what the future held for him? A cycle of watching people he loved grow old and die? Was that the price of the project?

And if so, was it worth it?

He was still grappling with that question a few weeks later, when he received an email telling him that he'd been accepted onto the trial. For the briefest moment, he hesitated. Maybe he should just forget the whole thing? Get his head down. Focus on his studies.

But just then, his phone vibrated on his bed and Sophie's number flashed up. For months she'd tried calling him relentlessly, but it had been weeks since she'd last called. As always, he refused to answer. But the damage was done. Just seeing her name left him overcome with memories of the morning outside her hotel room. Of Paul's naked body on the bed behind her.

With a violent jerk, he snatched up his laptop and replied to Dr Andersson's email, accepting his place on the trial.

And now, eleven years later, here he is.

He'd dared to hope he might be able to sneak in unnoticed and take a seat at the back. The moment the door creaks open, however, it's obvious his plan isn't going to work. As he enters, the assembled faces turn to look at him. They're seated in a loose circle in the middle of the room, with Dr Andersson standing in the middle, a weary expression on his face.

'Benjamin. How nice of you to join us.'

Ben crosses the room sheepishly. All of the other Evergreens are here, and he nods a silent hello to them as he takes a seat. Some he knows well. Pete and Michael, obviously. He's been out with Tom Hander a few times over the years. And Martin Hardridge, too. The others he knows less well. Christine, Iqbal, Nadia, Adaku, Tanisha, Sasha, Meredith. Half of them he hasn't seen since the very first year of the programme. For whatever reason, Dr Andersson seems a little reluctant to get them all together. And yet here they all are, like one big happy family.

'For the benefit of our latecomer, I'll run through the key points again before I hand out the new medication.'

Ben turns to Pete, frowning. 'New meds?' he whispers.

Pete shakes his head. 'Just listen, will you?'

'Now, as I have *already* explained,' Dr Andersson continues, 'it has come to our attention that there is a small issue with your current treatment. Nothing serious. But out of an abundance of caution, we're asking you to discontinue taking it. Instead, we have decided to replace your regular oral treatment with a single intravenous shot. To be clear, that is one dose for life. No more worrying about forgetting your dose. Think about it as a vaccine shot against ageing.'

From the other end of the circle, Nadia asks a question. 'What about side effects?'

Dr Andersson shakes his head. 'Well, unless you count not getting old as a side effect.'

There's a chuckle from the crowd.

'But seriously, other than a sore arm and a little fatigue, you'll be fine. The new vaccine has been subject to the most rigorous testing. It's perfectly safe.'

'And when are we getting this vaccine?' Ben asks.

'Today. Although first, we have a couple of pieces of paperwork we need you to sign. And then there's a few routine tests we'd like to run, just to ensure that everyone is nice and healthy. Now if you'd all follow me down to the waiting room…'

Somewhat predictably, 'a couple of pieces of paperwork' turns out to be half an encyclopaedia's worth of forms, all of which need to be read, signed and dated. Meanwhile, 'a few routine tests' turns out to be a prolonged and exhausting examination by a team of nurses, who force Ben to change into gym gear and undertake a range of exercises while they monitor his responses. He runs on a treadmill, cycles on a static bike, lifts weights, performs star jumps and squats and lunges. By the time he is eventually led through to Dr Andersson's office, he is dripping with sweat.

'If you'd warned me you were going to make me work out, I'd have worn my leotard,' he says.

Dr Andersson doesn't acknowledge the quip. Instead he stares at Ben's notes, frowning slightly. 'And how have you been feeling lately, Benjamin? Any issues I should be aware of? Loss of appetite? Changes in sleep pattern? Depression or anxiety?'

'Come on, you know me, doc. I'm fine. Fit as a fiddle.'

The doctor makes a non-committal sound, his eyes still on Ben's notes. 'Mmmmm.'

'Is there a problem?'

He shakes his head. 'I'm just keen that you take care of yourself. I know you tend to think you're indestructible, but I can promise you, you're not. You've been given a gift here. It's important you remember that.'

Ben rolls his eyes. He's been receiving this lecture every few months for a decade now. He actually finds Dr Andersson's concern quite sweet. 'I am looking after myself,' he tells him. 'Sure, I might blow off a bit of steam now and then, but that's all it is. I promise.'

The doctor nods but makes no further comment. Instead, he snaps a fresh needle from its packaging and then pushes it into a small vial, drawing up a clear liquid into the syringe.

'So this is it?' Ben asks. 'No more pills to worry about?'

'No more pills. It's the beginning of a whole new chapter, Benjamin. Now, if you just relax your arm for me, you may feel a small sting…'

Ben grits his teeth at the bite of the needle. An ice-cold sensation courses its way through his veins and down his arm. For a moment, he feels light-headed. Stars scatter across his vision. But then, just as quickly, he feels fine again. Yet he's still not permitted to leave. First, he must go back up to the conference room, where he sits with the other Evergreens so they can be monitored for adverse reactions. Then there is more paperwork to complete, and then another round of tests, heart rate, pulse rate, oxygen, before he is finally – *finally* – told he can go home.

By the time the train pulls into Slough station, the sky is dark. Ben is tired and more than a little disorientated. He nodded off on the train, and as he staggers down his street, all he can think about is climbing into bed. Dr Andersson hadn't been lying when he said they might feel a little fatigue as a result of the injection. He's ready to drop.

When he finally makes it home, he's surprised to find Sophie waiting for him in the hallway, sitting on the bottom step, her phone in her lap. As he pushes open the door, she looks up expectantly. He stares at her, confused for a moment. And then he remembers. Their anniversary. The meal he'd promised.

He's forgotten it all.

She stands up.

And then, without a word, she turns, climbs the stairs, and closes their bedroom door behind her.

17

Sophie has always prided herself on the fact she isn't materialistic. She doesn't care about the fact they live in a small, grotty house. Or that they don't have a car. Or that they never go on holiday. So why does the lack of an anniversary card bother her so much? It's not like he usually gets her one.

But of course, it's not about the card. It's everything. She's unhappy. More than unhappy.

She's miserable.

Her parents have always disapproved of Ben. On the rare occasion she's managed to drag him over to their house for dinner, they've interrogated him mercilessly. Where did he see himself in five, ten, thirty years? Did he really want to work in that kitchen forever? Didn't he want to go back into law, where there was more money and stability?

Of course, what they really want to know is why he hasn't aged a day in all the time since they first met. At Ben's insistence, Sophie has only ever given them the lightest sprinkling of information. A few vague references to a mysterious medical condition – the same condition that prevents them from having children of their own. Thankfully, etiquette has always prevented them from openly prying. Although lately, as the gulf between their physical appearances has become more apparent, Sophie has noticed them being more combative than usual. They speak in a weird, slightly patronising tone, as if talking to a child. Or share secret glances with each other when they think he's not looking.

To his credit, Ben has somehow always managed to be civil to them, simply smiling and nodding and making vague noises of agreement whenever they start lecturing him about his life choices. Sophie, on the other hand, has shown no such restraint. She's had several blazing arguments with them over the subject, particularly with her dad. The last time they fought about it, she accused him of being a snob who was more concerned with the contents of Ben's bank account than his character.

'You don't get it, sweetheart,' he'd fired back. 'It's precisely his character I'm worried about.'

She'd stormed home that night, refusing to speak to either of them for weeks.

Yet recently, she's begun to wonder if her dad might have a point, after all. It isn't only Ben's inability to hold down a job for more than a few months at a time that's getting to her. Although admittedly, never having any money isn't exactly fun. No, what is hard to take is his carelessness. There are a million little examples, which individually aren't much. A missed birthday here. A forgotten anniversary there. But taken together, they paint a picture of someone who is essentially selfish. Who doesn't value or appreciate her.

Who doesn't love her.

And if they don't have love, what do they have?

A few days after their anniversary, Ben and Sophie are sitting in a fancy burger joint on the outskirts of Spitalfields Market. The meal is a peace offering. Ben has taken her to London for the day in an attempt to make up for the missed anniversary. To his credit, he's trying really hard. He's been sweet, funny, charming. All the things she loves about him. Yet Sophie is distracted, barely able to muster the energy to respond. As he talks, she looks past him, across the restaurant, where the teenage waitress who'd served them earlier is staring back at her. She'd noticed the double-take the girl had given them when they'd first walked in. Sophie could almost see the cogs in the girl's brain turning as the waitress tried to figure out their relationship.

She's too young to be his mother, so are they... aunt and nephew?... Older sister and younger brother?... Some old bird and her male escort?

It's not an unusual reaction. Recently, Sophie has noticed more and more people giving them sideways glances. Even her own friends and family have begun to get in on the act, referring to Ben as her 'young man' or her 'boy', despite how many times she reminds them that he's a month and a half older than her. It doesn't help that she's under strict instructions not to tell anyone about the Evergreens Programme. She tries not to think what it will be like a decade from now, when the difference between them will be unmissable. How on earth will she explain that? Not that she should *have* to explain. If it was the other way around, a thirty-something guy and a twenty-year-old girl, she suspects no one would bat an eyelid. Or if they did, it would only be to congratulate him. It's infuriating.

She scowls at the girl, before shifting her attention back to Ben, who appears to have just asked her a question.

'...It's amazing, isn't it?'

'What's that?'

'How these posh burger places have taken off. When I was a kid, burgers meant junk food. Processed, mass-produced muck. Yet you get rid of the creepy clown mascot and the moulded plastic booths, and expose some brickwork and air-conditioning vents, maybe add some graffiti and neon signs, and bingo, you can sell them for more than the price of a steak.'

'Uh-huh.'

'It's got me thinking. What's to stop me opening a place like this? Or something along the same lines? Gentrified Pies. Or, I don't know, Deluxe Doner Kebabs? You're always telling me I should open my own restaurant someday. I could take a bank loan. Start a pop-up? Street food's huge at the moment...'

'Yeah. Sure. Maybe. Whatever.'

'Hey, is everything OK? You've been a little... I don't know. And you haven't touched your food.'

'I'm fine.'

'You're sure?'

'I just said so, didn't I?'

A pointed silence stretches between them, before Ben gets to his feet and heads in the direction of the bathroom.

Once he's gone, Sophie looks up to spot the waitress staring over again, a faint smirk pulling at the corner of her lips. It takes all of her self-control not to fly over there and slap the teenager. Desperate for a distraction, she reaches for her bag and retrieves her phone. There's an unread message from Sinead. She opens it up and a blurry black-and-white picture springs from the screen, a single word underneath:

Surprise!

For a second, she has no idea what she's supposed to be looking at. A vampire bat? An astronaut?

But then she sees it.

The bulbous head. The coiled body. The crumpled legs.

It's a baby. Sinead is having a baby.

Surprise!

It's the final straw. Sophie puts down her phone. And then she bursts into tears.

It's not a conscious decision to cry. She doesn't feel it coming. It just happens. An explosion of salty tears and snot and sobs. Then she catches herself. She will not, *will not*, give in to self-pity. She sucks it up. Takes a breath. Dabs her face with a serviette.

And then she gets up and walks out of the restaurant.

She's halfway down the road when she hears Ben calling after her. She doesn't stop. She doesn't want to talk. If she does, she's scared she'll say something she'll regret. Or maybe she won't regret it? Maybe it will feel good to have the truth out in the open at last.

That she wants to call it a day.

She keeps walking, dipping into the clamour of the covered market, with its boutique stalls selling artisanal bread and vinyl records and vintage clothing and hand-cobbled shoes.

Behind her, she can hear Ben calling. Begging her to stop.

People are staring now. Staring at the young boy shouting after the older woman.

Sister and brother?
Aunty and nephew?
Client and escort?

She doesn't care. She keeps walking. Head down. Deeper into the market. The store fronts giving way to trendy food stalls, the air filled with the sizzle and smoke of Taiwanese pancakes and Hawaiian poke bowls and French crêpes and Peruvian barbecue. In the centre of the market, there is a makeshift dining hall, long tables filled with tourists and locals and families and couples. All of them craning their necks to watch the free slice of domestic drama unfolding in front of them. Meanwhile, Ben keeps yelling, imploring her to stop. Please. Just for a second.

Wait.

Until finally, she's had enough. More than enough. If he

wants to talk, they can bloody well talk. She will tell him *exactly* what's on her mind.

Only when she turns, ready to scream, to shout, to cry, she finds he's no longer standing behind her. No. Instead, he's on one knee. Looking up at her.

'Listen, I know I messed up,' he begins.

'What… What are you doing? Get up.'

Around her, she can sense the crowd leaning closer in anticipation, their smartphones already levelled to capture the moment, as if the two of them are engaged in an elaborate piece of street theatre. As if at any moment, they'll send round a hat, asking for coins.

'And I'm sorry. I really am….'

She should finish it. She knows she should. If she doesn't say something now, then when? But already the words are disappearing. Her anger, dissipating. Replaced instead by bewilderment. 'Ben?'

'Let me finish. Now, I know I've treated you terribly. And I know you deserve better. Which is why… It's why I'd like you to do me the honour of becoming my wife, Sophie Edwards. I want us to get married.'

She looks at him. At his lost-puppy-dog eyes set in his sad, smooth face.

No, she thinks. Not like this. Not now.

Maybe not ever.

'I…' she says. 'I…'

2070

V

Sophie steps out of the taxi and looks down Harley Street. It's been a long time since she was last here. More than fifty years. Ignoring the pain in her knees, she begins to make her way down the street, desperately trying to remember where the hell the building is.

It's easier said than done.

Whereas bricks-and-mortar retail has been in terminal decline for decades, demand for private medical treatment has never been greater. As a result, Harley Street remains as busy as ever. Although the clinics that line the street today look nothing like they did half a century ago. Gone are the sash windows and black railings of the Georgian town houses, their traditional frontages replaced by digital cladding, each of them spewing retina-scalding holographic adverts into the afternoon air, each treatment seemingly more extreme than the last.

Scalp transplants.

Elbow implants.

Iris recolouring.

The constant dazzle of adverts quickly leaves Sophie utterly disorientated. She keeps her head down, swatting away the virtual salespeople and ploughing forwards until she finally accepts that she has no idea where she's going. She begins to panic. Even if she does miraculously stumble across the right building, what are the chances the clinic will still be here? Or Dr Andersson, for that matter? Sophie has only ever met him once, at that fateful university lecture, more than sixty years earlier. He wasn't young back then. If he's still alive, he'll be at least a hundred now. Of course, that's not impossible. Especially considering his line of work. Yet she remains doubtful. After all, the Evergreens Programme was disbanded long ago. There was only ever the original twelve.

Who, if the police are to be believed, are now beginning to drop like flies.

She fights her way down the street, assailed by evermore aggressive holograms.

Shin contouring.

Hand resizing.

Neck lengthening.

'No, no, no,' she huffs, dodging past the offers of complimentary initial assessments and interest-free payment packages. It was a mistake to come here. She knows that now. Her energy is fading. The pain in her joints too bad to ignore. She needs to sit down. To lie down. To curl up on the pavement and go to sleep. She should be back in the hospital, with Ben. What if he wakes up while she's here? He'll be all alone. Confused. Frightened. Even if he doesn't wake up, surely she'd be more use there than here, stumbling through this ghoulish carnival in search of a man who, in all probability, is dead.

She gives up. Fumbles in her bag for her deck so she can call a taxi.

And then she stops.

Because directly opposite where she is standing, positioned between a clinic offering forehead reduction surgery and a place that specialises in racial reassignment, is a building that looks strangely familiar. Like the other buildings, the front has been remodelled, the old black railings torn out.

But if she squints...

She tells herself she's being ridiculous. That there's no way it can be the right place.

Yet all the same, she crosses the road to investigate. Sure

enough, next to the doorway is a small silver plaque. The logo of a pine cone just about visible through the layers of tarnish.

She hesitates for a moment. And then she presses the buzzer.

Nothing happens.

And then, there is a faint electronic click. Followed by the dry crackle of a man's voice.

'Hello?'

Sophie freezes. She's been so focused on finding the right building she's given almost no thought to what she will say now she's actually found it.

'Oh, hello,' she stalls. 'I'm hoping you can help me? I'm looking for someone. On behalf of my friend. Mr Ben Walker.'

Silence.

'Ben Walker,' she repeats. 'He was part of the Evergreens Programme? I believe he was treated here. At this clinic?'

More silence.

'It was a long time ago now. Fifty? Maybe sixty years? Anyway, Ben's not very well. He's in the hospital. And I was hoping... I don't know, if there was someone I could talk to about his condition? Hello? Are you still there?'

There's no response.

'He was treated by a Dr Andersson?' she says desperately. 'If there's anyone there who might have contact details for him or his—'

She doesn't finish.

She doesn't finish, because at that moment the electronic lock buzzes and then the intercom crackles again.

'Why don't we discuss this inside?'

2019

18

'Oh my God, he's *gorgeous*. I can't believe how much he's grown.'

'I know. It goes so quickly. He's five months now, I think.' Sinead shrugs.

Sophie raises an eyebrow. 'You think?'

'Fine. He's twenty-one weeks, four days and... eleven hours. Jesus, I promised myself I'd never become one of *those* mums.'

'Oh, come on. It's perfectly normal to be obsessed when you've got someone so cute to look after. Although if you start telling me about the contents of his nappy, I may have to erase your number from my phone.'

'Deal. Just as long as *you* promise not to ask me if I'm getting much sleep. Or how I'm getting on with losing my baby weight. Or "helpfully" remind me that breast is best.'

Sophie laughs and looks down again at the tiny baby that's nestling in the pram. Sinead had given birth to Jacob a couple of days after Sophie and Ben's wedding, having somehow managed to waddle her way through her maid-of-honour duties. Aside from a brief hospital visit, Sophie's only seen her friend one other time since, back during the early post-baby-bedlam phase, where both she and her partner Ashley sat there like shell-shock victims, eyes glazed, hair frazzled, their clothes flecked with vomit.

To her shame, Sophie secretly enjoyed seeing Sinead struggle with Jacob, schadenfreude that she knew in her heart was driven by her own lack of babies. Not that she'd ever admit it to anyone. After all, she'd known from the very outset that she and Ben wouldn't be able to have children of their own. Sterilisation had always been part of Andersson's deal, his unhinged attempt at squaring the ethical issues at the heart of his project. And it wasn't as if Ben had concealed anything from her. He'd been upfront about his infertility from the start. In fact, it was one of the main issues that had threatened to derail their relationship before it had even really begun, with each of them fretting for months about what it might mean for their future together. He desperately didn't want her to end up with regrets. In the end, she decided the positives of being with Ben outweighed everything else. Besides, the concept of having a baby was so abstract, so *grown-up*, it was hard for her to seriously consider it. After all, she was still practically a child herself.

As the years have gone by, however, and she's watched her friends start families of their own, she's come to recognise a gnawing sense of loss about her own futile prospects at becoming a mum. Recently, she'd even tentatively touched on the idea of adopting a child with Ben, just to see what he'd say. Of course, he'd completely freaked out, mumbling something about not being in the 'right place' in his life to even *consider* anything like that. Which is a reasonable enough response, she supposes. Although she suspects he'll probably never be in the right place, no matter how long he lives.

Either way, she's pleased to see that Sinead is back to her usual, effortlessly stylish best. If anything, she looks better than she did before the baby, radiating a warm, contented energy that would come off as smug if it belonged to anyone else. They are sitting in their favourite old haunt, the same Portobello Road cocktail bar where they had met after Sophie's last advert shoot. This time, however, she has joined Sinead in ordering a peppermint tea. Ever since the wedding, Sophie has been on a health kick, forgoing all of her favourite sins – alcohol, red meat, caffeine, processed sugar – in favour of early nights and probiotics and yoga classes and everything else she is forced to pretend to enjoy in order to prevent her body from prematurely falling apart.

'So,' Sinead begins, fanning her fingers expectantly. 'Tell me about the new house.'

The new house.

At their wedding, her parents had surprised Ben and Sophie by presenting them with a cheque for fifty thousand pounds, to be used as a deposit for a place of their own. Though she'd sensed Ben's reluctance to accept such an extravagant gift, there was no way she was turning down the chance to escape their miserable little hovel in Slough. Yet, as soon as they'd booked their first viewings, Ben began trying to talk her out of it.

'Look, why don't we just take the money and run?'

'What are you talking about?'

'I mean, it's a lot of money, Soph. More than we're ever likely to see again. We could go backpacking. India? South America, maybe? We could probably keep going for three or four years. More if we picked up work along the way.'

Sophie was bewildered. 'But what about my career? I don't want to drop that just to go bumming around Goa like some teenager. I've been there, done that.'

'You might have done that, but I haven't. The most I managed was half a week in Melbourne, remember?'

'Since when has seeing the world been such a priority for you? In the ten years we've been together, we haven't once been on a foreign holiday. You haven't even got a valid passport.'

'Yes, but we didn't have this opportunity before. We might never have it again.'

'And what about when the money runs out? What do we do then? We'll be back in Slough in some crummy rented house again, with cobwebs on the windows and black mould on the walls.'

'At least we'll have made some memories.'

'But that's exactly what we're doing now, silly. We are making memories. The memory of buying a house together.'

After half a dozen more conversations like this, Ben eventually relented and they began actively looking for somewhere, eventually settling on a tiny house in Winchmore Hill, a leafy suburb of North London. It was further out than she would have liked, but the area was nice, and it was great to be back in the capital, especially for work. Not that there's been much work lately. Though she's attended more auditions than ever, she hasn't received a single callback since the wedding. Even the mum roles seem to have dried up. She'd voiced her frustrations over lunch with her agent, Linda, who gently brought up the issue of her age.

'You're stuck in a funny place, that's all. It happens to everyone. There just aren't many roles for women in your bracket.'

'My bracket? I'm thirty-fucking-three. I'm in my prime.'

'Yes, yes. I know you are. But from a dramatic perspective, roles tend to be aimed at either younger or older women. It's a bit like singers. You can either be a great big fat diva or you can be a skinny slip of a teenager shaking your barely-there booty. Anything in between can be a little... difficult to market. It's like, *what are you exactly?*'

Sophie swallowed down a reflexive spasm of shame about her own body. Unlike Linda, who weighed about seven stone and seemed to subsist exclusive on vodka martinis and itsu sushi, Sophie falls slap bang in the middle of the 'what are you?' category, something she knows only too well from years of brutal auditions where directors praise her performance and then, in the same breath, ask about her willingness to slim down for a role.

'But it's not like I have to play women the same age as me. It's acting, for fuck's sake. I can put on a wig and make-up.'

'Of course you can, darling. I know how versatile you are. I love that about you. And you must remember that, even if those dramatic roles aren't there right now, there are still plenty of commercial opportunities out there for *experienced* women like yourself. Did I tell you that Bisto are casting for a new campaign?'

'Oh, great. So I'm gravy girl now?'

'Whatever pays the bills, right? And the good news is that, in a couple of years from now, you'll find all sorts of exciting new things will start opening up for you. Ranevskaya in *The Cherry Orchard*. Martha in *Who's Afraid of Virginia Woolf?* The stage is awash with great roles for slightly tragic middle-aged women.'

Sophie stared down at her lunch and frowned. 'Tragic and middle-aged? I can hardly wait.'

Still, at least the lack of work has freed her up to focus on the house. She and Ben have decided to renovate the place themselves, spending their evenings stripping wallpaper and painting ceilings and sanding floors. To her surprise, Ben has thrown himself into the task, despite having never previously shown the faintest interest in DIY.

'And how is Ben?' Sinead asks when she tells her this. 'Apart from being fucking gorgeous, obviously.'

Sophie laughs uncomfortably. Despite her being one of the few people she has confided in about Ben's involvement in the trial, Sinead has always had this slightly weird running joke about the way he looks. 'Oh. He's fine.'

'You can say *that* again. What I wouldn't give to go to bed next to a hot young thing like that every night.'

'Yes, well. I mean, Ben isn't actually young, is he? We're the same age. Listen, are you going to get another cup of tea? Actually, I might see if they have any camomile…'

'Don't get me wrong. Ash is great. I love him to bits. And he's a brilliant daddy, he really is. But he's pushing forty now. I'm lucky if I get so much as a peck on the cheek at night before he rolls over and starts snoring. Especially since this little bundle of joy arrived. That's the problem with these older guys. No stamina. Whereas I bet Ben still keeps you up half the night…'

Sophie is squirming now. Why the hell does Sinead have to be such a creep about this stuff? Hasn't she made it perfectly clear in the past that she has zero interest in discussing her sex life? Not that she has much of a sex life to discuss. Maybe that's unfair. It's not like her and Ben *never* do it. And it's not that she doesn't find Ben attractive any more. Far from it. As Sinead points out, he's still as handsome as the day they met. It's not even that there's been any great dip in her sex drive. She still feels desire. It's just that, by the time her head hits the pillow most nights, it's outweighed by the desire to pass out.

Not that Ben really complains about the situation. Sure, he might occasionally attempt to entice her. But mostly he doesn't bother any more, perhaps sensing her unwillingness to reciprocate. And although she feels vaguely guilty about the situation, in the way she used to feel guilty about maintenance jobs that needed doing around the house, like cleaning the oven or descaling the kettle, somehow the guilt is never quite enough to give up the prospect of eight hours of uninterrupted sleep. Of course, she has never told any of this to Sinead. Or anyone else for that matter. And so she sits there and grits her teeth as her friend makes increasingly lecherous comments about Ben until finally the waiter comes over and asks them if they'd like another drink.

Before he can take their order, Jacob stirs, then abruptly explodes into a fit of rage, his previously angelic face transformed into a mess of snot and tears. As the waiter scurries away to another table, Sinead hauls the wailing boy onto her lap and begins the whole pantomime of trying to find out what's wrong with him. Nothing will placate him, and his screams rise to reach a whole new level of intensity, to the point Sophie begins to worry he'll do permanent damage to his vocal cords. Or her eardrums. Sinead, meanwhile, has begun to look increasingly desperate. There's a haunted, harried look in her eye that Sophie has never seen before. Around them, she senses other patrons staring pointedly in their direction.

In the end, Sinead gives up. Actually, she looks like

she's in danger of bursting into tears herself. She makes her apologies to Sophie, drains the last of her tea and bundles the still howling child out the door.

Once she's alone, hers ears still ringing, Sophie marvels at the sudden calmness of the room. *Look at all these sophisticated adults enjoying a quiet afternoon drink*, she thinks to herself. Free to relax and do as they please without fear of anyone demanding anything of them. Smiling to herself, she waves the waiter over.

'Pinot Grigio, please. Large. And a slice of the carrot cake I spotted on the counter.'

To hell with the diet.

19

Ben is trying. He's really trying.

He goes to work. He comes home.

He cooks dinner, cleans dishes, does laundry.

He paints walls, grouts tiles, hangs shelves.

He goes to bed.

He wakes up and does it all over again.

He does this for months. And really – *honestly* – it's fine. Fine.

Life is like a treadmill set to a comfortable speed. No ups or downs. No changes in scenery. Just the same thing day in and day out. Over and over again. One foot in front of the other. Again and again and again.

This is what being an adult is all about, he tells himself.

I am a reliable, responsible *married* man.

This is my life now.

His job is a breeze. He's in a new kitchen, a middle-of-the-road pub that serves standard English fare. Steak and kidney pies and bangers and mash. Lamb shanks and stews and ploughman's lunches. Roast dinners on a Sunday. He can do it in his sleep. It's busy enough to keep him on his toes, but nothing like some of the relentless conveyor-belt gigs he's worked in the past. Not only that, but for some reason the head chef has a soft spot for him, and more or less allows him to pick his own shift pattern. As it stands, he only works one weekend in four, a luxury that is practically unheard of in the hospitality industry.

And then there's the house. Admittedly, he hadn't been too keen at first. He didn't fancy rooting themselves to one spot. Or saddling themselves with debt. And he certainly wasn't interested in the endless hours of DIY that the place would undoubtedly require. Yet after watching a few YouTube videos, he found he could turn his hand to pretty much anything. He's plastered walls. Plumbed sinks. Fitted windows. While it's not exactly fun, there's a certain sense of satisfaction that comes with each task he completes. And there's no denying it's helped fill the time. Between work and fixing up the house, whole months have slid by. And isn't that what being an adult is about, really? Finding something to pass the days without giving him too much time to think?

He goes to bed.

He goes to work.

He comes home.

He could lose decades like this, he thinks. Centuries. There will always be meals to cook. Walls to paint. Rooms to rearrange. And is that so bad, really? Sophie certainly seems content with it. After so many years of squabbling, they have finally arrived at an accord. He can't remember the last time they argued. And while things aren't exactly passionate, they keep each other company. In the evenings they watch Netflix. They talk about the news. The weather. The house. They sleep side by side in the same bed. *So, this is marriage*, he thinks. A comfortable chair. A lukewarm bath. A rerun of a favourite TV show. Who wouldn't want that?

He goes to bed.

He goes to work.

He comes home.

The only real deviation from his routine are his monthly appointments to the Evergreens clinic. Yet even here, he is a reformed character. He is organised. Punctual. He no longer goes out drinking afterwards with Pete and Michael.

His good behaviour hasn't gone unnoticed. Rather than offering him an eye roll and a telling off, Becky the receptionist seems genuinely pleased to see him, smiling as she waves him through to Dr Andersson's office.

Ever since he received the age vaccine, his monthly check-ups have become far more gruelling affairs, longer and more involved than ever. Today is no different, and once Ben has undertaken the usual battery of physical tests, the doctor moves on to the dreaded psychological survey. Over the last month has Ben had any of the following:

Difficulty falling or staying asleep?

Trouble concentrating?

Feeling afraid as if something awful might happen?

He's supposed to score each of the questions from zero to three. As ever, he assigns a big fat nought to each statement. It's all so ridiculous. He's recently married. He's in perfect health. He's staying out of trouble. Why on earth would he be depressed?

At the end of the survey, Dr Andersson puts down his tablet and stares hard into Ben's eyes, a look of deep concentration on his face, as if he is trying to read something written on his retina.

'Are you happy, Benjamin?' he asks at last.

Ben chuckles at this. 'Sure,' he says. 'I'm ecstatic.'

'I'm serious. Are you happy with your life?'

Ben grows a little uncomfortable. He's unsure what the doctor is driving at. He's answered his stupid survey. What more does he want?

'Because I have to be honest,' Andersson continues. 'You seem a little off to me. A little low.'

'Low?'

'Not your usual self. I just wondered if everything was OK at home?'

'With Soph? Everything's great. Better than great. We've bought a house and...'

He trails off unconvincingly.

'Well, if you're sure,' Doctor Andersson says at last. 'Just know that if you ever need to talk, you can come to me, OK? That's what I'm here for.'

As Ben leaves the office, he feels a little shaken. A little angry, too. What the hell was the doctor talking about? Sure, there might be a few small issues at home. But that's true of any marriage. And anyway, what business is it of his? Essentially, he's perfectly happy.

Isn't he?

He's still on Harley Street when he feels a familiar rumble in his coat pocket. It's a message from Pete. He and Michael had their appointments earlier this morning. Does he want to join them for a cheeky one?

Sorry, I can't, he types back automatically. *Work this evening.*

He hits send but doesn't put his phone away. Instead he stands still on the pavement for a moment. All around him, he can feel the city thrumming with opportunities. As if it has a pulse. As if it's alive.

Then he unlocks his phone.

Actually, scratch that.

I'll be there in five.

2070

VI

As the door clicks shut behind her, Sophie finds herself standing in a small reception room. White walls. White lights. A few potted plants. The room is clean and bright, but dated, as if it hasn't been decorated for decades. Ahead of her is a reception desk, on top of which sits an old-fashioned telephone and computer, both of them antiques now. But it's the woman sitting behind the desk who is really jarring. She's wearing a cotton blouse and cardigan, a Bluetooth headset nestled in her ear. She looks like she's stepped straight from the set of a period drama.

Sophie clutches her handbag to her chest like a security blanket and tiptoes towards the desk. The receptionist looks up from her work. Smiles.

'Hello, welcome to Evergreens. How can I help you today?'

There is a name badge pinned to her chest that reads:

Becky

Sophie swallows. Tries to remember what the hell it is she's doing here. In this strange room. Speaking to this strange woman. 'Oh. Yes. Hello. I'm a friend of Ben Walker. He used to be a patient here. I was hoping I could speak to—'

'Hello, welcome to Evergreens. How can I help you today?' *the receptionist repeats.*

Sophie stares at her hesitantly. 'Oh, sorry,' *she tries again, raising her voice.* 'I was just saying that I'm here to speak to—'

'Hello, welcome to Evergreens. How can I help you today?'

The receptionist's grin grows wider. Threatening to split her face in two. Her eyes bulge manically from her skull.

'How can I help you today? How can I help you today? How can I—'

There is a sudden burst of light as the receptionist explodes into a cloud of swirling pixels. They hover there for a moment like digital confetti, before disappearing altogether, leaving the desk deserted.

Sophie has hardly had time to process the fact that the woman was only a hologram, when a dark shape fills the glass door at the back of the room.

And Dr Andersson walks in.

2020

20

How many hours of her life has Sophie spent sitting in the run-down reception of some low-budget production company, waiting to be called through to audition? Weeks? Years? Certainly enough to have lost any sense of expectation that she will get the part. Nowadays, she attends these things out of habit more than hope. That, and loyalty to her long-suffering agent, who continues to line up these auditions despite all evidence pointing to the fact that Sophie is, at this point in her career, pretty much unemployable. Although looking around the waiting room today, she feels less sympathy for her agent and more frustration that she would, once again, put her up for something for which she is so obviously unsuitable.

Of the dozen or so other girls who are sitting in the waiting room of Number 26 Eastman House, Sophie is by far the oldest. Most of them look as if they have stepped straight from the classrooms of RADA. Their heads poised, shoulders back, eyes brimming with confidence. Ready to go out there and win the part that will kick-start their long and illustrious careers on the silver screen.

A bitter streak in Sophie wants to grab them and wring the enthusiasm out of them. Tell them that most of them don't stand a chance. Not really. Because no matter how well they've memorised their lines, or immersed themselves in the character's backstory, or understand their motivation, their chance of landing the role will ultimately depend on whether their face – or their body – fits. In other words, if they don't *look* the part, they won't *get* the part.

End of story.

Perhaps she should try being less cynical. After all, the new year is still only a couple of weeks old. And it's not just a new year. It's a whole new decade. *The twenties.* Just the sound of it is glamorous, with all its intimations of decadence and free expression. Wild jazz and sequined flapper girls and illegal speakeasies serving teapots full of bathtub gin and rotgut moonshine. Of course, it's still far too early to guess whether *these* particular twenties will roar or not. Politically, the omens aren't too good. And then there's the endless existential threats queuing up to wipe everyone out: climate change, microplastics, superbugs, weapons of mass destruction, the rise of artificial intelligence... The world has never seemed in such peril.

Closer to home, things aren't much better. Following a promising start to their married life, Ben has very much slipped back into his old ways recently. He managed to lose what was probably the most comfortable job he's ever had after once again getting drunk and failing to show up. Now he's back to hopping from kitchen to kitchen across the city, stumbling home wasted in the early hours. And she doesn't want to be uptight, she really doesn't. But at the same time, she wonders just how long he plans to live like this for. Will she be fifty, sixty, seventy years old and still living with a perpetual man-child? Because even now, she's not sure how much longer she can take it. She feels stuck in a miserable cycle. Last time they were here, he'd literally had to marry her to stop her leaving. She's not sure there's anything left he can offer to make things better this time round, other than...

Well, grow up.

Her phone trills. It's Sinead. Lately, it's always Sinead. She's been going through something of a crisis since discovering that she's accidentally pregnant again. When they'd had lunch together a few days later, Sinead looked broken. Jacob, who still isn't one yet, spent almost the whole time screaming again. That was when he wasn't performing his new trick of taking everything out of Sinead's handbag and hurling it as hard as he could across the room. Sinead had blinked and twitched her way through their conversation, losing her train of thought whenever Jacob sent another limited edition lipstick or concealer clattering to the floor.

'We always said we'd have them close together,' she garbled. 'It makes sense at our age. I just didn't think they'd be *this* close together.'

By the time Sinead left, her back bent under the sheer weight of toys and changing gear and bottles and beakers, and Jacob once again wailing at lung-shredding volumes, any remaining sense of smugness had evaporated. Sophie actually felt sorry for her friend.

Today, Sinead's message is a single syllable cry for help:
Cake?
Sophie taps out an equally terse reply:
Can't. Audition. Tomorrow?
Three dots bounce on the screen.
Sure.
Then:
Assuming I make it that far.
Poor Sinead.

Before Sophie can send her a message of solidarity, a grey-haired man in a crumpled suit appears in the waiting room carrying a clipboard.

'Sophie Walker? I'm Matthew. We're ready for you now.'

The audition is like every audition. Sophie is led into a nondescript studio space, where a panel made up of four people sits facing her behind a long desk. The director, the casting director, the writer, and Matthew, who turns out to be the producer. They all beam at her when she enters and take turns to shake her hand warmly.

'Hi, Sophie,' they chorus. 'Great to meet you. Thanks *so* much for coming in.'

Sophie nods. Sophie smiles. Sophie thinks:

I'm never getting this fucking part.

The audition is for a minor role in a low-budget movie. Some half-baked sci-fi screenplay about a man who has a chip implanted in his brain so that he can live-stream his thoughts to the world. 'It's very edgy,' her agent had insisted. 'Very *now*.' As far as Sophie can see, it's also very underwritten. Particularly the female characters, who only really seem to exist in order to propel the male lead's narrative. In the scene she's been asked to perform, her character, a young dominatrix-cum-secretary called Katya, meets the protagonist and gives him a guided tour of her company's building. There's not a lot to work with.

Still, Sophie gives it her all. As always, she's done her homework. She knows her lines by heart, projecting them earnestly while the casting director reads the other parts in a halting monotone. Sophie does well. She disappears into the role, actually becoming Katya. At least, she does for a while. For as immersed as she is in the part, the slightly glazed expression from the panel keeps pulling her out of the moment. They don't look bored, exactly. Although God knows how many times they must have sat through this particular scene already today. No, it's more as if they too are actors, engaged in a piece of site-specific theatre. Each of them playing the part of interested interviewer. They say the right things. Pull the right faces. But no matter how convincingly they nod their heads or stroke their chins, they are only pretending. Because, from the second that

Sophie walked into the room, they knew they weren't going to cast her. How long does it take to make a first impression? Seven seconds? Well, this was much quicker. This was instantaneous.

All it took was a single glance.

In the script, Katya is described as being in her twenties. She is described as having dark hair. She is described, though Sophie can't see how it is in any way relevant to the character, as being thin with big boobs. Sophie is none of these things. She is evidently unsuitable for the role. But what choice does she have? Or any of them, for that matter? And so they all keep going, her pretending to act and them pretending to watch, all of them secretly willing it to end so that everybody can get on with their lives.

At last she reaches the end of the scene. The panel parrot their predictable lines. Thanking her. Telling her she was *wonderful*. Promising they'll speak soon. All of them playing their part to perfection. Just as Sophie plays hers. She is gracious. Humble. Grateful. She is about to head for the door. And then, for some reason, she stops. She decides not to play her part. Not today. She thinks:

Fuck it.

'Well, that was a waste of everyone's time, wasn't it?' she says.

The casting director looks up sharply from her notes. She looks confused. As if she might have misheard. 'Excuse me?'

'Well, I just mean that we all know I'm not getting it.'

All four of the panel look up now. They shake their heads incredulously. All of them rushing to offer reassurance. All of them still acting. 'You were good,' the director insists.

'You were *very* good,' someone else offers.

'Thank you,' Sophie says. 'But we all know that *good* has nothing to do with it. Anyone can be good. Although I have to admit, with dialogue this bad, you're not exactly making it easy to shine.'

The panel look mortified now. The blood drains from their

faces. Their eyes widen. Mouths pucker in distaste. Sophie knows she should probably leave. That she's just burning bridges. That word will get back to her agent. But she can't stop. For the first time in years, she feels genuinely exhilarated in an audition.

'I mean, honestly, guys, I don't know why you can't just cast the role with a headshot. Or a body shot. Because let's face it, we all know what you're looking for. Some nubile young lollipop with airbags for tits. Or better yet, just get a cardboard cut-out to play her. That would be pretty appropriate actually, considering the part is so thin.'

The director and casting director both look furious, while Matthew the producer is staring at the desk, refusing to meet her eye. Meanwhile, the writer, a young man with a receding hairline and an elaborately groomed beard, looks anguished. 'I think you're being *very* unfair,' he stammers.

But Sophie isn't listening. She's too busy laughing. She laughs like a maniac. And then she turns to leave. 'Don't call me, I'll call you,' she says as she marches towards the door, leaving a stunned silence in her wake.

It's only once she gets out onto the street that she really starts to panic. Now that the adrenaline has drained away, she's horrified by her little performance back there. What the hell was she thinking? For the sake of a self-righteous sugar rush, she's pulled the plug on her ailing career. For she knows how these things work. The microscopic circles these people move in. It won't be long before word gets out about her.

That she's rude.

Unprofessional.

And very possibly deranged.

Part of her wants to go back in and apologise. But that would only make it worse. Maybe she should call her agent now? Get ahead of the story? Jesus, she needs a drink. She needs several drinks.

Before she can make up her mind about the best course of action, someone calls out to her. She turns to see that Matthew has followed her outside. Probably to demand she hands over her Equity card right now, lest she darken the door of any other unsuspecting audition again.

'Sophie? Are you OK?'

'Aside from being hideously embarrassed?'

'That was quite some speech you gave in there.'

'I'm sorry. I didn't mean it. I'm just having a bad day I guess and… I hope I didn't offend anyone too badly.'

To her surprise, she realises he's smiling. Not a spiteful smile. Rather, he seems to be pleasantly amused by the whole miserable scenario. 'Not at all. Well, Lee looked a little bruised. But he'll get over it. He'll have to. Because, by and large, I think what you said is totally fair. The female parts in the script *are* pretty two-dimensional. And there are *way* too many references to their… Well, their chests.' He laughs. 'Look, the whole script is a fucking mess. All of it needs tightening. Characters. Plot. Dialogue. It could all be better. So why don't you help us?'

Sophie stares at him, bewildered. 'Help you?'

'As a script consultant. You clearly have some strong ideas about where it's not working. And we've already established you're not afraid to speak your mind.' He laughs again.

'You're joking, right?'

'I'm deadly serious. Privately, we've all felt there were issues with the script. But you're the first one with the guts to voice them. Don't stop there. Help us fix it, Sophie. Help us make this film as good as it can possibly be. What do you say? Are you up for the challenge?'

'I don't know what to say. I'm an actress, not a writer. Am I even qualified?'

Matthew smiles again. 'I tell you what. Why don't you think about it? Take my number. If you're interested, give me a call. If you're not, well, no hard feelings either way. What do you say?'

21

For a few months, things are good. Things are very good. Perhaps the best they've ever been. In spite of her scepticism, Sophie takes Matthew up on his offer and sets to work fixing his terrible film script. To her surprise, she finds she loves the process. Every second that she's not working or acting, she spends tucked away in the makeshift office she creates in their spare room. And while things continue to unravel domestically, with Ben staying out after work almost every night, it hardly matters to her. Because the script eclipses everything else. Even when she's not actively working on it, she thinks about it constantly. Taking it apart scene by scene so she can see how it works. Tinkering with plot and characters and dialogue. It obsesses her. Possesses her. And she gladly lets it. For the first time in her life, she begins to consider a career other than acting. That perhaps it was the stories she was attracted to all along, rather than the performance of them. Because the truth is, she can see herself doing this forever.

And then, as is the case in so many of the dramas she loves, there is a plot twist.

And everything goes spectacularly wrong.

There has been talk of a new virus for months. Some new thing that had started in China. Sophie is too busy with the script to pay it any real attention, even when she receives a call from her mum, who appears to be frantic with worry. Apparently, her parents have been stockpiling food for weeks now, like some kind of demented survivalists, while her father watches the news channels pretty much twenty-four hours a day. She wants to know if she and Ben have been taking suitable precautions.

Sophie laughs and tells her they're fine. Besides, isn't there always some apocalyptic doomsday bug brewing out there? Bird flu. Swine flu. Zika. And hadn't they all turned out to be a false alarm?

'Seriously, Mum, it's nothing to worry about. A storm in a teacup, I promise.'

But by the beginning of April, the country – the whole world – is upside down. People are dying. Supermarkets are rationing basic supplies. Hospitals are falling apart. The prime minister is on the TV every night telling people they must stay at home.

Fear is everywhere.

It almost goes without saying that Sophie's career lies in tatters.

Thanks to The Virus, and the national lockdown it has precipitated, the performing arts are in free fall. Concerts are cancelled. Shows shut down. An entire summer's schedule of festivals pulled in the time it takes to tap out a tweet.

Most devastatingly of all, the film is no longer happening.

'So that's it?' she asks when Matthew calls to tell her that funding has collapsed. 'It's over?'

'Well, not *over*. We still have your drafts should anything change in the future. But at the moment… Maybe we should think of it as being on involuntary hiatus?'

Sophie nods, doing her best not to scream, swear, burst into tears, or all three at the same time. She knows she has no right to be upset. Every day, there is news of more people in hospitals. More families destroyed. The numbers of dead doubling, trebling, quadrupling. And here she is worrying about a piffling *film*.

'Don't be too disheartened,' Matthew continues. 'I know things look bleak right now, but the night's always darkest before dawn. Just hang in there, OK? I'll be in touch soon.'

Somehow, she manages to hold it together long enough to say goodbye. It's only once he's gone that it really hits her. She stares at the wall above her desk. At all of her futile notes. Plot arcs. Character studies. All of her grand ambitions. Her new career. Her future.

Gone.

With a sudden jerk, she jumps up and begins tearing it down. Months of work, shredded in an instant. When she's finished, she collapses back into her chair, the torn-up strips of her dreams like confetti at her feet. She stares at the bare walls.

And then bursts into tears.

For weeks, she fears the clouds will never part. She enters a weird zombie state, the rules that have governed most of her adult life suddenly rendered meaningless. She doesn't get dressed. She subsists on three meals of breakfast cereal a day, eaten dry from the packet. She showers infrequently. Time loops and warps. She loses track of the date and the days.

Things with Ben, meanwhile, have gone from bad to worse. She'd dared to hope that the enforced time at home together might improve things. But Ben seems to go out of his way to avoid her, the two of them engaged in an unspoken game of hide-and-seek around the house. If she's in the living room reading, he'll be upstairs in the bedroom. If she's in the kitchen, he'll be out in the garden. As for the nights, he's basically nocturnal. While she's asleep, he's up most of the night playing computer games. It isn't as if he's openly cruel to her. In some ways, that would be easier to take. No, he's still the same old Ben. And that's precisely the problem. His interests and outlook have essentially stayed the same since the first day they met. Which would be fine, if she was the same person. But she's not. And every time she tries to pin him down to have a serious conversation, about the house, about the pandemic, about her career, about adoption, about anything at all, she can feel him either squirming or stifling a yawn, looking to escape the clutches of this boring old *grown-up* he's somehow found himself stuck with. He simply doesn't want to spend any time with her. And that's hard.

Because time – endless, horrible time – is all they have any more.

It's not until early May that she finally spies a chink of light. By now, lockdown has become a way of life for her. She has accepted this will go on forever. That her career is over. That trips to the shop have been replaced by a soul-destroying scrabble for supermarket delivery slots. That her one hour of prescribed exercise, during which she listlessly traces the deserted pavements of her neighbourhood, is the only time she will ever leave the house. This is just how she lives now.

But then a phone call from Sinead changes everything.

Sophie's been avoiding her old friend for weeks. Ignoring her messages. Refusing to like her artfully posed baby bump photos on Instagram. But one morning Sinead calls early and Sophie, who is still half-asleep, accidentally picks up.

After a brief hello, Sinead launches into a tortuous twenty-minute tirade, bludgeoning Sophie with a shopping list of her own pandemic-related complaints, while Sophie grunts an occasional response, barely able to disguise her disinterest.

'And how are things with *Ben*?' she asks once she finally finishes talking about herself.

Sophie sighs. She can't – won't – go into any of that with

Sinead. And so instead, she tells her about the whole miserable business with the film. How she'd finally found her calling, only to have it snatched away. How she almost feels bereaved.

'Is this why you've been avoiding me?' Sinead asks once she's finished.

Sophie feels her cheeks burn. 'OK, so I admit I have been feeling a bit sorry for myself. I just feel cheated, you know? What if this pandemic goes on for another year? Or five? I just keep thinking that this is all the time I have allotted on earth, and I'm being forced to waste it lying around on the sofa all day. It's not fair.'

'So why don't you just write your own script then?'

The way Sinead says it, it sounds like the simplest, most obvious solution in the world.

'What do you mean?'

'Well, you said yourself the film you were working on was terrible. That's why they needed you to come in and fix it in the first place. So why not just do your own thing from scratch? Why do you even need them?'

'But who in their right minds is going to want to read my script?'

'I don't know. Maybe no one? But you won't know unless you try. And it's not like you've got anything else to do, is it?'

After the call has ended, she thinks about Sinead's advice. The idea of going it alone terrifies her. But then again, working on the rewrites for Matthew had terrified her, and she'd ended up loving that. And Sinead's right. It's not like she's stuck for time.

From here on in, things start to look up. The next day, she goes back to her office for the first time since the job fell through. She clears up the mess. Wipes everything down, making it clean and new and fresh. She lights a candle. Then she opens up her laptop and starts a fresh document.

And she begins to write.

At first, she has no idea what she's doing. It's more like auto-writing than anything else. Little unconnected fragments bubbling up from the depths of her subconscious. But she persists. Every day, she forces herself to go up to her office and spend at least a couple of hours working. Even if that 'work' mostly consists of staring at a blank screen. Gradually, the outline of a story begins to fall into place. A strange plot about a woman stuck in quarantine. Only this quarantine is a hundred times worse than the pandemic she's in now. Rather, it's set in a world where people had become so infectious to each other that they can't even risk being in the same room, let alone touch each other.

Not entirely unlike her marriage, she thinks glumly.

Alongside the writing, she takes up running again, just as she had in her final year at university. The first time is horrendous. Her lungs burning, heart hammering, legs so wobbly she fears she won't finish. She limps back home, broken and embarrassed. How has she let herself get so unfit? But, just like the writing, she keeps at it. Morning after morning. Day after day. By the end of May, she can make it round a three-mile circuit without wanting to throw up. By mid-June, she can do five.

This morning, she's aiming for eight.

As she heads downstairs, already dressed in her trainers and running gear, she passes the living room. She pauses. Inside the room she can hear the roar of a digital football crowd. She opens the door a crack to see Ben staring dead-eyed at the TV, a controller clamped in his hand, the floor around him scattered with empty beer bottles. As usual, he hadn't come to bed last night.

'Hey,' she says.

It takes him a moment to register she's speaking to him.

When he does respond, he doesn't look at her, instead keeping his eyes firmly glued on the screen. 'Hey.'

A silence stretches between them. Not a pointed or angry silence. Just an empty space, created by two people who no longer have anything to say to each other. And in that vacuum, an idea comes to Sophie. Not an idea. A *certainty*. She understands that their marriage is over. Not simply broken, but unfixable. And though it might not be made official anytime soon, that is only a detail.

She's going to leave him.

She examines this realisation further. She expects to be sad. Angry. Distraught. The great love of her life has imploded. Not in some raging fire, either. No. It has simply fizzled out.

To her surprise, she feels oddly at peace with the idea. In truth, she knows it's been over for a long time. Way before the lockdown began. It started before they were married. Perhaps even before they officially began? She could probably trace it back to that disastrous night with Paul. Or Ben's decision to join the Evergreens. For as long as she can remember, they have been in trouble. Now all she is doing is facing up to that fact.

'I'm heading out,' she says. 'Round the park. I'll be back later.'

'Right,' he says, still not looking up from the screen. 'Sure. See you later.'

'Bye.'

'Bye.'

And then she is turning away from him. Out of the front door and onto the pavement, the fresh air stinging her cheeks, rather than the stubborn tears that still refuse to come.

And it's a beautiful morning out here. A bright new day.

22

Just when it seems the lockdown really will last forever, it finally lifts. But things don't go back to normal. Not completely. While pub beer gardens fill up with socially starved drinkers, people still keep their distance, obsessively massaging sanitiser into their palms, wary of one another. Face masks, once the exotic preserve of East Asian tourists and health-conscious cyclists, are now as common as hats and sunglasses, and mandatory in most indoor spaces. Paranoia hangs heavy in the air. Because no one truly believes it's over. Not really. It feels more like a pause. A moment for people to catch their breath, before the virus roars back. Maybe this is what people mean by 'the new normal'. That while at a glance things look pretty similar to the way they were before, beneath the surface everything is different. And as much as people might want it to, nothing will ever truly be the same again.

Ben is on his way to Harley Street. For the last three months, his regular meetings with Dr Andersson have been virtual, taking place over video call. While Ben had been pleased at no longer having to trek across the city, Victor had complained bitterly about the arrangement. Now that the world was beginning to reopen, they were to revert to their monthly appointments at the clinic.

But this is not Ben's monthly check-up. That isn't due for another fortnight. Rather, he has once again been called to attend the clinic at short notice, along with the other Evergreens. He doesn't know why. Nor is he particularly curious. Another tweak to his medication? Another lecture from Andersson about taking care of his health and making the most of his opportunities? It hardly matters. His mind is on other things.

Mostly, Sophie.

The last few months have been the hardest of their entire relationship. It's now undeniable that they have very different visions of what their shared future should look like. Sophie wants stability. A successful career. Children, even.

Whereas Ben wants… anything but those things. At least not yet. Unlike her, he doesn't feel the need to try and squeeze everything in before he runs out of time. He has time. The only thing he wants to squeeze in is fun. And as much of it as possible.

Talking of fun, their sex life is not what it once was. If he's honest, that's probably more his fault than hers. It's not that he no longer finds her attractive. Although it's true that he's recently begun to notice physical changes he hadn't detected before. A stray grey hair (or three, or four). A fine line where it had once been perfectly smooth. A general softening of her features. All of which is totally normal and natural. He knows that. He does. And yet at the same time, he finds these changes slightly disturbing. Like a foreshadowing of what is to inevitably come, once the clock, and gravity, has its way with her. Once or twice, on particularly bad nights, he's caught himself lying in bed next to her and thinking about his nan. Remembering how she'd grown older as the years had passed. Her body faltering. Failing. It makes him shudder to think about the same thing happening to Sophie.

And so, wherever possible, he doesn't think about it. He

stays out of her way. Makes himself scarce. Dodges intimacy and hopes that she doesn't notice. Most of all:

He tries not to think about the future.

When he arrives at the office, Becky smiles at him from behind her face mask and directs him up to the conference room. The room is only half-full when he gets there, and he takes a seat next to Pete Meadows while he waits for the others.

'So what do you think?' Pete asks. 'Another tweak to the medication?'

Ben shrugs.

'Or maybe he's getting some new recruits?' Pete continues. 'I wouldn't mind some new faces joining us. Liven things up a bit, eh?'

One by one, the other Evergreens file in. There's a giddy, vaguely celebratory atmosphere in the air as they enjoy the novelty of being together in an indoor space after so many months apart. They chatter away as they take their seats, until at last Dr Andersson makes his entrance. To Ben's surprise, he looks terrible. Everything seems to have sagged and faded since he'd seen him last. His artificial tan no longer working to disguise his grey complexion beneath. His hair thinner than ever before. As the head of a research programme dedicated to prolonging youth, he looks conspicuously old.

The doctor trudges to the middle of the room, his eyes glued to the floor until the last possible moment, when he finally looks up and acknowledges them. 'Thanks for coming here at such short notice,' he begins. 'I know it's been an extraordinarily difficult year for everyone. Although I'm pleased to see you all look well. As the virus predominantly seems to harm the old, I like to think we can take a little credit for that.' Behind his mask, the doctor allows himself a glum little smile.

'Now I'm sure you're wondering why I called you here today?'

'You're increasing our stipend?' Pete calls out to a few half-hearted laughs.

'Sadly not. Although you'll be pleased to hear that your stipend will not be affected. At least not in the immediate future. You see, I'm here to announce that, as of today, Phase One of the Evergreens Programme is officially over…'

Ben waits for the next part of the sentence. But Dr Andersson doesn't continue. He just stops there, until Meredith Coleman calls out the question on everyone's lips. 'But what does that mean?'

'Exactly what it sounds like. Phase One is now complete. We have come to the end of the trial.'

'But what's next?' someone else asks.

'At the moment… Nothing. Despite the excellent data we have generated over the last decade, our funders have decided to step back from the project. Unfortunately, they've decided that the Evergreens Programme is not financially viable given the current global uncertainty.'

'So that's it?' Meredith asks.

Andersson nods. 'For the time being, yes. That is indeed it.'

For a moment, there is stunned silence.

And then mayhem breaks out, a dozen questions all shouted at the same time. Dr Andersson does his best to reassure people. He tells them that, for now at least, nothing significant will change. The original funding package will cover their ongoing financial needs. As for the treatment, the vaccine has proved to be incredibly effective. They are not all about to start suddenly ageing. The only real difference is that there will be no more monthly appointments.

'But what if something goes wrong?' Meredith asks. 'What if it does stop working?'

'You all have my personal contact details. I'm not going anywhere. If you need me, day or night, you only have to call. Although, I'll be honest with you, I'm not expecting to be inundated. After all, nothing's gone wrong so far. Has it?'

An hour later, Ben is on his way back home. It's only now that the shock has worn off that he realises how upset he is. He's been visiting Dr Andersson once a month since he was twenty-one years old. It's hard to contemplate life without him.

Yet as the train judders its way toward Winchmore Hill, his melancholy gives way to a tentative optimism. Maybe this could be the sign he's been waiting for? That it's time to change his ways. Prioritise Sophie. After all, with Victor gone, she's all he has left now. Sure, last time he'd tried to lead a domesticated life, he'd almost had a breakdown. But there must be some middle ground? He could go out less, she could come out more. It'll be tough. But he's certain they can make it work.

What other choice does he have?

By the time he reaches the top of his road, he's practically running. He feels manic, his thoughts racing too fast to keep track of them. He's going to start with an apology. Draw a line in the sand. He's going to tell her that he wants to start again.

That he's finally ready to grow up.

He's calling her name even before he's through the front door.

'Sophie!'

When she doesn't appear, he rushes into the living room, then the kitchen. There's no sign of her. He checks the garden, but it's deserted.

'Sophie?' he calls again.

Now that lockdown has ended, she sometimes goes out for a second run in the afternoon. Or maybe she's gone to meet Sinead?

Yet already, he has a creeping sense of dread that something is terribly amiss.

When he gets upstairs, her office door is slightly ajar. He nudges it open all the way.

Inside, her desk is clear. Her laptop isn't there.

He staggers through to the bedroom.

At first, it looks the same. It's only when he opens the wardrobe that he sees that her

clothes are gone, along with their biggest suitcase.

And that's when he spots it. The envelope on the bed. His name scrawled across the front.

He tears it open and takes out the letter.

Dear Ben, it begins.

2070

VII

'*A museum?*'

Sophie is sitting in the sleek open-plan office that lies behind the old-fashioned reception area at the front of the building. Opposite her is Andersson.

When he walked in earlier, she thought she was seeing a ghost. Or rather, another hologram. Any moment, she expected him to dematerialise, like the receptionist before him. There was no way Dr Andersson could be so well preserved after all these years. Unless, of course, he'd started treating himself?

Framed in the doorway, he looked exactly as she remembered. He even dressed the same way. Designer shirt. Shoes with no socks. Expensive watch.

It was Dr Andersson, alright.

Only it wasn't.

When he moved into the light, she saw the similarity wasn't as strong as she'd first thought. Nor was he a hologram; his first handshake settled that.

'*I'm Johan,*' *he explained once Sophie had got over her shock.* '*Victor was my grandfather. The poor guy died about twenty years ago now. Although people tell me all the time that I inherited his better qualities.*'

He flashed her a bright, artificially white smile. The same one he's wearing now as he explains his reasoning behind the reception area.

'*Perhaps museum is the wrong word,*' *he says.* '*It's not open to the public or anything. But we thought it would be cool to preserve the reception room as it was when my grandfather first founded the company. We see our heritage as an integral part of our brand.'*

Sophie shakes her head, struggling to understand. 'So Evergreens still exists?'

Johan grins. And as he does, Sophie once again catches a glimpse of his grandfather. The slick salesman, ever keen to reassure the customer. 'Yes and no. You see, the Evergreens Programme refers to the specific medical trial that your husband took part in. That project officially concluded back in the twenties, whereupon my grandfather's research sat dormant for decades. That was until around ten years ago, when I received financial backing to relaunch the project under the name Evergreens Limited.'

'Limited?'

'Yes. We've spent the last decade in R & D, tinkering with the product, but we're almost ready to launch. The plan is to offer a refined version of the original treatment to a select group of outstanding individuals.'

Sophie turns this phrase over for a moment, trying to decipher his marketing-speak. 'Outstanding individuals? You mean... rich people?'

Johan's smile widens. 'My grandfather was a visionary scientist, but a horrible businessman. His dream was to bring down the cost of our service so we could treat everyone on earth. To banish the misery of disease and decrepitude once and for all. It's a noble ambition, for sure. But there was a fundamental flaw in his thinking. I mean, the planet is massively overpopulated as it is. If people start living for two, three, four hundred years...'

'It would be a disaster for the environment. I said that to him the first time we met.'

'Precisely. It's a broken business model. What's the point in living for a thousand years if the world is falling apart? Disease? Famine? War? No, thanks. However, if we turn it on its head and make the treatment incredibly exclusive...'

'By which you mean incredibly expensive...'

He flashes her his ice-white smile. 'Well, then we have a viable proposition. CEOs of international corporations. World leaders. Movie stars. We have a diverse list of people on the waiting list, ready to undergo treatment the day we launch. Household names, many of them. Although naturally, they value their privacy. Hence no web or social presence, no listed building. You won't find us on any map. Discretion is everything in this line of work.'

'Oh, I'm sure it is. I'm sure the last thing you'd want is a public scandal. If, say, these prospective clients of yours found out that the business that's been wooing them for a decade has suddenly started killing off its original patients.'

Johan stares at her. For the first time since she arrived here, he seems a little wrong-footed. A little flustered. 'Excuse me?'

'Oh, come off it. One minute, Ben's perfectly healthy, and the next he's lying unconscious in a hospital bed? What's the matter? Did he know too much? Or maybe you decided you need a clean slate? Out with the old in with the new, is that it?'

'Hey now, listen—'

'And what about the others? Nadia, Martin, Adaku. All of them dead within the space of twelve months? That's a hell of a coincidence.'

'How did you...?'

'It's not just me who knows about them, you know. The police are out there, too, joining the dots. Sooner or later they're going to come knocking on your door to find out why you're out here attempting to erase every trace of the original trial, including the participants.'

By now, Johan looks furious. For a second, she fears he will attack her. Isn't that what happens to people who stick their noses in where they don't belong? Particularly where there's vast sums of money involved. Any moment, she thinks, the door behind him will fly open and a pack of burly security guards will set upon her. Suited thugs with a rope and a shovel. And what will she do then? Nobody knows she's here. Not her *family. Definitely not the police. She can't run. Not any more. She braces herself for the violence that is inevitably coming her way.*

But then Johan's expression changes. His eyes widen. His lips twist.

And this is even scarier than everything she has just imagined.

Because, to her immense confusion, she realises he is laughing.

2033

23

Sophie beams.

Dressed in a smart blazer and sensible blouse, she sits at an ordinary dining table in an ordinary kitchen, surrounded by her family. Two beautiful, blonde-haired, blemish-free pre-teens.

But this is no advert.

These are her children.

Orson, aged twelve, and his eight-year-old sister, Amelia.

Sitting opposite her is Matthew. Still dressed in a crumpled charity-shop suit. Still handsome, too, although his hair is almost totally grey now. Sophie occasionally teases him about it, although privately she thinks it rather suits him. It makes him look very distinguished, as her mother used to say.

On the table before him is a huge home-baked chocolate cake, on top of which a forest of candles is ablaze.

'Sorry, we couldn't fit all fifty-one on there,' Sophie says. 'We ran out of space at… How many, kids?'

'Thirty-one,' Orson says.

'No, thirty-two,' Amelia corrects him. 'Look. One, two, three, four…'

'OK, sweetie. There's no need to count them again. I think we can all agree there are a disgraceful number of candles on Daddy's cake.'

'Hey!' Matthew grins. 'There aren't *that* many. Anyway, you'll only have three fewer than me on your next birthday.'

'Ahem! Five, actually. You're not stealing two years from me.'

Orson shakes his head. 'I don't know what you're fighting for. You're both *ancient*.'

Everybody laughs.

After dinner is done and the remains of the cake cleared away, Sophie and Matthew decamp to the living room to watch the news while the kids run upstairs to play before bed. Last year, for Matthew's fiftieth, she'd gone all out and thrown a huge party. As the pièce de résistance, she'd got Emilio, one of the editors at their production company, to help her cut together a trailer for a fake biopic of Matthew's life. They'd spent weeks on it, splicing in real home video from his childhood alongside more recent bits and pieces they'd stolen from social media. She'd even gathered together a cast of actors in bad wigs to recreate the stuff for which they didn't have footage, hamming up the pivotal moments of his life. The now famous audition where Sophie had stormed out; their first fumbling kiss; the shock news that she was pregnant with Orson. She'd meant it as a joke, complete with fake title cards and a gravelly, pitched-down voice-over:

'He was the boy... who became a man... who became a legend...'

And it was funny. Everyone laughed. Yet somehow, accompanied by the portentous classical soundtrack Emilio had added, it was also strangely moving. Watching it back on the huge projector screen, surrounded by everyone they loved, she'd found herself unexpectedly choked up, a silent stream of tears sliding down her cheeks as she watched the life of the man she loved playing out on the screen.

This year has been a far more low-key affair. A takeaway with the kids. And, later on, a film. One of Matthew's favourites. *In a Lonely Place*. Or *Chinatown* maybe. That's the plan, anyway. But Sophie can already see him rubbing his eyes. She suspects they might have to defer the movie until the weekend, unless she fancies watching it with him snoring beside her on the sofa again.

She's not surprised he's tired. It's been a long week. A long couple of years, if she's honest. It was all so much simpler when they started on this crazy journey together. No staff. No offices. No big contracts to fulfil. No pressure, really. It was just the two of them, with nothing to lose.

Well, technically, it was just her. At least at first.

After she'd left Ben and moved back into her parents' house, she had no idea what she was going to do. It felt like everything was ending. Her marriage. Her career. The whole fucking world.

Yet somehow, in spite of all of the trauma and turmoil, she managed to keep writing. Hunched over her laptop in her childhood bedroom, she tapped away. Word after word. Scene after scene. Doing her best to block out the periodic lectures from her mother about needing to move on and rebuild her life ('Have you thought about teaching, dear?') and the endless news that poured from the TV and radio, the promises that a vaccine, and brighter days, were just around the corner.

She blocked out Ben, too. Declining his calls. Deleting his emails without reading them. She even refused to come to the door when he turned up outside her parents' house one Tuesday afternoon, demanding to see her. She'd stood at the top of the stairs, listening as her dad tried to let him down as gently and diplomatically as possible.

'Listen, son. She just needs some time to clear her head. She'll call you when she's ready, OK?'

It turned out Ben wasn't interested in diplomacy. 'You know what, Douglas? I'm not your fucking son. And I'm not a child, either. I'm an adult, and I need to have an adult conversation with my adult wife.'

Her dad wouldn't relent though, and in the end Ben stormed away.

She knew she couldn't avoid him forever. There was still much to do. The legal dissolution of their marriage. The selling of their house. All of the banal bureaucracy of a break-up.

But that could come later. For the time being, all she could think about was the script, which she finished late one night after a marathon writing session, exactly six weeks after she'd walked out on Ben. She remembers saving the document, closing her laptop, and then promptly bursting into tears. Rather than feeling relieved to be finished, she felt terrified. What would she do now that she no longer had a project to take her mind off the plane wreck of her personal life? And who the hell wanted a film script when no one was making anything?

In the end, she reached out to Matthew. He got back to her almost immediately. He loved her script. More than loved it. He'd sat up all night reading it and was *besotted* with the thing. What's more, he was convinced he could get it made.

Unfortunately, on this last point at least, he turned out to be utterly wrong.

'It's hell out there,' he said after a month and a half of virtual doors being slammed in his face. 'There's just no market for anything at the moment. Cinema's dying a slow and painful death. Everyone's terrified. No one's taking any chances.'

As he spoke, Sophie felt herself burning with embarrassment. She knew at once that Matthew was just being nice. That the script was terrible. Unsellable. After all these months of clinging to this idea that she'd somehow found her calling, it turned out to be just another dead end. She wasn't a writer. She was a failure. 'So I guess that's that,' she said, wishing he'd hurry up and kill the video call so she could throw herself onto her bed and scream into her pillow.

But Matthew only shook his head. 'That's not what I said. I said no one's making anything at the moment. But that doesn't mean we can't go ahead and make it ourselves.'

Sophie stared at him. This slightly stammering older man

in his crumpled tweed jacket. Was he just trying to console her? Was he simply too polite to walk away?

But it turned out Matthew was deadly serious. His idea was to reimagine her script as a low-budget web series. With just a few tweaks, he explained, the whole thing could be filmed for a pittance, with each actor remaining in isolation. 'We can film it on our phones,' he enthused. 'It's the perfect pandemic-proof piece.'

And so, once again, the writing began in earnest, as she desperately tried to adapt her story for the small screen. As the weeks went by, however, Sophie found being back in her childhood home was an increasing hindrance to her productivity. For one thing, both her parents appeared to have independently decided to make her their primary retirement project. Her mother's lectures now stretched to multi-day seminars, sprawling conferences during which she instructed Sophie on the steps she needed to take in order to set her drifting ship back on course ('…and teachers do have such good pensions, sweetheart.').

Her father, meanwhile, had taken her temporary move back home as an opportunity to re-establish the master/apprentice dynamic of her early childhood. There always seemed to be some little job around the house that he needed help with. Recaulking the bathtub or repointing some old brickwork or clearing out the gutters.

'It's important you learn how to do these things for yourself,' he'd say, while Sophie somehow managed to resist the urge to point out that she had recently bought and renovated an entire house.

'It's killing me,' she complained to Matthew, during one of their nightly video calls. 'They never stop telling me how I need to "stand on my own two feet", but then they don't let me do anything for myself. I feel like I'm regressing. Ageing in reverse. I can't even make a cup of tea without one of them leaping up to do it for me. I half expect them to start mashing up my meals and feeding me with a spoon.'

Matthew shrugged. 'So why don't you just move in with me?'

'Oh, right.'

'I mean it. It would certainly make writing simpler. I'm so sick of staring at my own bloody face on a computer screen all day. And it would give you the space you need to actually get some work done. I have a futon you can sleep on.'

She grinned wickedly. 'The old "I have a futon" routine, eh?'

'Victor-what?' he asked, his face turning a shade of scarlet.

'Oh, come on. I've been around the block enough times to know how it goes. You offer me a rickety wooden thing that's about as comfortable as a bed of nails, so that I have no option but to come and crawl into your luxurious memory-foam palace in the middle of the night. Yeah, I'm pretty sure I fell for that one at university. Several times, come to think of it.'

Matthew looked like he was going to be sick. 'I'm offering a practical solution here, Sophie. My motives are entirely professional. And I'll have you know that my futon is perfectly comfortable.'

'Calm down, Matty. I know you're no creep.' She laughed. The idea of her and Matthew being together like *that* was unimaginable. Not that she didn't like him. He was a nice guy. A little buttoned-up. But kind and sweet and funny. And attractive, too, in his own way. He reminded her of a down-on-his luck English lecturer who'd temporarily taken to sleeping in his car. His clothes creased, his glasses permanently askew, his hair sticking up in tufts. But the idea of another relationship – or even a one-night stand – was the furthest thing from her mind. Not with her break-up from Ben still so painfully fresh. No, the only thing she had room for at the moment was the work. And from that perspective, Matthew's offer was tempting.

And so she agreed, informing her crestfallen parents that she'd taken their advice to stand on her own two feet, before dragging the suitcase that contained what remained of her worldly possessions back to London and setting up shop in Matthew's tiny but immaculately tidy flat.

Where, of course, just three short weeks later, they found themselves in bed with each other.

'So it turned out I did fall for the old futon routine, after all,' she'd joke for years to come whenever anyone asked how they'd got together. Much to Matthew's intense discomfort.

Still, the fact they'd become an item didn't derail their film project. If anything, it drove them to work harder than ever before. As the old year rolled over and died, and the new one began with yet another lockdown, they created their own little bubble, their personal and professional lives folding into a single exhilarating blur of activity that occupied every waking second. And most of her sleeping ones, too.

They finished the script, recruited actors to film themselves at home, then stitched the scenes together into something coherent during a marathon month of all-night editing sessions. And then, once it was finally ready, they uploaded the whole thing for people to watch free, online.

To Sophie's amazement, the show was a success. Not the mind-boggling, seventy-full-time-employees-and-offices-in-Central-London kind of success they would enjoy just a few years later. But a success nonetheless. A 'zero-budget lockdown hit' was how it would come to be described, attracting a small but passionate audience. The writing was singled out for particular praise. Sophie was hailed as a vital new voice, an overnight sensation, despite the endless months she'd spent working on it. But it wasn't only the critics who were impressed. It wasn't long before the people with the chequebooks noticed, too. Before long, she and Matthew had a firm offer to make something a little bigger.

They've been riding that same wave ever since.

As for Ben, aside from a few emails, she had spoken to him just once since they split. A few months after she and Matthew had started seeing each other, she'd called him up. There was some legal stuff to clear up, some paperwork that needed signing. And although in truth she probably could have left it to the solicitor her father was paying, she wanted to check he was OK. After all, she hadn't left because she was angry with him. Not really. She'd left because it had become agonisingly apparent that he no longer loved her. Not sexually. Not romantically. Not even, and this hurt more than anything else, as a friend.

Still, as sad as the situation was, she accepted it. She was an adult. She knew that people grew and changed. Even if, in Ben's case, he didn't actually grow or change. But people move on. Which is exactly what she'd done. She had to. After all, she knew *he'd* never have the courage to end it. And then what? They'd have both remained stuck, going nowhere, indefinitely miserable as the months and years swirled down the sinkhole.

He might have *forever*, but she certainly didn't.

'Oh. Hey. Sophie.'

Ben sounded so small, so flat, so resigned to the fact that it was over, that it broke her heart all over again. Later, she would wonder if he'd said something then, begged her, pleaded with her, told her he loved her, well, then who knows what might have happened? Maybe she would have realised that the real reason she'd walked out was not that their relationship was over, but that she simply wanted him to notice her again? Maybe she would have gone back to him, and Matthew would have been relegated to a small blip in the history of their lives together. A brief fling before their inevitable reconciliation. Not that it mattered. Because Ben didn't beg or plead or proclaim his undying love. He just spoke very quietly and sadly. He apologised for dragging his feet and agreed to sign the papers and to forward the rest of Sophie's things.

'Well,' she said, as they reached the end of the call. 'I guess this is goodbye then.'

He was silent for a moment, long enough for her to dare to hope he might protest.

But he didn't.

Instead, he ended their relationship with a final, defeated mumble. 'I guess so.'

And then he was gone.

A few months later, much to her father's consternation, she fired her solicitor. The show was taking off online and she didn't have the headspace for a divorce or a house sale. She could arrange all that later, she thought. Although it turned out there was never any need. Matthew didn't believe in marriage, and she wasn't interested in going through all that fuss again. Anyway, she didn't want to be vindictive. If she insisted on selling the house, who knew where he'd end up? On a park bench, probably. So she sent him an email, offering him the chance to buy her out at a ridiculously low price, which he duly accepted. There were a few calls to the bank. A couple of documents to initial. And that was that. Their life together was over.

She hadn't heard from him since.

Of course, she's thought about reaching out over the years. Occasionally, late at night, after Matt's gone to bed and she's had one too many glasses of wine, she's been known to punch his name into various social media sites. But nothing ever comes up. It's crazy. He must be literally the last person left in the world who still doesn't have an online presence. She could call him, she supposes. Assuming he hasn't changed his number. Or send him an email. She could even go and visit, unannounced. Knock on the door of their old house and see if he still lives there. Tell him she was passing and see if he fancies a coffee for old times' sake.

But she never has.

She's always too busy with work, kids, Matt – life.

Besides, maybe it's better this way? It was all such a long time ago now. Things were different. They were different. She's changed. Grown up.

That's what she tells herself.

Yet in spite of all that, sometimes, like tonight, he still flickers through her mind involuntarily. She'll catch herself speculating about what he's doing. Who he's with.

If he's happy.

'Well, that's a bloody disaster waiting to happen,' Matthew says, pointing at the television screen.

Sophie shakes her head, swimming back into the present. 'What's a disaster?'

'The US elections. I just can't believe they've finally voted to make a rapper their head of state. I wouldn't mind, but he hasn't put out a decent album in about thirty years.'

'Oh, that. Right. Yes.'

He looks at her quizzically. 'Are you OK? You seem a little distracted.'

'It's nothing. I was just thinking it's funny the way things turn out.'

Before he can press her any further, there's a thunder of footsteps on the stairs. Seconds later an Egyptian mummy and a blood-splattered surgeon burst into the living room.

'Oh my goodness! You scared the life out of us!' Matthew says, laughing.

'We're getting ready for Halloween,' Amelia says.

'But Halloween's not for another three weeks,' Sophie says. 'Wait, did you use the last of the loo roll to make that?'

She nods. 'Orson said it was OK.'

'I'm not Orson,' says the surgeon standing beside her. 'I'm… Doctor Death!'

'Well, I think you both look marvellous,' Matthew says. 'Did you know that when Orson was a baby, we had to wear masks like that all the time? Even if we wanted to go to the supermarket.'

Orson rolls his eyes and makes the same disdainful grunt that Sophie used to make when she was his age. 'God, Dad. You've told us this story, like, *a hundred million times* already.'

'We're doing the pandemic in our topic in history next term,' Amelia adds.

'Yeah, in *ancient* history,' says Orson.

'Oh, really?' Matthew says, grinning as he hauls himself to his feet. 'Do you know what else is ancient history?'

'What?'

'You two, if you don't take those costumes off and get ready for bed right now,' he roars.

And then they are all off, the children running while Matthew chases, everyone screaming and clattering and laughing their heads off as they scramble up the stairs, while Sophie sits smiling and looking up at the ceiling, listening to the three of them as they sprint into their rooms and land with a thump, a tangled pile of limbs and tickles and kisses and screeches and blown raspberries. A cacophony of love filling the house, loud enough to chase away even the most persistent of ghosts.

24

Ben is panicking.

He is sitting in a small Italian restaurant off the Portobello Road, a glass of Primitivo in his hand. Opposite him is his date for the night. She's young, outgoing, funny and incredibly smart. Fresh out of university with a degree in cultural anthropology and a passion for tackling social inequality in Timor-Leste. Not that Ben is able to concentrate on anything she's saying. He's too busy trying to remember her name.

Sara? Sasha? Sahara?

Shit.

This is bad. Although not unusual. And certainly not surprising. How many first dates has he sat through over the last decade? Hundreds? Probably more like thousands. Each one a carbon copy of the last. Not that there's any sign of him slowing down. Not when there seems to be an inexhaustible pool of sexually liberated young people who are more than happy to slide across the screen of his phone and into his bed, before they slide out of it again just as quickly a few hours later. Which suits him just fine. He's not looking to make friends. As soon as the morning arrives, they're gone and he's on to the next. A perpetual conveyor belt delivering beautiful bodies to his bedroom. It's a revelation to him. Sex without emotions. All of the fun, without any danger of getting hurt.

It's like a risk-free bet.

Yet as the years have spiralled by, he's found himself progressively less satisfied by the encounters. Swiping through the endless list of potential partners, he feels he might as well be scrolling through a list of high-end coffee machines. They're all well designed. Aesthetically pleasing. *Functional*. But at the end of the day, they all do essentially the same thing.

And the longer it goes on, the less sure he is that he even *likes* coffee any more.

Across the table, Sara/Sasha/Sahara is telling him about her hopes and dreams for the future. She wants to establish a not-for-profit to empower young people in low- and middle-income countries. She wants to swim the channel to draw attention to environmental pollution. She's thinking about getting a puppy.

Ben nods. He feels utterly detached from the conversation. He's heard these monologues so many, many times before. Some bright-eyed young person laying out their dreams and ambitions. Telling him they're going to change the world. Go down in history.

And how many of them ever go on to do it?

Although there is always Sophie. Sophie with her wild success. Sophie, who's achieved everything she set out to do, and more. Though he's had no contact with her for more than a decade, her career is inescapable, her interviews splurged across the newspapers and the internet, so that even when he's not actively thinking about her, suddenly there she is, smiling at him from the screen, compelling him to compare his latest conquest with her perfect life.

Just as he is now.

Thankfully, the waiter arrives before he can become too maudlin, furnishing the table with a selection of small plates of antipasti. Parmigiano, gamberoni, calamari, along with a basket of bread and another healthy glug of red in his glass. A candle flickers between them.

It's perfect.

Only he no longer feels the slightest bit hungry.

'So what about you?' the girl across the table asks. 'What do you want to do with your life?'

Ben resists the urge to laugh. Like all of the first dates who have come and gone before her, she assumes they're the same age. Why wouldn't she? He looks the part. And he deliberately leaves his date of birth blank on his dating profile. Not that this omission feels like a lie. He never mentions the programme to anyone. It just doesn't seem relevant any more. It's not like he's kept in touch with any of the other Evergreens. Nor has he heard from Dr Andersson, who hasn't sent him so much as an email in all the years since the trial ended. So no, he doesn't bring it up. He just goes along with their assumption that he's young, fun and up for a good time. Which, mostly, he is. Even in his mid-forties, he still thinks of himself as young. Not just physically, but in spirit, too. Partly, he suspects it's down to the company he keeps. Working in kitchens, the people under him tend to be those willing to settle for shitty minimum-wage jobs. Students. School leavers. Drug addicts and drunks and other assorted fuck-ups. People who hang around and wash pots or chop veg for a few months and then move on. He has a lot more in common with them than he does with people his own age. Those serious, grey-haired bores, whose conversation is leaden with talk of pensions and investment portfolios and holiday homes and kitchen extensions and their children's university choices and their new VR headset and the number of miles their electric car can travel between charges. Ben couldn't care less about that stuff. Give him the kitchen crazies any day of the week if it means avoiding death by a thousand yawns.

Only recently, something's changed. As with his sexual partners, he's found himself struggling to relate to the teenagers and twenty-somethings he counts as colleagues. At first, it was simply a case of missing the odd reference here or there. They'd mention a film he hadn't seen, or a band he hadn't heard, or an app he hadn't used. No big deal. But then suddenly there were whole sentences he couldn't decipher. New slang that had somehow passed him by. Entire subcultures that meant nothing to him. It's like they've started speaking another language. And even when he can follow what they're saying, he frequently struggles to care about it. It's as if a chasm has opened between their generation and his. In fact, the more time he spends with these so-called *young people*, the more closely they seem to resemble the serious, sour-faced grown-ups he's always sought to avoid. All they ever want to talk about is the latest archipelago to be swallowed by rising sea levels. Or the surge in private companies mining the moon for minerals and precious metals. Or the worrying number of jobs being made redundant by artificial intelligence. Or, in the case of whatever the hell her name is sitting opposite him now, child poverty in Timor-Leste.

'Oh, I'm still figuring things out,' he says with a smile. 'I figure I've still got plenty of time.'

Eventually, dessert arrives. Panna cotta for him, zabaglione for her. Ben is glad of the distraction. Over the course of the meal, the lights have dimmed and the candle has melted into a waxy puddle, casting them both in shadows that he hopes are helping to mask the disinterest on his face whenever she talks.

He's about ready to make his excuses and call a premature end to the evening, when he feels something under the table. The girl's knee accidentally brushing up against his. He mumbles an apology and moves his leg. But then he spots her tongue tracing her bottom lip. Her eyebrow arching. The bloom of her pupils in the dark. And how many times has he seen this expression over the years? This pantomime played out at dinner tables across the city as the evening moves towards its inevitable conclusion. The suggestion of one more drink back at his place. The sofa fumble followed by the drunken stumble from living room to bedroom. The clash of teeth and the awkward angles and the clumsy attempts to unlock the secrets of a stranger's body. The excitement turning into disappointment turning into an awkward goodbye the next morning. The flood of nausea and self-loathing that arrive with the first strains of daylight, before the whole sorry cycle starts again an evening or two later.

Well, not tonight.

'Listen, Sara,' he begins.

'It's Saskia,'

Saskia. Fuck.

'Saskia. Sorry. I just want to say this now so there isn't any misunderstanding. About what happens later…'

It feels as if all of the air has been sucked out the room. Saskia's mouth puckers as she waits for whatever bombshell Ben is about to drop.

'I… er…'

And how can he even begin to explain? To tell her that he is actually a jaded middle-aged man masquerading as a twenty-one-year-old. That he's so lost and empty that he feels as if one more meaningless night of sex might be enough to break him permanently. That he would simply crumble and turn to dust.

He can't tell her any of that. So he does what he always does when he feels cornered.

He lies.

'I need to get an early night. I have a flight to catch in the morning.'

At this, Saskia's expression turns from defensiveness to confusion. 'A flight?'

'Yes. I'm going travelling. Around the world. I tried to go when I was… Well, a while ago. But it didn't work out. I feel like I've got unfinished business. So I decided to quit my job and just… do it.'

She stares at him, trying to decide if he's joking or not. 'So you're off on a round-the-world trip and you thought it was a good idea to go out on a date the night before?'

Ben grimaces. 'I probably should have mentioned something earlier, shouldn't I?'

'Do you think?'

The exchange that follows is excruciating. Though he offers to pay the bill, she insists on splitting it down the middle. They part ways without so much as a goodbye, Saskia storming off towards a taxi rank before he even manages to get his coat on.

Yet as he walks out of the restaurant and into the cool night air, he feels oddly exhilarated by the unexpected turn of the evening. As it happens, he does have to be up fairly early tomorrow morning, the purgatory of the brunch shift awaiting him.

Unless he doesn't go in...

An idea emerges. Fragile at first, but quickly crystallising. What if he really does go travelling? After all, he has the Evergreens money to tide him over. It's not a lot, but it would probably go a bit further in Southeast Asia than it would here. He could look for work along the way. Maybe he'd even make it as far as Australia again?

It's a preposterous idea. One born of equal parts desperation and Italian red. Yet even as he tells himself this, he takes his phone out and begins browsing budget airlines.

Just to see what's possible.

2070

VIII

'I must start by applauding your imagination, Mrs Walker.'

By now, Johan Andersson has stopped laughing, although he still looks amused.

'I always feel there's something admirable about conspiracy theorists. Their boundless creativity. Their determination not to let facts get in the way of a thrilling narrative. But then, you're a writer, are you not? And writers nearly always save the best stories for the ones they tell themselves. However, I'm afraid that no matter how good the story is on this occasion, it simply doesn't stand up to scrutiny. Here, let me show you.'

As he reaches into his jacket pocket, Sophie half expects him to produce a pistol. Instead, he brings out his deck, a sleek, high-spec model, and caresses the screen, sending a sprawl of photographs into the air between them. Six girls, six boys. Beside each picture is a name. Some written in green, others red. Scanning the list, she sees that Ben is number ten. His name is green.

'Of the original twelve Evergreens, seven are still alive,' Johan says, gesturing to the photographs. 'Including, for the next few days at least, your husband. Now the reason they are alive is simple. They are alive because they chose to be.'

Sophie stares at him, unable to hide her confusion. 'What?'

'Before my grandfather was forced to shut down his trial, he was still in the process of perfecting the treatment. There were various iterations of the medication, right up until the *intravenous vaccine he settled on right before the plug was pulled. The vaccine was incredibly effective. It was the best treatment he'd developed yet. But there was always a risk that it could become unstable. In fact, that was one of the reasons his backers got cold feet. There was no way they could have gone to market. He was still years away from getting it right.'*

'So you're saying the drugs your grandfather gave Ben weren't safe?'

'You must remember, this was a drug trial involving experimental medication. Of course it wasn't safe. Anything could have happened. Were the participants aware of this fact? Absolutely. Did they choose to participate anyway? Yes, they did. And, for the most part, they were absolutely right to do so.'

'How can you say that? Three of them are dead.'

'But not because of the treatment. Or at least, not only because of it. That's what I'm trying to explain. When I relaunched Evergreens, I knew there were issues with the vaccine. It's all there in my grandfather's research. He hypothesised it would eventually fail. Although he assumed there would be a gradual tapering off, rather than the cliff edge the participants are facing now.'

'Cliff edge?'

'If you picture a leaking dam, Mrs Walker. You might not notice the cracks appearing until it is too late and the whole thing comes crashing down. It's the same thing here, unfortunately. At some point, the body simply rejects the vaccine, sending it into catastrophic shock. The subject loses consciousness and begins rapid degeneration. They die. Unless...'

'Unless?'

'I'm pleased to say that things have moved on a lot in fifty years. We have access to technology that my grandfather could have only dreamt about. As a result, we have developed a new treatment. A booster shot, if you will. Which is precisely what has allowed me to bring my product to market. As long

as the subjects receive a regular top-up, there's no reason that any of this unpleasantness needs to happen.'

Sophie stares at him, outraged. 'Well, if it's so great, then why are three of them dead? And where the hell was Ben's booster shot?'

'This is what I mean when I say that some of them chose to live. As soon as we'd developed the booster, we wrote to all the Evergreens, inviting them to come in to receive their booster. Some of them decided not to pursue further treatment. Ben was one of them.'

'You wrote to Ben? When?'

'The first time? Almost a year ago, now. And then every month since. We were desperate to help him. From a PR perspective, this whole thing is a nightmare for us. We can't have ex-Evergreens dropping dead all over the place, no matter how long ago they began treatment. It's a disaster. And so, naturally, we did everything we could to reach Ben. To reach all of them. We wrote, called, emailed. But unfortunately, some simply never responded.'

Sophie is struggling to process everything Johan has told her. Was it really possible that Ben had turned down the opportunity to continue his treatment? That he'd chosen to die?

'So these people. The ones who never got back to you. You're saying they decided to commit suicide?'

'In a sense. They may not have seen it in those terms, of course. But the messages we sent were unambiguous. The treatment is failing, you must come in. If, for whatever reason, the subjects choose not to act on that information, then there's very little we can do, no matter how much we'd like to help. It really is a terrible shame.'

Sophie sits in silence. She knows that Ben has been unhappy. But this? She never thought in a million years he'd do something like this. 'A shame? These are people's lives we're talking about. Surely you have a duty of care to them? A legal responsibility? Or...'

Johan shakes his head sadly. 'Not if they don't want to be helped. It's a terrible situation.'

'So you're saying that's it? I'm too late. That Ben just has to lie there, wasting away, until...'

She trails off.

Johan looks at her. His lips are pursed, as if he's hesitant to speak again. 'Actually, that's not quite right,' he says at last. 'There may be something we can do. To help him, I mean. Although from an ethical perspective, it may be a little... problematic.'

2045

25

She'll never get used to these cars.

As Matthew swivels around to rummage around on the back seat, leaving the vehicle to steer itself, Sophie fights the urge to lurch for the unattended wheel, so as to stop them veering off the motorway towards a fiery death. This despite the fact that car crashes have been more or less confined to history books for over a decade now. Along with so much else.

'Here you go, love,' he says, handing her a travel mug filled with synthetic coffee.

She takes a sip, grimacing slightly at the taste.

'No good?'

'It's fine. I just always forget and expect the real thing. Who'd have thought I'd end up missing Nescafé so much? And don't get me started on tea. You know sometimes I still dream about a proper cup of Yorkshire Tea?'

'With real cow's milk? And sugar? Remember sugar?'

'Stop. I'll cry.'

They both let out a sigh in tandem.

It's a stiflingly warm Wednesday morning in February, and both of them are sweating in their seats as they make the journey from London to Birmingham. The last time Sophie made this trip was almost forty years ago, when she'd attended Mal's disastrous birthday party. Considering everything that happened that night, she's been in no hurry to return. Yet it is precisely because of that party that she finds herself heading back there now. For today, they are on their way to a funeral.

'So remind me again how you knew this poor chap?' Matthew asks.

She rolls her eyes. She's told Matthew this story dozens of times before. How she'd first met Darren in Australia at the same time she'd met Ben, and then briefly again a few years later at a party in Birmingham (she tactically neglected to mention Paul and skipped the part about how the night had ended). That how, after not hearing a peep out of him for twenty-five years, he'd sent her a friend request on social media and they'd reconnected, staying in touch intermittently ever since.

What was more difficult to explain was exactly *why* she was going to his funeral. While it was true they'd been friends online, in reality their friendship consisted of liking each other's posts, and very occasionally adding a single-word comment underneath.

Nice!

Great!

Beautiful!

Like everyone else she knows, Sophie has thousands of 'friends' like this. Colleagues. Former classmates. People she once shared a glass of wine with at a movie premiere. Many of whom she's seen in the flesh far more recently than Darren, and whose funeral, if she's honest, she wouldn't dream of attending.

So why him?

Partly, it's down to shock. At fifty-eight, death has begun to become an unwelcome visitor in her life. Both her parents are gone now, her mother to cancer, her father, finally, to dementia, having spent the last eighteen months of his life staring at the walls of a care home. Farida, her old housemate, died of breast cancer around ten years ago, leaving behind a young family. Her cousin Mark, three years her junior, had a heart attack while on holiday in Greece. And more recently, a young production assistant she worked with had somehow managed to electrocute himself while installing a set of garage doors at his house. Yet for all of these losses, she knows she is relatively lucky, in that her experiences of tragedy have been mercifully small. She hasn't yet reached the miserable age her dad had once described, before he got really sick, where 'you wake up one morning and realise all your friends are dead'.

Sophie hadn't even been aware that Darren was ill. On the fast-flowing stream of her social media channels, she'd managed to miss the various posts he'd made over the previous eleven months. Photos of him looking increasingly gaunt in hospital waiting rooms, where he bemoaned the crippling cost of treatment and missing the old NHS. Or sitting in a wheelchair, surrounded by his grown-up children. It was only when she spotted a comment from his wife thanking people for their support that she realised he was gone and scrolled back through his posts to see what had happened.

'Such awful luck,' Matthew said when she told him. 'To think they can send a person to Mars, but people still die every day because of a few out-of-control cells in their liver. I'd have thought we'd have cured all this shit long ago by now. I guess it just goes to show where our priorities lie.'

Still, it isn't only shock that has sent her hurtling up the motorway to Birmingham today. If she's honest, she hardly knew the guy. No, it isn't so much Darren's death that upsets her, but what it represents: another link to her life with Ben disappearing.

And perhaps, secretly, she's hoping that maybe she won't be the only one to have been shaken by the news. That Ben will have heard, too, and choose this moment to make a miraculous reappearance, returning from wherever he's been hiding all these years to pay his final respects to his old friend.

Not that she says any of this to Matthew. Instead, she

takes another swig of her awful fake coffee and pats her husband's leg.

'He was just someone I used to know.'

As soon as they pull off the motorway, Sophie suspects she has made a terrible mistake returning to Birmingham. The glimpses of the city she spots from the car window are nothing like the thriving metropolis she remembers from her youth. The buildings they pass are mostly abandoned, their windows shattered, their walls daubed with graffiti. Some have been burned down altogether. As they pause at a set of traffic lights, Sophie sees an entire shanty town has been constructed on the side of the road, with hundreds of homeless people lying under bent sheets of corrugated steel. Others mill around the pavements and spill into the road, tapping on the windows of cars and holding up their battered deck readers in the hope of a quick donation. While some are English, many have the telltale look of climate refugees. Whole families who have been forced to flee from floods and famines and fires, as well as other things too terrible to name. Up ahead, a small boy weaves between the traffic, moving from car to car, attempting to wash windows. He can't be more than seven years old. Sophie watches him for a while before, like Matthew, she glances down at her deck and begins to scroll through her social feed until the lights turn green and they pull away.

The crematorium is already packed when they arrive, the cramped chapel barely big enough to contain the multitude of black-clad mourners who fill the benches and jostle for spaces in the aisles. Sophie and Matthew stand at the back of the room, feeling very much strangers at what is clearly a family affair. Sophie glances around the room, wondering if Ben might be here, but the place is too full to make out much more than the backs of people's heads.

Moments later, the service begins. To her surprise, a priest leads the ceremony. Sophie was brought up an atheist, and no one in her circle is remotely religious. She'd always assumed organised religion would go the way of Facebook or Apple or Disney, and all those other old-fashioned institutions that at one point in time seemed utterly dominant. Yet religion is actually growing around the world, the various crises that have engulfed this century creating a boom time for gods of every persuasion. Still, she finds it hard to picture Darren praying. The loud-mouthed party boy knocking back shots of Jägermeister never struck her as particularly pious. But then again, she reminds herself, that was an awfully long time ago now. Almost an entire lifetime.

While the priest drones on, she finds her attention drawn to the coffin, which sits on its catafalque at the front of the stage. Sophie isn't squeamish about death. She accepts it as a sad but inevitable part of life. Even so, it's a strange thought that Darren's body is lying there, less than thirty feet away. That his journey is done. How can it all go so quickly? One moment she was sprawled on St Kilda beach with a beer and book and now she's sitting here. She remembers her poor dad, in one of his final lucid moments, bemoaning how fast it all goes. That how just yesterday he was a young man, kicking a football in the park with his friends. And then he blinked and found himself hardly able to bring a spoon to his mouth without food dribbling down his chin. With every passing year, she understands more clearly what he meant. She can still feel that Australian sun beating down on her, forty years later. Still hear the gulls wheeling overhead. Still smell the sea. Her whole life ahead of her. Until suddenly it wasn't.

Quite unexpectedly, she finds herself crying, a small sob breaking loose from the back of her throat.

'I know,' Matthew whispers, sliding a protective arm around her waist. 'It's OK to be sad. It's a sad day.'

What she doesn't tell him, however, is that she's not crying for Darren. Not really.

She's crying for herself.

At last the service is over. Music is piped from concealed speakers. Some saccharine pop song she doesn't recognise. The coffin is transferred onto a trolley. People begin to drain away. Once they're outside, Matthew goes to the car to make a phone call, but Sophie lingers a while outside the chapel, watching the faces of the mourners as they stagger out into the light. There's no sign of Ben. She smiles bitterly. She's an idiot to think he might be here.

She turns to leave. Before she can move, however, she senses someone approaching. A bald man with a huge belly, a wide grin spread across his face.

'Sophie?' he says. 'Is that you?'

Sophie stares blankly, struggling to place him. 'Oh, hey,' she says, stalling.

'Paul,' he prompts. 'We met in…'

Jesus. This is *Paul*? An image of a hyperactive teenager with a blonde mohawk and gym-jacked body tumbles through Sophie's mind. She could pass him in the street and not know it was him. He's utterly unrecognisable.

'…Melbourne,' she finishes, forcing a laugh. 'You've hardly changed a bit. Gosh, how long has it been?'

'Must be almost forty years?'

'That long? Wow. The last time I saw you…' She trails off, flushing as she thinks back to that mortifying morning in the hotel. Ben's unexpected arrival at the door. And then those awkward, hungover moments between them after he'd stormed off. Paul hunting around on the floor for his boxer shorts. Sophie sitting on the bed, waiting for him to go so she could throw up or burst into tears or both at the same time. Their weird, fumbling goodbye once he was finally dressed. A kiss? A handshake? In the end, they'd settled on a hug. A brief, passionless squeeze, before she bundled him out of the door. Both of them promising to speak soon. Both of them knowing they would do no such thing.

Paul is obviously remembering the same thing. 'Well.' He coughs. 'A long time ago, anyway. But it's great to see you. Although, obviously, I wish it was under different circumstances. I didn't know you and Darren had stayed in touch?'

'Only online. You know how it is. I was so sad when I heard. He was what? Fifty-eight?'

'Yeah. Poor sod. It's no age.'

'Did you two stay close?'

'A bit. I mean, we'd see each other now and then. But he got married and had kids and all the rest of it. Life just runs away from you, doesn't it? How about you? A little birdie told me that you and Benny tied the knot? You know, I always knew you two would end up together. So where is your other half?' His face lights up as he glances around expectantly.

Sophie shakes her head. 'We split up years ago. I haven't seen him in… Gosh, I don't know. Twenty years?'

'I'm so sorry. I shouldn't have said anything.'

'It's fine. It's all in the past now. Although, I must admit, part of me was hoping he might show up here today.'

'I know what you mean. Whenever I did manage to catch up with Darren, we'd always end up talking about Ben. I was gutted we lost touch. We saw him at Mal's funeral and then… Well, that was that. Neither of us ever heard from him again.

It's sad, really. I know I was a total nightmare when I was a kid, but we went through so much together. I thought after all these years he might have…'

Before he can finish, Matthew arrives, and Sophie introduces them.

'Great to meet you,' Matthew says, holding out his hand. 'I bet you could tell me some stories. I hear Sophie was quite the wild child back in the day.'

'You don't know the half of it…'

'And on that note,' Sophie says, 'we actually have to get going.'

Paul frowns. 'You're not coming to the wake?'

'Sadly not. Our youngest is going back to university tomorrow and I'm dropping her off. No rest for the wicked, eh?'

They say their goodbyes and exchange numbers. 'Let's not leave it another forty years, eh?' Paul says as they part ways.

'I'm not sure we *have* another forty years.' She laughs.

In the car on the way back to London, Matthew and Sophie discuss their plans for the next few weeks. While Matt has talked about retiring for years now, Sophie suspects it is little more than an empty threat. After all, things are busier at work than ever. Currently, they are working on a pet project of Matt's: a semi-biographical drama, loosely based on a little-known singer from the tail end of the twentieth century. A girl called Susan Swan, who died in mysterious circumstances, just as her career was on the verge of taking off. Matthew has recently been sent a batch of unheard demos by her family, one of which he thinks might be perfect for the closing credits. He hits a button on the dashboard, and a woman's voice fills the cabin, sad and lilting:

I slipped overboard, fell into hell,
Bruised, battered and broken, I lay where I fell,
Washed up on the shore, I uttered a spell,
My mind is an ocean, my body's a shell...

As she listens to the music, Sophie's mind wanders back to the funeral. She's still disappointed about not seeing Ben. Perhaps he simply hadn't heard the news? As impossible as it seems, her late-night trawls indicate that he's still not on social media. And how else would he find out? For all she knows, he might not even be in the country any more. Or maybe he's in prison? Or dead? This last thought troubles her most of all. Could he really have passed away without her knowing? It was perfectly possible. Yet she doesn't believe it. As ridiculous as it sounds, she's always imagined she'd feel it if something happened to him. That even now, all these years later, they still shared an invisible connection on some level, even if they were no longer physically present in each other's lives.

The song finishes, the car fills with silence. They pass signs for:

Banbury.

Buckingham.

Bicester.

'Are you OK?' Matthew asks as they reach Oxford. 'You're very quiet.'

'It's just been a funny day. And it makes you think, doesn't it? When people your age start dying. You begin to worry about how much longer you've got left. And how you can possibly fit in all the things you still want to do.'

'You know, when I was in my early twenties, I went to Japan for three months. I had a minimum-wage job on the ticket counter at my local cinema and I saved up for eighteen months for the ticket...'

Sophie smiles to herself. She's heard about this famous Japanese trip a thousand times over the last twenty-five years. Each time, the duration it took to save up gets longer.

'This is back when you were in your dyed-black-hair-and-eyeliner emo phase?' she says.

'I mean, I wouldn't necessarily describe myself as *emo*. But guilty-as-charged on the eyeliner front. Anyway, the point is, even after all that saving and hard work, I really didn't enjoy that trip.'

'And you don't think that has anything to do with the fact you spent your time visiting super-depressing places like Hiroshima and the suicide forest on Mount Fuji?'

'I'm serious. Going to Japan was all I'd thought about for so long. I was desperate for it to be life-changing. And it was, in a way. But I never really *enjoyed* it. At least, not while I was there. I just kept thinking about how the clock was ticking. I knew it would take years to properly explore Japan, but I *only* had three months. It overshadowed everything I did. I took the ferry to Okinawa, and instead of appreciating how beautiful it was, I ended up scolding myself because then it meant I didn't have enough time to go to Yakushima. It was horrible.'

'They used to have a word for that when I was a kid. FOMO. Fear of missing out.'

'Exactly. But in a way, that's why the trip ended up being so life-changing. Because when I got home, I vowed I wouldn't fall into the same trap again. And for the most part I haven't. What I'm trying to say is that nobody knows when their number's up. This car could swerve off the road and kill us both right now.'

'Except cars don't swerve any more.'

'That's very true. But you take my point. Anything can happen at any moment. And when it does, I promise, it won't be neat and tidy with a nice little bow wrapped around it. There will be unfinished business. Things you could have said or could have done. But you can't spend your life worrying about that. Otherwise it's all you'll ever think about. All you can do is enjoy the things you do get to do and let the rest... remain unsaid.'

They're silent for a while then, until eventually Matthew

leans forward and puts on another track. And as the singer's quiet, mournful voice fills the car, calling out to them across the decades, Sophie slips her hand into Matthew's. And she thinks about how warm and soft it is.

And how lucky she is to love and be loved.

26

It's strange to be back in London. For the longest time, he thought he was done forever with England. Why on earth would he return to this bleak little island when he could go back to Sri Lanka or Kerala or Palawan or Fiji, or any one of the other sun-soaked tropical paradises he's spent the last twelve years? Looking out of the taxi window at the rain-lashed city streets, it's not an easy question to answer. Maybe he was simply homesick? Although he's not entirely sure if he really has a home any more. He has a house, which until recently had been let out to tenants. But a home?

That's different.

The car turns a corner, and the street lights leave him looking at the ghost of his own reflection in the window. His hair is long now, streaked blonde and pulled back in a messy bun. That aside, he looks the same as he ever has. His skin smooth. Eyes bright. His attempts at growing facial hair as pathetic as they were when he was twenty-one. Only he isn't twenty-one any more. Friends he went to school with are probably thinking about retiring now. Darren, Paul. Whatever happened to those guys? He doesn't know. Even in this age of ubiquitous interconnectivity, he is still stubbornly old-school. While most people have transitioned to these new 'deck' things, he still lugs around his ancient smartphone. He just doesn't have the energy to learn something new. Not at his age.

The car turns again, and his reflection vanishes.

He disappears.

Though his decision to leave the country had been spontaneous, actually getting away took a little longer than he'd expected. There was the house to sort out. Some financial bits to put in place. He even ended up working his notice at the pub. In all, it was almost two months after his ill-fated date with Saskia that he found himself sitting on an aeroplane to Bangkok with a wallet full of baht and zero idea what he was going to do once he got there.

For the first few weeks after he arrived, he was convinced he'd made a terrible mistake. Rather than being enthralled by this brand-new culture, he felt alienated by it. The food, the smells, the language. All of it was overwhelming. He could hardly figure out how to cross the road without getting himself run over. Yet gradually, things began to improve. His first breakthrough was moving out of the hotel and into a backpacker's hostel, replacing the air-conditioned isolation of his Radisson suite with the sweaty confines of a mixed-bed dormitory. What he lost in comfort, he made up socially, and he quickly met a community of travellers from all over the world. Israeli, South African, Canadian. Some of them were as young and green as he was when he took his first doomed trip to Australia all those years ago. Others were older and had been out on the road longer. Five, ten years some of them. The lifers. They'd hop from country to country, picking up odd jobs, living cheaply and partying hard. It was these people he latched on to. Sharing beers and plates of pad thai in the low-rent restaurant opposite the hostel, he listened carefully to their advice. Where to go and where to avoid. The best places to catch a wave or look for work.

It was at this first hostel that he met a French couple, Michelle and Jean-Paul, who he spent the next six months travelling with. They explained they were on their 'now or never' tour, visiting places that were at threat of disappearing altogether due to climate change. Bangkok had been badly affected by rising sea levels over the decade, with whole sections of the city now uninhabitable. At their suggestion, he followed them to the islands along the east coast: Ko Chang, Ko Mak, Ko Samet. From there, he took a flight to Vietnam, picking up work as an English teacher in Ho Chi Minh City for a few months, before parting with the couple and heading to Hanoi alone, and from there to Halong Bay.

Before he knew it, a year had passed in this way. And then another. He wasn't particularly fussy about where he visited. Unlike most of the people he met, he didn't have a bucket list. Why would he? He went wherever the wind blew him, partying with other backpackers, picking up work here and there, moving on when jobs dried up or he fancied a change of scenery.

Was he happy?

That was difficult to say. He was certainly occupied. The weather was good, the people were interesting. And there were always new things to see. Waterfalls. Mountains. Beaches. Sure, sometimes it could be a little lonely. But his bed was rarely empty. As in London, there was always an unlimited supply of young people willing to share it for a night. Sometimes even longer. Although nothing that ever lasted for more than a few months.

He'd been travelling for almost a decade before he began to feel the first stirrings of disillusionment with his lifestyle. A constant feeling of being adrift. He could literally go anywhere. Do anything. But after all these years doing precisely that, indifference had begun to creep in. How many ancient temples or endangered rainforests or stunning sunsets could a person realistically be expected to see before they all blurred into one? Yes, they were all objectively exquisite. But the more he saw, the more they left him cold. He'd started to grow bored of his fellow travellers, too. As with the landscape, he realised they were all essentially interchangeable. Sure, they might come from different places and speak different languages, but in the end they were all the same. He found himself withdrawing, no longer interested in listening to these strangers' stories, or even bothering to learn their names.

Still, in the end it had been rather more practical reasons that had driven him back to England. Things had always been tight financially. His monthly stipend from Evergreens still dropped into his bank each month like magic, but it only ever took him so far. The gap needed to be filled with casual work. Recently, however, that work had become increasingly difficult to come by. It had been obvious for a while that the world was beginning to come apart at the seams. Especially in the developing countries that he'd made his home. Everywhere he went, there seemed to be an ever-deepening anti-foreign sentiment, even in places where tourists had traditionally propped up the economy. Visas had become ever trickier to obtain, as had the flights themselves, the costs of which skyrocketed due to local taxes designed to offset their emissions. And so it came to be that Ben was almost relieved when he received an email from his property management company to say that his tenants were moving out and they were struggling to find suitable replacements. He was in Indonesia at the time, working at a bar in Sumatra, when the message came through. He didn't hesitate. He quit on the spot, took what little money he'd managed to save and bought a one-way ticket back to England.

It was only once he was on the plane, sitting on the tarmac in Jakarta airport, that it occurred to him he had no more idea what he was going to do when he got back than he did when he had made the reverse journey twelve years earlier.

The taxi comes to a pause near Camden Market. Though the traffic is nowhere as bad as he remembers, London is still

London. With almost eleven million people calling it home these days, all the smart technology in the world can't prevent it grinding to a halt now and then. As he stares out at the churning pavements, his mind once again goes to Sophie. Save for a few emails untangling their shared finances, he's not spoken to her for over twenty years. Yet, he's still never really lost track of what she's doing. He knows from interviews that she's still based in London, somewhere south of the river. For all he knows, she could be on this very road, in another car. They might pass a few feet from each other and never know. He daydreams about dropping her a line. He still has her email address. Now that he's back in the city, he could invite her for coffee.

Only he knows he never will.

From what he's read, she's happy now. Married, children, a successful career. As for him, what has he got to show for the years that have passed? The thought of her seeing what a mess he has made of his life makes him feel physically sick. No, he'll never call.

The taxi starts moving again, speeding north towards Winchmore Hill and whatever it is that awaits him there. An old house. A strange bed. A million days to somehow try and fill.

The thought fills him with dread.

IX

'How long has he been out?'

'Two days.'

Johan Andersson nods. 'OK, that's good. That means the majority of cellular damage should still be reversible.'

'Reversible? But how? Your grandfather said it couldn't be done. Pure fantasy, he called it.'

'And he was right. Until recently, that is. Even two years ago, we didn't have the technology to do it. But today, we can go further than we ever imagined would be possible. We're no longer just stopping the clock; we're turning it back. And thank goodness we are. Otherwise, we'd be no more viable than my grandfather's original project.'

'Viable?'

'As a business, I mean.'

'I'm not sure I understand?'

Johan smiles. 'Do you know the median age of the world's billionaires, Mrs Walker?'

Sophie shakes her head.

'Sixty-three. Sure, there are a few upstarts who grab all the headlines. Young tech prodigies. The odd social media star or music mogul. But most are older. Generally, it takes decades to accumulate that kind of fortune. Almost all are already born rich, of course. Then they dedicate their lives to becoming even richer. But it's not until they reach what was traditionally seen as the final third of their life that they become truly, obscenely, private-island-in-the-Bahamas *wealthy. If the Bahamas wasn't underwater, of course. But I digress. The point is that even if we'd been able to make the original treatment safe sooner, we'd never have sold it to anyone. No one is interested in forking out millions only to spend centuries trapped inside their failing bodies. And who can blame them?'*

Sophie raises an eyebrow. 'I'm trapped inside a failing body, and you don't hear me complaining about it.'

Johan laughs. 'True. But you aren't a billionaire. And if you were, and you could afford to pay for a treatment that took away every ache and pain with a promise it would never return, are you honestly telling me you wouldn't take it? Because that's the pitch we are making to our prospective clients. Finally, after years of intensive research, we've done it. We can take a sixty-year-old, a one-hundred-year-old, and reset them to their biological peak. We can make them twenty-one again. And we can keep them there indefinitely. It truly is a miracle.'

'Just so long as you can afford it?'

He grins. 'Well, nobody ever said that miracles come cheap. Besides, I like to think that our project will provide peripheral benefits for the whole of society, rather than just our customers. Take the space race in the middle of the last century. Sure, only a select few ever got to go to the moon. But we all benefited from the technology that was created along the way. Freeze-dried food, memory-foam mattresses, portable computers. The work we're doing could lead to new treatments for cancer, dementia, arthritis. Even if not everyone gets to live forever, they can still live happier and healthier lives because of us. And that's without considering what we're already doing for the planet.'

Sophie snorts. 'You sound just like your grandfather. So, explain to me how contributing to overpopulation is going to help the planet?'

'Have you considered that our product might actually be the one thing that convinces those in power to start taking

action on the environment? Think about it. The ultra-rich have never cared about the earth. Sure, they might have paid lip service to it when it suited them. Bleating on about their green credentials and commitments to sustainability and all the rest of it. But they never really meant it. Why would they? They assumed they'd be in the ground long before the shit really hit the fan. Meanwhile, they were content to make hay while the planet burned.

'But we're changing that. Ever since they found out about our product, they've started realising they're going to need somewhere to live for the long haul. Once this second phase of treatment is approved by the regulators, people will be queuing up to join the programme. Just think about the impact on the—'

'Wait... Once it's approved?'

Johan grimaces slightly. 'This is the problem I mentioned. While the authorities here in the UK have been incredibly accommodating, *our cellular rejuvenation therapy is still waiting to be officially endorsed by any of the world's major health bodies.'*

'So you want to use Ben as a human guinea pig?'

'Not at all. Numerous animal trials have confirmed it's perfectly safe. This is simply a matter of red tape. I'm sure you appreciate how slowly the wheels of bureaucracy tend to turn. It could be months or even years before we can take this thing to market. But that doesn't mean it's not ready. And just think, he'll be making history. The first person in the world to not only defy ageing, but to reverse it. Of course, we'll have to get you both to sign a waiver...'

'But Ben's not even conscious.'

Johan shrugs. 'The decision is between you and your conscience. But from where I'm sitting, it doesn't sound like Ben has many other options right now...'

2063

27

Six months to the day after Matthew dies, Sophie's son Orson arrives, carrying Angel in his arms. Angel, Orson explains, is a Papatzu. A cross between a Papillon and Shih Tzu. Good-tempered and fully trained. Well, partially trained. He still chews things. And wees in the house. And barks at everything. But he's getting there.

It is, Sophie thinks, the most preposterous-looking creature she has ever set eyes on. A bat-eared ball of fluff with the snub face of an Ewok.

'Well, what the bloody hell are *you* doing with her?' she asks as she leads her son down the hallway.

'Angel's a boy, Mum.'

'Fine. What are you doing with him?'

'What's that?' Orson shouts. 'It's a bit loud in here. Do you have to have all this on?'

He's talking about the TV. And the stereo. And the radio. All of which are blaring at full volume in various rooms in the house, blending together to create a dissonant wall of noise. This is not an accident. Since Matthew died, Sophie has found the house to be almost oppressively quiet. She's not sure why. It's not like they used to sit around chatting to one another all day. Particularly not these last few years. Most of the time, they occupied different parts of the house. Sophie tucked away in her study, still doing bits of writing, while Matthew had finally embraced retirement. Mostly, he spent his days reading, gardening and rewatching his favourite films. Although he had also, rather improbably, decided to try and learn Japanese at the grand old age of eighty. While they might not have spent much time in the same room, he was nevertheless a comforting presence in the house. She would listen out for the pad of his footsteps upstairs, his frantic muttering as he attempted to memorise useful words and phrases.

'Konnichiwa.'

'Konbanwa.'

'Oyasuminasai.'

With him gone, she soon learned to despise the sound of her own breathing, or the clatter of her fingers on the keyboard. Even the smallest sounds seemed enormous in the empty house, echoing off every hard surface and reverberating around her brain. And so, she uses the noise as a comfort blanket. Even at night, cold and lonely in the too-big bed, she leaves the radio on low, some late-night talk show burbling away in the background, helping to drown out her melancholy thoughts.

'That's better,' Orson says as she snaps off the flat-screen TV in the living room. 'By the way, what the hell even *is* that thing? It's an antique. I've told you before, I can get you a holographic set from work. Just say the word.'

'And I've told you before that I hate those things. There's nothing wrong with two-dimensions, thank you very much.'

He rolls his eyes. 'Also, I think I need to take you for another hearing test. You know a double drum replacement costs practically nothing these days? You can be in and out in an hour.'

She stares at her son. When did the power dynamic between them shift? One minute he was totally reliant on her for everything – food, warmth, changing his nappy – and the next he's this hulking forty-something telling *her* what to do. And that tone he uses with her. Slow and slightly irritated, as if he's giving directions to someone who doesn't speak the language. It's the same voice he uses with his teenage children, her grandchildren, Zayden and Ellery. Each of them the apple of her eye. Even if their parents did insist on those ridiculous names.

'I can hear you perfectly well, thank you very much. Maybe I should come round to your house and start criticising your life, eh?'

'Here we go,' he says, laughing. 'Anyway, I didn't come here to argue, Mum. I came here to give you this.'

He holds up the ridiculous dog so that it's eye level with Sophie.

As the penny drops, so does Sophie's expression. 'Oh shit. You've bought me a grief puppy, haven't you?'

'Well, he's not a puppy. He's a rescue dog. He's five years old. And it was either this or one of those companion robots. And I know how you feel about those things.'

She pulls a face. 'You mean at best creepy, at worst a terrifying invasion of privacy designed to further erode our sense of humanity? You know people are using those things as nannies for their children now? How the hell are kids supposed to learn to interact with another flesh-and-blood person if they spend their formative years talking to a bag of circuitry? And to think we used to look down on people who'd plonk their kids down in front of Netflix all day.'

'What the hell's a Netflix? You know what, never mind. The point is, Asheni and I got you Angel because we're worried about you, Mum. Since Dad's gone… Well, you're all alone in this house every day. It's not healthy. It'll be good for you to have some company. It'll make you feel better.'

Sophie sighs. But before she can reel off her objections, Orson puts Angel on the floor and then embraces her in a huge bear hug. The physical contact, her first in weeks, is almost too much to take. She breaks away from her son, determined not to cry in front of him.

'Fine,' she says, swallowing hard. 'I'll take the stupid dog.'

'That's great,' he says, scooping up the squirming ball of fur and handing him to her.

'So what the hell am I supposed to do with him?'

Orson shrugs. 'I don't know. Walk him?'

So she does.

She starts small. Ten minutes around the block. Once in the morning, once after lunch.

'That's all you're getting,' she warns the whining animal whenever it scratches the door outside of its allocated walk times. 'I've got too much work to do, so you can stop that noise at once and sit down. Sit. Sit. *Siii-it.*'

As the weeks pass, however, she relents. They go out for an hour. Then for half a day. Rambling through the city, finding new paths and parks they've never explored before. Walking, walking, walking, until Sophie's not sure who's leading whom any more.

To her vague disgust, she finds that Orson was right. It does feel better to have some company. She finds herself talking to Angel incessantly. Worse, she gets the sense that he actually understands her, those big, wet eyes she'd initially taken to be dumb transformed into wise and sensitive pools, an oracle into which she can whisper any secret. He's the perfect partner, she decides. Sure, she has to feed him and wipe his pee off the floor and, occasionally, put up with him humping her leg. But that's no worse than any other man she's known. And at least this one listens without answering back.

Yet despite Angel providing companionship, sometimes she still craves human contact. On these days, she reaches out to Sinead, the one friend she's remained consistently close to over the years. Well, they call each other friends. In truth, Sophie isn't really sure how much they actually like each other any more. Most of the time, Sinead irritates the hell out of her, and she suspects the feeling is mutual. Still, when you get to their age, it hardly seems worth falling out. Not when they have so much shared history behind them. And so, one morning, Sophie invites her to join her on a walk.

At Sinead's suggestion, they meet in Hyde Park. It's almost a two-hour trek from Sophie's home, but she doesn't mind. At seventy-six, she's still fit. She doesn't run any more, of course. Arthritis in both knees has put paid to that. But she can still get around fine, *thank you very much*, and her daily walks with Angel have helped her build up her stamina. Besides, it's a beautiful day. Whereas London used to be a miserable, traffic-choked hellhole, recently things have begun to change for the better. Around ten years ago, there had been an abrupt shift in government policy. Vast swathes of the city have been pedestrianised. Public transport is free. Acres of new urban nature reserves have been created across the city. It isn't just London that's changed. Over the last decade, forests have been replanted at an astonishing rate around the world. More than forty per cent of the planet has been designated as protected. Fossil fuels have been outlawed, as archaic as asbestos and tobacco. It's astonishing, really. As if the penny finally dropped for leaders around the world. Although, for some places, change came too late. The Maldives. Vanuatu. Samoa. The Solomon Islands. All now missing from world maps. And, of course, most of California, Southeast Australia and Central Africa are uninhabitable due to a combination of fire and drought. Yet slowly, very slowly, there are signs the planet is beginning to heal. The thought fills Sophie's heart with hope. It seems there will be a world for Zayden and Ellery to inherit, after all. And whoever comes after them.

Sinead is already waiting in the park when Sophie arrives. As ever, she is startled by her old friend's appearance.

Unlike Sophie, who long ago accepted, and even embraced, her silvery hair and wrinkles, Sinead has for decades now attempted to wage war on the ageing process, submitting herself to evermore radical procedures and cosmetic surgeries in a quest to look the way she did fifty years ago. Which, from a distance, in the right light, with a dash of age-related myopia, she almost does. It's not until she gets close that the illusion falls apart. Sinead has had so much work done over the years that Sophie sometimes imagines anthropologists using her face like an archaeological dig, each layer revealing the history of cosmetic procedures from over the last half-century or so. There are the little scars from old-fashioned treatments: facelifts and Botox injections and collagen fillers. And then there are newer developments: stem cell injections, laser sculpting, gene therapy, ultrasound, right up to her most recent surgery, which apparently involved having, at great expense, a nanorobot permanently inserted under the epidermis of her face to correct flaws and sagging in real time.

Yet for all the money and energy she has invested in trying to look young, to Sophie's eye, she still looks a little off. Or rather, she looks like a woman in her seventies desperately trying to look like a woman in her twenties.

Which is to say, she looks a little tragic.

She understands, of course. Once her children were old enough, Sinead had attempted to restart her career, something her agent had warned her would require, at the very minimum, a boob job and a tummy tuck. She's been fighting an uphill battle since. The roles getting smaller and less visible, to the point where she's lucky to get work as an extra these days. Sophie has found similar issues with her own projects over the years. While she isn't considered personally offensive, so long as she's tucked safely behind the camera, whenever she writes a role for a woman over forty, she finds the producers begin to get nervous, pushing her to rewrite the part, or else casting someone younger and then ageing them with make-up or CGI. It seems that for all of the social breakthroughs over the last few decades, to show a surgically unaltered older woman on the screen remains the ultimate taboo.

'Hello, my love,' Sinead coos, throwing her arms around Sophie, before stopping to pet Angel. 'And look at *this* little cutie pie. I might just have to kidnap you when your mummy isn't looking. What do you say?'

'Please for the love of God take him,' Sophie deadpans.

'And how are you, my love? Are you coping with… *things*?'

'You don't have to tiptoe around it, Sinead. I'm a big girl. You can just ask me outright if I've adjusted to Matthew being dead yet.'

Sinead looks pained. 'Sorry. I bet you're sick of euphemisms by now. When Ash died, I lost track of how many people apologised for my loss. Loss? I didn't put him down and forget where he was. He had a fucking heart attack.'

They both laugh.

'I'm fine. Seriously. Although, nobody believes me. My kids are so worried about me they got me this bloody mutt, so he takes up half my life, now.'

'Well, you can't blame them for caring. Having your husband die on you is about as awful as it gets.'

'It is. Although Matt wasn't technically my husband, remember?'

'No, of course not. And who can blame you for not wanting to go through all *that* again? I seem to recall your first marriage wasn't exactly a picnic. That bloody Ben. Talk about immature.'

'Immature is an understatement.'

'Although, he was gorgeous, as I recall. I wonder what he looks like now?'

'I wouldn't know.'

'You mean you've never been tempted to look him up online?'

'I don't think he *is* online.'

Sinead looks utterly horrified. 'Not online? Are you sure he's even alive?'

Sophie shakes her head. 'I'm not, actually. I mean, the last I heard from him I was signing over our old house to him. But that was… I don't even know when? A long time ago.'

'Your old house? The one in Winchmore Hill?'

She nods.

'Well, why didn't you say? That's less than half an hour from here.'

'And?'

'You could just hop on the Hyperloop. Knock on the door. See if anyone answers.'

'And why the hell would I go and do something like that?'

Sinead shrugs. 'I don't know. Curiosity, I guess? And we're not getting any younger, are we? It might be a case of now or never.'

Sophie shakes her head dismissively. 'If it's all the same to you, I think I'll stick to never. Let sleeping dogs lie. Speaking of which, I'd better get this lazy pooch walking or he'll never settle tonight.'

Later on, after the walk is finished and Sophie has allowed her arm to be twisted into a second gin and tonic for 'old times' sake', she says goodbye to Sinead and heads off towards the station. As fit as she is, her knees are starting to ache, and Angel has started to whine. She's not sure either of them can face the long walk home. When she arrives at the Hyperloop station (which she still insists on calling the Tube), she looks uncertainly at the digital board, trying to work out the right platform. It is at times like this that she feels her age. It's not that she doesn't like the new technology. Far from it. Whereas the old trains were generally cramped, rattling, bedbug-infested health hazards, the new carriages are bright and airy, and whisper-quiet, too. It's just not always easy to keep track of how things work any more. Take paying for her ticket. In her lifetime it has gone from cash to Oyster card to chip and PIN to Apple Pay to the crypto chip that is currently embedded in her arm.

'It does your head in, doesn't it?' she says to the whimpering dog under her arm. 'All this constant change. How is a woman ever supposed to keep up?'

She stares at the board, attempting to decode the timetable, when she happens to spot a train going to Winchmore Hill, leaving in less than five minutes.

And maybe it's the gin, or maybe it's just the wild coincidence of hearing that name twice in the space of a few hours, but she decides to make an unscheduled visit.

Half an hour later, Sophie stands on her old street. At least, she's fairly sure it's her old street. It's changed a lot since she was here last. As with most major cities in the Global North, England underwent a period of unparalleled civil unrest midway through the century. London was hit especially hard. First there were the Climate Riots and then, in the early forties, a series of violent protests, which the tabloid press at the time christened the Great Levelling. Essentially, these were a prolonged, and ultimately unsuccessful, attempt by those living below the poverty line – which by then accounted for around half the country – to force the wealthiest in society to contribute more and help shrink the gap between those who had everything and those who could hardly afford to eat. It was, of course, a conflict that had been decades in the making, with social mobility falling from around the beginning of the century onwards, as richer families feathered their own nests, passing their money and property from one generation to the next, and generally hoovering up everything else they could get their hands on, leaving nothing for the rest. Not even, it seemed, a habitable planet, having proved themselves as committed to trashing the environment with their endless long-haul holidays and gas-guzzling vehicles and bottomless consumerism as they were to hoarding the country's collective wealth. As standards of living fell through the floor, accelerated by the Plague Years, the European Troubles, and mass redundancies due to automation and A.I., protests broke out across the country. Middlesbrough. Liverpool. Burnley. Birmingham. And then, as these things are prone to do, these disparate disturbances turned violent and joined together. A few stray sparks rapidly become a raging fire. In this case, a very literal fire, as arsonists set England alight, torching the houses of the conspicuously rich. With its sprawling stately mansions and detached houses, Winchmore Hill had been badly hit. Not that you'd know it now. Unlike everywhere north of London, which had essentially been left to rot once the flames had eventually burnt themselves out, most of this area had been rebuilt in the late forties, the buildings carrying the characteristic retro-futurism that was briefly popular twenty years ago. Lots of Plexiglas domes and transparent walls and silver paint, all of which looks a bit naff now.

She keeps walking, trying to get her bearings, until she abruptly realises she's here. This is the house. *Their* house. The first place they ever owned.

The sight of it makes her feel unexpectedly nervous. It's been so long since she's been here she almost stopped believing it ever existed. It was like a half-forgotten story from her childhood. A fairy tale. Unlike the neighbouring properties, it's totally dilapidated. The front garden a jungle. Roof tiles mossed. Guttering cracked. The windows fogged with filth. The place looks derelict. Abandoned decades ago. Surely no one lives here any more?

But she hasn't come all this way for nothing. And so, she

gathers up the whimpering Angel into her arms and makes her way down the drive. Battling brambles. Nudging past nettles. Until finally she reaches the front porch.

Up close, the place looks even more run-down. Paint flaking from the walls. Brickwork bleached and cracked. The only indication that anyone lives there is a small security camera that points down at her from above the door, its red light blinking on and off. She takes a deep breath and reaches for the doorbell.

It doesn't work. The button rusted and seized. Again, she considers leaving. Instead, she takes a deep breath and knocks on the front door.

Her mouth is dry now. The gins she had with Sinead seem a very long time ago. In her arms, the dog whines more loudly.

'I know, sweetie. There's no one here. It was a silly idea. I just wanted to check if…'

She doesn't finish.

She doesn't finish because there is a noise from behind the door. Footsteps. A chain being drawn back. A lock turning. Then another.

And then the door eases open.

28

Sophie sits in the living room of her old house, clutching a glass of water. She'd have preferred coffee. Or better, brandy. Something to take the edge off her shock. But Ben doesn't have anything in. She's not surprised. She'd glanced in at the kitchen earlier. The washing-up bowl was stacked with festering cutlery, the bin overflowing, the surfaces piled with takeaway cartons. She's not convinced there's been any fresh groceries here for years. Even if he did have anything else to offer her, she's not sure she'd risk it.

It's not just the kitchen that's a mess. The whole house is a state. Every corner clouded with cobwebs, the floor sticky, the furniture and appliances coated with dust. Yet beneath the layers of grime, she's amazed by how little has essentially changed since she was last here. The sofa, the bookshelves, even some of the art on the walls. It's all almost exactly as she left it. Only older. Worn out. Faded.

But then again, aren't we all? she thinks.

Apart from Ben, obviously.

'I'm sorry about crying on your doorstep earlier,' she says. 'I was just overwhelmed. I didn't expect you to be here. And you look... I mean, you look great. Just as I remember you. But it caught me off guard. I was overwhelmed. I'm just so happy to see you, Ben.'

He smiles. 'It's fine,' he says. 'Really, I get it.'

To be honest, he'd almost burst into tears, too. Although he suspects for very different reasons. He's shocked by the way she looks. More than shocked. Appalled. Of course, he was aware, in an abstract way, that Sophie had aged. The internet is awash with images of her. If he'd ever wondered what she was up to, he only had to hammer her name into a search engine and he'd immediately be greeted with photographs of her on the red carpet of some awards ceremony or other, looking regal in her glittering black gown. But nothing has prepared him for seeing her in the flesh. To open the door to find a little old woman standing in the place his lover once occupied. These days, she wears her white hair in a short pixie cut which only seems to draw more attention to her weathered face: the deep lines, the dark bags, the age spots. She's smaller than he remembers, not just shorter, but gaunt, too, so thin that she is lost in her clothes, her bangles hanging on stick-thin wrists. It's like something from a nightmare.

'So what's with the dog?' he asks, desperate to keep things light. 'Has she got a name?'

'She's a *he*,' Sophie says. 'Angel.'

He raises an eyebrow. 'Angel?'

'Don't start. He was called that when I got him. My son picked him up for me.'

'You know, I still can't get used to you saying that. *Your son*. Orson, right?'

She nods. 'My eldest. And if you think that's weird, just wait until I tell you about my grandchildren. That will really make you feel old.' She frowns, looking at his line-free face. 'Or maybe it won't?'

'Trust me, I feel old,' he says. 'I don't think I've ever felt older.'

As the afternoon unspools, Sophie sets about updating Ben on everything he's missed in the intervening decades. There's a lot of ground to cover. Her life with Matthew. Their children. Her career. He already knows much of it, of course. He still remembers how shaken he'd been when he'd read that she'd ended up marrying the stiff, slightly pretentious producer who'd asked her to work on that awful screenplay all those years ago. If he's honest, he still feels a pang of jealousy when he thinks about the two of them together.

'But how about you?' she asks when she finally gets back to the present day. 'Are you seeing anyone?'

She shoots him a sly smile, but Ben shakes his head. 'There have been one or two people over the years. But no one serious. And not for a long time now.'

'Well, I don't blame you. No point getting too close to anyone. They only go and die on you in the end.' She laughs wickedly. 'I'm joking, of course. But I do see the appeal of flying solo. I bet you've had all kinds of crazy adventures while I've been gone, haven't you?'

Ben shrugs. Has he had crazy adventures? There were his travelling years, of course. But they seem like a distant memory now. These days, he doesn't really do much at all. He doesn't work any more. His mortgage is paid off, and while the state pension is hardly enough to live on, when combined with the Evergreens money, which still miraculously drops into his bank account each month, he has just enough to get by on. It's not like he has expensive hobbies. He plays old video games. Listens to old music. Watches episodes of old TV shows he tracks down online. The more time that passes, the more he finds he gravitates to the things he enjoyed in his youth, rather than attempting to interact with a modern culture he no longer understands or cares about.

'There have been a few adventures, I guess,' he says. 'But I'm retired now. It's the quiet life for me. Unlike you. Speaking of which, tell me about this new film that you have coming out...'

As Sophie talks, Ben marvels at the sheer amount she seems to have squeezed into her life. More than she could ever hope to unpack into a few stolen hours on a Tuesday afternoon. It seems every story spins off in a dozen directions, every life that intersects hers taking on its own narrative arc. Friends, family, colleagues. She knows so many people that he feels as if he could sit and listen to her for a year and he'd still be no closer to scratching the surface of everything she's done. Everything she's achieved. Everyone she's loved.

'My goodness,' she says eventually. 'Will you look at the time? My daughter's coming over this evening. Weekly welfare check, I call it. If I'm not there, she'll assume I've topped myself.'

She puts her untouched glass down on the grime-caked coffee table – a table they'd picked together at a vintage market, back when they lived in Slough – and then stands up.

'Sorry again for the waterworks when I arrived,' she says as he walks her to the front door. 'You know me. Always the drama queen. But I've had a really great time. I can't believe I left it so long. You know, I always meant to visit, but… Well, life gets in the way, doesn't it?'

'It's been lovely,' he agrees. 'We should do this again. You know you're always welcome here.'

She smiles. 'You know what? I might just take you up on that offer, Mr Walker.'

2070

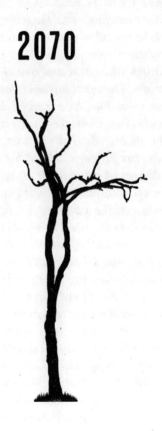

X

Sophie goes back to the hospital.

Back to the machines and the white walls.

Back to the mystified doctors and the sympathetic nurses.
Back to Ben.

With his ash-white hair and wrinkled features, she hardly recognises him. Though it has been less than thirty-six hours since she last saw him, he has aged decades. He has finally caught up with her. Overtaken her, even. His body shrunken beneath the sheets, his limbs so thin that the electronic ID band the doctors fastened around his wrist when he arrived is now in danger of slipping off altogether. Sophie can't see how he'll make it through the next couple of hours, let alone another few days. She's arrived just in time.

Settling by his side, she reaches for her bag and rummages through it until she finds the small plastic case she'd been given once she'd accepted Johan's offer and signed the paperwork on Ben's behalf, releasing Evergreens of all liability for the procedure she is about to perform.

She takes out the case and examines it. Considering its immense value, it's surprisingly small, the size and weight of an old-fashioned tobacco tin, its sleek black surface embossed with a silver pine cone. She takes a deep breath, then thinks back to the video Johan had made her watch before she left his office. A shimmering holographic nurse had instructed her on what to do. Inside the case, she explained, Sophie would find a vial of medicine, a syringe, an antiseptic swab and bandage.

Once the dose had been administered, the patient's response would be almost instantaneous.

'And Ben will be perfectly fine? Just as he was before?' she asked Johan.

At this, he offered her a stilted smile. 'Well, nothing in life is certain. But he certainly has a fighting chance. Which is more than he has without treatment.'

By now, Sophie's hands are shaking. Carefully, she rolls back the sleeve of his gown, stretches out the wizened folds of his arms and swabs the skin with an antiseptic wipe, before she takes the needle and jabs it into the vial. A light pink liquid fills the syringe. It looks a little like diluted blackcurrant squash. As she turns back to Ben's arm, she pauses to gather herself. She hates needles. This one seems particularly long, a thick spike glinting under the harsh hospital lights. With all this technology they have today, it seems positively medieval that they still rely on steel piercing flesh. Johan had told her they were working on an oral version of the medication, but for now there is only this. A syringe full of experimental medication and a scared old woman.

Ben's only hope.

She takes a deep breath. And then, just as the hologram had shown her, she tilts the needle to a ninety-degree angle and, with a darting motion, jabs it into his arm. She depresses the plunger. And...

Nothing happens.

She leans over him and examines his face.

It looks the same.

She's not sure what she'd expected. For all of Johan's bluster, she knew in her heart it was a million-to-one shot. Yet still, she's devastated that it should end like this. Ben wasting away to nothing. His beautiful face barely recognisable beneath the sag of flesh and spidery lines...

His face.

Sophie leans closer still, squinting through the cloud of her cataracts. And then she does see something.

Or does she?

It's hard to tell. It's not the rapid magic she'd been expecting. The abrupt reversal from old to young. No. This is subtler. The way the night can sneak up on you sometimes, so that one moment it's day, and the next you're sitting in the dark.

But now there's no mistaking it. Ben's face is definitely smoother. His hair darker. Fuller. Even his body seems less emaciated than it did only moments before, so that seconds later, he no longer looks like an old man at all, but merely middle-aged. And then younger still. The last of the white hairs now a deep black, his wrinkles giving way to a smooth complexion.

And then his eyes flicker open.

And he's back.

He's really back.

2070

29

'Mr Walker? Is this a good time?'

Ben has been awake for just over a week when a pair of young detectives arrive at the door of his hospital room, each of them dressed in gleaming white uniforms. Though by now he's able to sit up and talk, he's still severely depleted by his experience. Thankfully, Sophie has been present at his bedside almost constantly, acting as friend, counsellor and mediator all rolled into one. The role comes naturally to her. She's been doing something similar ever since she'd appeared on his doorstep seven years earlier. Back then, it had started with gentle encouragements to clean up the house. And once that was done, maybe he could redecorate? Get some colours on the walls. Brighten up the old place. Before long, she was calling him every day to make sure he'd showered and got dressed. Within a month she was regularly forcing him to come into London to join her on her circuitous dog walks around the city, forcing him to get some much-needed fresh air.

Here in the hospital, she's put this assertiveness to good use, liaising with the medical team on his behalf, helping to put a rehabilitation plan in place and ensuring he sticks to it, despite his constant threats to discharge himself and return home. She's also helped fill the gaps in his memory, explaining to him how he ended up in hospital in the first place. How, after years of speaking to each other on an almost daily basis, he abruptly stopped answering her calls. After a few days with no word, she'd decided to drop in on him, just to make sure he was OK. When he hadn't answered the door, she called the police, who broke in and called an ambulance. He'd been in hospital for a few days when the police arrived to ask her questions about the Evergreens Programme. And the other participants who'd died. At the mention of their names, Ben's face turned ashen, though he made no comment.

'I thought you were going to die, too,' Sophie said. 'Until I tracked down Johan...'

When she explained how he'd offered to treat him, Ben had grown irritable. 'So you just signed everything he put in front of you?'

'What choice did I have? You were wasting away. A couple more hours and there'd have been nothing left of you. And technically, I'm your next of kin. Like it or not, I'm responsible for you. I was doing what I thought was best.'

He nodded but looked far from convinced.

Sophie wondered if it might be a good time to broach some of the other stuff that Johan had mentioned. That Ben knew the vaccine was failing. That he'd been offered additional treatment and turned it down. That he'd *chosen* to end up here. But as forthright as she usually was, she couldn't seem to find the right words. It was too soon, she decided. There would be time for explanations later. For now, the important thing was that he got better.

'Now is the worst possible time,' Sophie says to the detectives, standing to block them from entering the room. 'He's just woken up from a coma. The last thing he needs is you lot bothering him.'

'It's fine, Soph,' Ben says, his voice still hoarse from the feeding tube. 'Actually, I asked them to come here.'

Sophie stares at him in confusion, before she spots his battered smartphone lying on the bedside table. 'You called them? When?'

'Yesterday, when you popped home to get some fresh clothes. You said they wanted to talk to me. I thought we might as well get it over with,' he says, before waving to the detectives. 'Come in, come in.'

Keeping a safe distance from Sophie, who continues to glare menacingly at them, the two young detectives creep in and take up a position at the foot of his bed.

'Thanks for seeing us, Mr Walker,' Detective O'Rafferty begins.

'Call me Ben, please.'

'Thank you, *Ben*. It's great to see you looking so much better.'

Sophie braces herself for the inevitable storm. 'Ben, are you sure you want to do this *now*?' she says. 'You're still recovering. Why don't you at least wait until you're back home? You could talk to somebody. Find a lawyer.'

He shakes his head. 'I don't need a lawyer. I'm tired of secrets. People have died, Soph. I can't live with that. Their families need to know the truth. The whole world does. Whatever happens after that is out of my hands.'

By now, Sophie is struggling to breathe. She thinks about the paperwork Johan made her sign before agreeing to treat Ben. The waivers and non-disclosure agreements and everything else designed to prevent them from talking about the programme under pain of horrendous legal consequences. Is Ben really so naïve that he thinks Johan won't come after them?

'Listen, this isn't right,' she says, turning back to the police. 'There are procedures you're supposed to follow. Ben is a sick man. He almost died a few days ago. He doesn't know what he's saying. He has the right to proper legal advice.'

At this, Ben's smile fades. 'And what about Nadia? Martin? Adaku? Don't people *deserve* to know what really happened to them?'

Sophie gasps. When she looks over at the detectives, however, she's surprised to find that neither of them look particularly surprised at Ben's outburst.

'Actually, we're not here to conduct an interview today,' Detective Gilligan says. 'This is just a courtesy call. We came here to inform you that we're closing our investigation into the Evergreens Programme.'

Both Sophie and Ben stare at him.

'What?' says Ben. 'But that's ridiculous. How can it be closed?'

Gilligan shrugs. 'Some new evidence came to light,' he says. 'From an unexpected source.'

'You see, it turns out that we weren't the only ones investigating this case,' O'Rafferty says. 'As it turns out, some of our colleagues – our *superiors* – have been following the Evergreens Programme for quite some time.'

'In fact, Commissioner Steele has taken a close interest in the case. I believe he knows Johan Andersson personally.'

'He knows Johan?' Ben asks.

Gilligan nods. There's a slightly sour look on his face, his nose wrinkled as if there's a bad smell in the room. 'Apparently, Mr Andersson is a very generous donor to the Police Benevolent Fund. And then there's the matter of Commissioner Steele recently becoming a shareholder in the company.'

Now it's Sophie's turn to act surprised. 'You're telling me that the head of the Met holds shares in Evergreens?'

'That's correct,' O'Rafferty says. 'And as such, he assures us that there's no case to answer regarding Miss Howley and the others. Unfortunate as their deaths undoubtedly are, we're now confident that they were the result of a legitimate medical trial.'

For a moment nobody says anything. Nearby, heart monitors beep and ventilators whir, while in a distant room, a Virtual Assistant barks its maddening chorus.

Please let me know how I can be of further assistance!

Please let me know how I can be of further assistance!

Subconsciously, Ben's fingers come up and tug at the silver pine-cone pendant around his neck. 'So that's it?' he says at last. 'It's as simple and predictable as that? Johan pays off the police and now he's free to do what he likes, no matter who gets hurt along the way?'

'Almost,' Gilligan says.

'Almost?'

'Yes,' O'Rafferty says. 'There's just one more thing. When Commissioner Steele heard that you'd reached out to us, he asked us to remind you of your legal obligation not to disclose any of the details pertaining to your participation in the programme. Just in case you were thinking of talking to… well, anyone.'

Ben stares at them. 'Is that a threat? Are you threatening me?'

'I think that about covers everything,' Gilligan says.

'Thanks again for taking the time to speak to us, Mr Walker,' O'Rafferty adds. 'And once again, we really are very pleased to see you looking so well.'

'You tell Steele that this isn't the end of this,' Ben shouts after them. 'Do you hear me? It's not over.'

But the two detectives are already gone.

30

In total, it takes more than six weeks of physiotherapy before Ben is deemed to have made enough progress to leave the hospital to continue his recovery at home. Sophie laughed the first time he staggered out of the therapy room, his face dripping with sweat as he gripped onto a steel walking frame for balance. 'We make a right pair. You know you might be about the only person left in the world who I could actually beat in a race.'

Unlike Sophie, however, Ben's mobility improves by the day, so that by the time he's ready to leave the hospital, he can walk as well as he could before his coma. Indeed, it is he who helps Sophie, looping his arm through hers to keep her steady as they make their way to meet the taxi.

Once Ben is safely back home, he is eager to slip back into their old routines. Long walks and endless talks over mugs of terrible fake coffee. But Sophie is evasive. She makes excuses about seeing her family. Cuts their calls short. Stays away. At first, Ben is understanding. She's been by his side for the last month and a half. It's natural for her to need her own space. But as the weeks go on, his patience wears thin, and he decides to address the situation outright.

'Have I done something to offend you?' he asks on one of the rare evenings he's managed to pin her down to a video call. 'Because you seem to be avoiding me.'

Sophie blushes. It's true, she has been avoiding Ben. For now that he's recovered, she knows they need to discuss the reason behind his collapse before they can move forwards. Had Ben really known there was a problem with the vaccine and refused the treatment? If so, then why? And more importantly, why hadn't he told her?

It all comes tumbling out of her. The questions. Her feelings of betrayal. When she's finished, Ben doesn't answer right away. He simply stares at the floor, like a little boy who's been caught out in a lie.

'Johan did write to me,' he admits at last. 'More than once.'

'Christ, Ben. Then why didn't you take him up on his offer? Do you know how close you came to dying? Another day or two and that would have been it. The damage would have been irreversible.'

Ben looks up. When he does, she's shocked to see he's on the verge of tears. 'How can you ask me that? I did it because of you.'

'*Me?*'

'I just thought... Jesus, Sophie. You must know I still love you?'

'Of course. And I love you. That's why I was so upset when—'

He stops her. 'No. You don't understand. I *love* you.'

As his meaning becomes clear, Sophie's eyes widen. 'Oh.'

'Oh? I declare my undying love for you and that's all you've got? Oh?'

She swallows hard, desperately searching for the right words. 'Look, Ben. Don't get me wrong. I do love you. I've loved you almost my whole life. You're my best friend in the world. But I'm an old woman. That part of my life is over.'

Ben shakes his head. 'You see? That's the whole thing right there. That's why I turned down Johan's treatment.'

'You thought killing yourself would help?'

'No, not that. I didn't know that was going to happen. When Johan wrote to me, he said the treatment was failing. I just thought he meant it was wearing off. That I'd start ageing again. That I had a chance to be *normal*. That's the whole problem with the programme. Dr Andersson didn't get it. Neither does Johan. The way they sell it, you think you're the luckiest person in the world. Staying in your prime? Never getting old or sick? It sounds like a dream. But the reality is a nightmare. What's the point in staying young forever if you have to watch everyone you love get old and die? It's awful. And I just thought if there was a way to stop it working, that maybe things could go back to the way they were when we were kids. That I wouldn't be this... freak. That you'd want me again...'

She shakes her head sadly. 'Oh, Ben. But don't you see? Even if you stopped the treatment, things can never go back to the way they were. And thank *God* for that. I was miserable back then. We both were. But these past few years with you have been some of the best days of my life. I wouldn't trade them for anything. So why don't we just enjoy them? For however long we've got left together, why don't we just try to be happy with what we have?'

So, they do try.

And, for a few years, they are happy.

Until, quite suddenly, things take a terrible, terrible turn.

2072

31

It begins with her losing the odd word.

Names, dates, places.

Then she starts losing things. She'll misplace her glasses or forget why she went to the fridge. Simple, everyday mistakes. But then quickly, it becomes more than that.

A lot more.

Whole sentences disappear, the thread of her point evaporating midway through her making it. She finds the narratives of books and TV shows impossible to follow. She's not sure of the year, let alone the day of the week. Her mind is like a house ransacked by burglars. Everything a jumbled mess. Yet miraculously, the past is protected. With almost unnerving accuracy, she can tell Ben the name of a hostel she stayed at in Jakarta sixty-five years earlier. Or the title of the book she was reading on St Kilda beach when her friend interrupted her to tell her she'd just met a group of boys.

And so that's where Ben and her stay. In the past.

She's no longer well enough to see him in person, and so they switch exclusively to video calls, which frequently last for hours. They reminisce about their days in Greenwich, mostly. Nonsensical plays they'd seen. Exhibitions they'd visited. They talk of family and friends, too. Samantha and Mags. Melissa and Farida. Sinead. All of them gone now. As is her brother, Christopher.

She's the last one left standing.

'Apart from you, of course,' she says with a sad smile. 'The boy who never grew up.'

And then one day, two years after he'd returned home from hospital, Sophie stops talking altogether.

Sophie's been even more tired than usual. Sometimes she's so sleepy she can hardly make it through a call. Her eyes flickering shut while Ben is mid-conversation. Later, he finds out that she's suffering a series of what the doctors called transient ischaemic attacks. Mini strokes. That it is likely these attacks that have triggered her rapid memory loss. If only he'd acted sooner, he could have called a doctor. Arranged a scan. But he didn't and he hadn't. And so they simply struggle on, with Ben putting Sophie's decline down to the indignities of old age. Until one afternoon, her daughter Amelia calls to tell him that her mum has collapsed with a suspected stroke. That she's been taken to hospital. That things don't look good.

'Which hospital?' he asks. He's frantic, his voice shredded with worry.

Amelia explains that she isn't allowed visitors right now but promises to keep him updated. As soon as she can see people, he'll be the first to know.

But almost as soon as she's admitted, Sophie is on her way back home again, the doctors deciding that she's out of danger and that she'll be better off recovering in familiar surroundings. She's lucky, Amelia explains. The stroke could have killed her instantly, the way it had Ben's grandmother all those years ago. It was Angel who'd saved the day, his barking so incessant that her neighbours ended up calling the police.

'It's a miracle,' Amelia cries.

Ben's not so sure that 'miracle' is the word he'd choose.

The first time he calls her, he's almost too devastated to

talk. Amelia had warned him beforehand that Sophie might have some difficulty speaking. However, nothing has prepared him for the way she looks. The stroke has ravaged her body, the left side of her face drooping like a dripping candle, her left eye hanging open, her mouth askew. Amelia explains that Sophie's suffered some brain damage, and though her cognition is essentially fine, she's unable to form words properly. Instead, she makes a low groaning sound, like an animal in pain.

It's almost too much to take. As soon as he sees her, he wants to hang up. He doesn't want to see this *person*, this Edvard Munch parody of the woman he loves. Surely, it's better to walk away now and keep what memories he has of her?

But somehow, he forces himself to talk, engaging in a stilted, one-sided conversation. Monologuing about the trivialities of his life. Smiling for the both of them. Cracking terrible jokes about her always making herself the centre of attention, while uncertain if she even understands a word he is saying, let alone finds them amusing.

It isn't until the call ends that he allows himself to fall apart. He curls into a tight ball on the floor of the living room they'd painted together and cries until it feels like there isn't another tear left in his body.

Yet despite his distress, he calls again the next day. And the one after that. And then every day. So that gradually, they find a rhythm. Just as they always have. Though her speech doesn't return, they develop their own private language. The tiny click of her tongue indicating pleasure. The flaring of her nostrils telling him she is unimpressed or disagrees. And, most frequently of all, the sparkle in her eyes that tells him she's listening. That beneath her ruined, mutinous body, it is still her in there. The same girl he'd fallen in love with seventy years earlier.

Again, he finds himself returning to the past, telling stories of their shared life together, so well worn now that they begin to feel like fables.

'Do you remember?' he begins one day. 'That night we first met in that pub. What was it called again? The Esky?'

Her nostrils flare.

'You're right. The *Espy*,' he corrects himself. 'And you stormed off? Not that I blame you. Those guys, Darren and Paul, were such a nightmare, weren't they? I thought you'd gone home. Can you imagine if you had? Or if I'd never followed you out to the balcony? Or if Mags hadn't thrown up all over that bouncer? That would have been it. We'd never have seen each other again. It's so crazy, isn't it? How your whole life can change like that. And you don't even know it's changing at the time. It's only later, when you look back, that you see how close you came to missing the best thing that ever happened to you.'

They are quiet for a while after that. There's no need for any words. They just look at each other instead. Eye to eye. Through the air and across the city.

Through the years.

That night, after his call with Sophie, Ben can't sleep. He lies awake, staring at the ceiling. He wonders how long things can go on like this. Privately, Amelia has warned him that her mother is unlikely to improve much more than she already has. So this is it then? At least, for however long it is she has left. One, three, five years? Stuck in bed, reliant on others. Trapped in the prison of her malfunctioning body. That was no life for a dog, let alone for someone as vivacious as Sophie. And he's just supposed to accept it?

Well, he won't.

Because as he lies here, unable to sleep, it occurs to him that the answer to all of this has been right in front of him all along.

And all it will take to make everything better is a single phone call.

32

Nestled on one of the few stretches of English coastline that hasn't been swallowed by rising sea levels, Umberslade Luxury Resort and Spa is an engineering marvel, an elegant concoction of steel and glass. Its silhouette is low and sweeping, designed to mirror the ocean that lies beneath it, so that it almost disappears into the landscape itself. Almost, but not quite. Because at the same time, it's so grand, and sprawling, it's impossible to miss.

It is also, Ben discovers, almost impossible to work out how to find the entrance.

After standing outside for ten minutes, running his hands along the smooth walls of the building in the hope of locating a secret door, he gives up and calls Johan, who apologises and offers to come and meet him. While Ben waits, he runs over his pitch for what must be the twentieth time today. He's still not quite sure what he's going to say. All he knows is that Johan holds the key to saving Sophie's life. It's his job to find the right words to get him to agree to use it.

Before last week, Ben had last spoken to Johan around two years ago, just after he got out of hospital. Sophie had warned him that he might want to talk to him, and sure enough almost as soon as he was home, Johan had reached out, offering to make Ben a brand ambassador for Evergreens Limited.

'As part of the company's lineage, I think you can really help sell the message that what we're doing here is perfectly safe.'

'Perfectly safe aside from almost killing me?'

'I'm not sure that's fair. If anything, we saved you, *despite* you wilfully ignoring our advice. Not that we'd necessarily want to share that narrative with potential clients. In fact, I'd prefer to gloss over the incident altogether and focus on the positives. There's such a feel-good story here. And of course, we'd be more than happy to compensate you handsomely for your involvement…'

At the time, Ben had made it clear he had no wish to tell his story, or help Johan become even richer. He just wanted his old quiet life back.

And so, Johan had been more than a little surprised when Ben had called him out of the blue to find out if the offer was still on the table. Did he still want him as an ambassador? And if so, would Johan agree to treat Sophie in return?

'Your timing's perfect,' Johan had enthused, while pointedly agreeing to nothing. 'The treatment has finally been approved. Our annual meeting is taking place next week. Why don't you come along and we can talk in more detail then?'

And so here he is, standing outside this preposterously space-age hotel, dressed in a second-hand tuxedo. He fears it may be a wasted journey. Unlike his grandfather, who at least paid lip service to the programme's altruistic aspirations, Johan makes zero pretence of wanting to help humanity. From the marketing videos he's sent Ben ahead of the meeting, it is clear that Johan's interest lies in making as much money as possible, as quickly as possible. His target market isn't starry-eyed students, but the obscenely wealthy. That privileged slither who could afford to pay to become immortal. Why would he agree to treat Sophie for free?

On the other hand, he'd invited him here, hadn't he? And wasn't it Johan who had originally made the offer to make Ben brand ambassador? Even if that was a couple of years ago now, he clearly believes Ben can be of value to the company. Helping Sophie is simply the price of his support. What was one more jab in the arm in the scale of things?

'There he is. The man of the hour.'

Ben looks up to see Johan emerging from a doorway that has miraculously appeared in the previously smooth wall. Like Ben, he's also dressed in a tuxedo, though the cut and the cloth indicate his is many times more expensive. This is the first time Ben has seen him in the flesh, and though Sophie had mentioned the family resemblance, he's startled to see just how much he looks like his grandfather. Other than the designer glasses perched on the end of Johan's nose, the two men could be twins.

It's not until he steps out to greet him that Ben notices the two other figures lurking behind him at a discreet distance. Two hulking security guards, each of them clad in black combat fatigues.

'There you are,' Johan says, shaking Ben's hand so forcefully that he's worried he'll dislocate his arm. 'It's so great to finally meet you in person. When I was younger, my grandfather used to talk about you all the time. He saw the Evergreens as his children. It was his biggest regret that his vision for the project was never completed. Which is why it's such a thrill, all these years later, to get it over the finish line for him. He'd be over the moon if he was here.'

Ben's not so sure. Still, he keeps the thought to himself, mindful of his need to keep Johan happy. Instead, he looks to change the subject. 'You must be relieved now that everything's finally been approved?'

Johan sighs. 'Well, I will be.'

Ben raises an eyebrow. 'But I thought you said…?'

'More delays, I'm afraid. We're expecting it to be rubber-stamped any day now. There are just a few more bureaucratic hurdles to navigate. While the police have been incredibly understanding, the FDA have been… less cooperative, shall we say?'

Ben snorts. 'By which you mean you can't buy them off?'

'Oh, believe me, we've tried,' Johan says, missing the dig. 'But these people just insist on doing everything by the book. One minute everything's fine and the next… Well, anyway, you know how these things go. It's not like there's any issue with the product. It's exactly the same treatment we gave you. And look at you. Fit as a fiddle. The only difference is that we've tweaked the format slightly. Our research shows a strong preference for an oral format, rather than the intravenous treatment you had, so we're now offering it in pill form. All very exciting. And we're close enough to FDA approval now that we can begin taking orders without any issues. The rest is just a matter of paperwork. But enough about all that stuff. I've got people in here that are just *dying* to talk to you. You're a bona fide rock star in these parts, Mr Walker. Are you ready to meet your adoring public?'

Ben swallows hard. He thinks of Sophie, her ravaged body. 'Oh, I'm ready,' he says, forcing himself to smile. 'I can hardly wait.'

33

'So, what do you think?'

Ben looks again at the bottle of mineral water Johan has just handed him. He's confused. 'About what? The water?'

'This was my original baby before I got into the life extension business,' Johan explains. 'BergWater: a drink twenty thousand years in the making. It's gone from strength to strength these past few years. It's produced from icebergs harvested from inside the Arctic Circle. No pollutants or contaminants. Very little mineralisation. It's about the purest fresh water left on earth.'

'And presumably in increasingly short supply?'

'That's the best thing about it,' Johan gushes, apparently without a trace of irony. 'Demand has just skyrocketed over the last few decades. These days, it goes for over five hundred dollars a bottle. Isn't that incredible?'

'Who knew melting ice caps could be so good for business?'

Johan beams. 'Exactly!'

Ben takes another swig from the bottle. It's the blandest thing he's ever tasted. 'Listen, can we talk? About the situation I mentioned on the phone. About Sophie…'

Johan's smile strains slightly. 'Absolutely. Totally. Just give me a couple of minutes, OK? There are a couple of things I need to take care of before my speech.'

And then he's gone.

Ben sighs. He's utterly exhausted. For the last couple of hours, he's allowed himself to be paraded around the conference like some living art installation. Making small talk with prospective clients. Posing for selfies. Grinning until his cheeks hurt. When Johan mentioned attending their annual meeting, Ben had pictured a stuffy, grey-suited affair. Shareholder votes. PowerPoint presentations. But the vibe is more like a rock concert. There are around three hundred guests in attendance, nearly all of whom have a sizeable security detail with them. Most of them are seated around the huge stage at one end of the hangar-like hall, on which various warm-up acts perform for the crowd. Earlier there was a stand up-comedian. A free-jazz quartet. Holographic dancers. At one point, a famous rapper appeared, changing the lyrics to his biggest hit to reference Johan and Evergreens. It was excruciating.

Those who aren't watching the entertainment mill around the various bars that are dotted around the hall which, alongside the ubiquitous bottles of BergWater, serve complimentary glasses of genuine vintage French Champagne, something Johan must have sourced at great expense, given that France's climate has left it bereft of vineyards for more than two decades. While Ben was being led around the hall, he noticed that the other guests all seemed to have one key feature in common. While at first glance they appeared young, closer inspection revealed the telltale signs of heavy-duty cosmetic surgery. Faded hairlines had been restitched to scalps. Previously crinkled faces pulled back and smoothed out. Yet none of it was really convincing. Unlike Ben, who is young at a cellular level, these people are fighting, and losing, an expensive battle against the inevitable.

Which is presumably what has brought them here in the first place.

Certainly, Johan has made a point of introducing him to every potential client they pass, Ben's perfectly preserved features a walking billboard for Johan's services. Indeed, as word spread about who he is, he began to feel a little self-conscious at the eyes that followed him around the room, a hungry expression on the face of every guest that crossed his path, so that he was grateful when Johan had eventually led him backstage to freshen up.

He takes another sip of his ridiculous water and looks around. In contrast to the gaudy chaos of the exhibition hall, the lighting is ambient back here, the furnishings a muted palette of creams and whites. Nearby, presenters hover over the vegan buffet, speaking in hushed tones. He'd half hoped he might bump into one or two of the original surviving Evergreens here. That maybe Johan had managed to twist their arms to join him with the promotional push. But there is only him.

'Jesus, Ben. Don't look so morose. This is supposed to be a celebration.'

Ben looks up to see Johan is back, a leather briefcase in one hand, a wide grin on his face.

'I'm having a great time,' Ben says. 'Actually, now that you're here, could we have a quick chat about my proposal?'

'Dude, I'd love to. But after my speech, OK? In fact, that's why I'm here. I was thinking it might be cool if you joined me on stage?'

'Me?'

'Relax. There's a teleprompter set up. All you have to do is stand there and read. I think people would really dig it.'

'I, um…' Ben stalls, before reminding himself why he's here. 'Sure. I'd love to.'

'Excellent. In that case, follow me.'

In the dark, cramped corridor behind the stage, Ben and Johan wait for their cue from the compère, whose voice booms out around the hall. It's unbelievably hot back here. Rivulets of sweat run down Ben's forehead and soak into his shirt. After a while, one of Johan's lackeys squeezes between them and tapes a discreet, flesh-coloured microphone to his jaw and straps a receiver to his belt.

Once they've gone, Ben tries speaking to Johan again.

'Listen, about Sophie…'

Johan shakes his head, cupping his ear. 'Huh?'

'Sophie,' he repeats, raising his voice. 'She's in a really bad way. I don't know how long she has left.'

Out on the stage, the compère has begun his introduction. Cheers from the audience punctuate his every word, making it even harder to hear.

'Can we talk about this afterwards?' Johan shouts.

'No. We need to talk now. All I'm asking for is that you offer her the same treatment you gave me. I know you can do it. I just want her to be better again. She doesn't deserve what's happening to her. She's a good person, Johan.'

Out on the stage, it sounds as if the compère is welcoming a pair of prize fighters to the ring. A rumble of applause echoes around the hall.

Johan sighs. 'Listen, Ben. I'd like to help you. I really would. But I can't justify the expense to our shareholders.'

'The expense? What are you talking about? You helped me and I didn't pay you a penny.'

'That was different. With you, it made sense. You're an Evergreen. You're part of our DNA. But Sophie. I mean, she's nothing…'

'Nothing?'

'I just mean—'

Before Johan can finish, another stagehand appears at the top of the stairs, beckoning them forwards. The compère has finished his speech now. The crowd noise lifts yet another level. It sounds like thunder. Like a bomb going off.

'Listen, I'm sorry, man,' Johan yells. 'But it's not going to happen. Now come on, let's get out there and give them a show they'll never forget.'

Ben doesn't move. He's tempted to turn and leave. Before he can make up his mind, however, there is a firm hand between his shoulder blades, forcing him forwards.

And then, before he even really knows what's happening, he is following Johan up the steps and stumbling out onto the stage.

34

The lights are blinding. So bright that Ben can't see the audience. There is only a dense darkness before him. In a dark corner of his mind, an ancient memory flickers. Of him following a strange girl down a pier at night.

Like stepping off the edge of the world.

At the front of the stage, Johan has already begun his presentation. He paces around, working the crowd, his grandfather's showbiz grin wedged on his face. He looks totally relaxed. Cool. Confident. In control. He certainly doesn't look like someone who's just condemned an innocent woman to death.

'Now as you know,' Johan booms. 'Evergreens Limited is a family business. It was founded by my grandfather over half a century ago. But of course, the story goes back a lot further than that. In fact, it goes all the way back to almost the beginning of time itself. Right back to my earliest ancestors. You see, like each of you, I am the custodian of a burning torch, passed from one generation to the next. But I'm here to tell you that today, after countless millennia, the journey is finally over. We have arrived.' He pauses, relishing the control he has over the room. 'Do you know what that means? I get to keep the torch. We all do.'

Applause erupts. Volcanic. Deafening.

Ben wonders what the children of these rich, old people must think. Some of them will have been waiting for years – *decades* – for their parents to finally die so they can claim their inheritance and take their place in the world. But now it won't happen. Not only will their parents outlive them, but they'll be biologically younger than them, too. They'll be younger than their grandchildren, even. Unless they plan on treating the whole family? He pictures dynasties of immortal billionaires stretching out across the globe, all of them frozen at twenty-one years old. A two-tier society, where those who can afford it get to live forever and everyone else is expected to wither and die.

People like Sophie…

Johan is talking again. Working the crowd. He tells them they are reaping the reward for their hard work in life. He's telling them that they have *earned* this opportunity. That they *deserve* everything that is coming their way.

By now, Ben's despair has been replaced by a burning rage. Fuck Johan. If he won't treat Sophie voluntarily, he'll force him to help her. He'll take Johan hostage. Drag him backstage. Make him hand over the treatment. Threaten him. Blackmail him. Whatever it takes. Then he remembers the security guards who shadow Johan everywhere he goes, and he knows he's dreaming. He'll never save Sophie like that.

'…and that is why, ladies and gentlemen, I'm delighted to tell you I have a surprise for you. A very special guest…'

This is it, Ben realises. Any moment now, Johan is going to invite him to speak. And maybe this is his opportunity, instead? To hell with the teleprompter, he'll go off-script. Tell them about his coma. The dead Evergreens. That will shut them up, won't it? Let's see how many people sign up to be treated once they know the truth…

But then again, it will also obliterate any chance he has of getting Johan to change his mind. In that case, perhaps it's better to simply toe the line? Read his script and smile for the crowd and try to appeal to Johan's better nature?

He doesn't know. And he's almost out of time.

At the front of the stage, Johan holds up the briefcase he'd brought on with him. The crowd falls silent. 'But before I introduce him to you, there's something else I want to show you first. Actually, it's a bit of a world exclusive…'

Johan pauses and puts the case down on the lectern, then snaps it open. By now, the anticipation inside the room is unbearable. Ben can hear every cough. Every wheezing, elderly breath. Johan retrieves a small pill bottle from inside the case. He holds it up. Rattles it. Then he pops off the lid and shakes out a small pink pill, gripping it between his thumb and forefinger, so that it sparkles under the stage lights.

'It doesn't look like much, does it?' he says. 'But I promise you, this tiny tablet is about to change the world. It's a wonder drug that not only means you'll never get a day older in your life, but you'll actually get younger. A lot younger. We can return you to your biological peak. Just one of these little pink pills, and you'll be twenty-one again. Only this time, you'll get to stay there forever. Isn't that right, Ben?'

At the mention of his name, a spotlight swings into life, bathing him in a blinding white light.

'Ladies and gentlemen, Mr Ben Walker…'

A machine-gun barrage of applause rattles around the hall.

'Now I know a few of you have been fortunate enough to meet Ben already,' Johan continues. 'But for the benefit of those who have yet to have the pleasure, Ben is one of the original Evergreens. Eighty-six years old and still going strong. He is also one of the first people in the world to experience our new treatment. And I'm delighted to say there have been no side effects. Isn't that right, Ben?'

Here it is. Ben's moment. Already the teleprompter is flashing his line.

He opens his mouth, still unsure of what he's going to say.

But something isn't right.

His microphone isn't working. They've cut him off.

'Ah, what a shame,' Johan says. 'It seems we have a small technical difficulty, folks. But not to worry. I promise you'll all get a chance to meet Ben later. For now, we've got something even better than second-hand testimony.'

Johan pauses, milking the moment.

'A live demonstration. And I must say, it's a real honour to be the first person in the world to try this refined, oral version...'

Johan holds the pill up again, as if examining it.

And then, almost nonchalantly, as if eating a peanut, he tosses it into his mouth and swallows it down with a chaser of BergWater.

'Now, I want you to watch very closely,' he says. 'I know you've seen the brochures and the simulations. But I promise you, that is nothing compared to seeing it in the flesh. Because what you are about to witness is nothing short of a miracle. In fact, it's already begun.'

Like everyone else in the room, Ben stands transfixed as he waits for something to happen. At first, it appears Johan is mistaken. The pill is a dud. It doesn't work.

Or does it?

Because Johan's face is changing. It's slow at first. Almost unbearably subtle. His features gradually getting smoother, as if he is a photo being airbrushed in real time. Seconds later, however, the transformation is unmistakeable. His hair is fuller, thicker. The fine lines and dark circles around his eyes vanish.

Johan is getting younger.

Throughout these changes, there is an expression on his face that is difficult to read. At first, he seems overwhelmed by what is happening to him. But then he seems to remember where he is. The audience, the room, the job that he's there to do. And so, breaking from his trance, he peels off his glasses and blinks, taking in his surroundings with his newly restored vision. Then, with a dramatic flourish, he drops them to the floor and crushes them under his heel.

The crowd are cheering again now. Hollering and whooping.

But Johan hasn't finished.

By now he is standing taller. His shoulders broader. His complexion glowing, so that even Ben is forced to admit that he looks great. Stronger. Healthier.

Younger.

He steps forwards to the front of the stage, his arms parted as he soaks up the applause, until at last the crowd grows quiet again, waiting for their messiah to address them.

Johan opens his mouth to speak.

But then he stops.

A look of confusion crosses his face.

Then panic.

And, finally, fear.

For a moment Ben doesn't understand what's happening. But then he sees it. As impossible as it seems, Johan's clothes are growing. Whereas seconds earlier his tuxedo had strained against his newly muscular torso, now it hangs off him.

From the audience, a single horrified voice rings out. 'Look!'

But everyone is already looking. No one can take their eyes off Johan. And now Ben understands it's not the clothes that are growing. Rather, it is Johan who's shrinking. Gone is the robust-looking twenty-something, replaced instead by a teenager, complete with a rash of acne and greasy mane of hair. Ben wonders if he'll stop there, but still he keeps going. The sleeves of his jacket covering his hands, his trousers bunching around his ankles, his shirt heading towards his knees, until suddenly, he's a little boy, lost and frightened in the middle of the stage.

Johan lets out a scream. But the sound is buried beneath the roar of the crowd. Chaos has broken out in the auditorium. Johan's team of stewards and security attempt to offer reassurance, but it's too late for that. The audience are spooked. Terrified that Johan's affliction might be contagious. Or worse, that they'll be caught in the blast radius of the bad publicity this disaster will inevitably bring with it.

And so, the billionaires scramble to flee the scene. Security guards form protective bubbles as they jostle them towards private helicopters. Chairs are knocked over. Gift bags are abandoned. Brochures are left in crumpled heaps. Somewhere an alarm rings out as a fire door is kicked open.

Ben is hardly aware of any of it. Instead, he keeps his eyes firmly on the toddler who is standing naked in the middle of the stage, a heap of clothes piled around him like the shell of a discarded cocoon. The little boy stares desperately at Ben, trying to speak. But all that comes out is a mangled sob.

This must be it, Ben thinks. *Surely, he's finished.*

But still Johan keeps shrinking, growing smaller and smaller, until his legs abruptly give way beneath him, sending him tumbling onto his bottom. His hair thins out, lightening, curling, then vanishing altogether, as if sucked backwards into his follicles, leaving a smooth scalp in its place.

Baby Johan is wailing harder now, his pudgy cheeks twisting to let out a loud, fire-siren cry as one by one his teeth disappear, retracting into angry-looking gums, leaving nothing but a wailing red mouth behind.

And then Johan is collapsing backwards, no longer able to keep his body upright, or even support his head. He wriggles and writhes and roars, flailing his miniature limbs.

For a second, Ben makes eye contact with this newborn version of Johan. As he does, he sees a flicker of understanding behind the baby's huge, tear-filled eyes. And in that moment, he's convinced that the adult Johan is fully conscious in there, trapped inside this tiny, wrinkled body. The same way Sophie is still Sophie, even though she can no longer speak.

But unlike Sophie, there is no peace in Johan's eyes. There is only terror.

And then the moment is gone. Because Johan is still changing. Pulling back into himself. Hunching into a foetal ball as he continues to shrink at an alarming rate. His eyes scrunch tight, then disappear, followed by his nose, his mouth, everything, until there is nothing left but a rubbery mass of cartilage and skin. A little pink worm, not much bigger than a kidney bean.

After that, Ben loses sight of him altogether.

He squints against the spotlights. By now, the auditorium

is almost completely empty. Just a handful of Johan's staff remain, frozen amidst the rubble.

Ben crosses the stage and stoops down to inspect the spot where, just a few minutes earlier, Johan had been standing. But there's nothing there. Ben keeps looking, but there's no sign of him at all. All that's left are his clothes.

A watch, a suit, and an expensive pair of shoes.

2073

35

Ben stands on Sophie's porch, clutching a condolence card so tightly it curls at the edges. He feels stupid. Do people still give cards at funerals? Or will he just end up offending someone? Didn't he read somewhere that paper is deemed unethical these days? Destined to go the same way as all the other embarrassing artefacts from the dirty, destructive past. Like oil. Or dairy. He feels like he doesn't understand anything any more.

He'd skipped the crematorium earlier. He couldn't face it. Not that it was really a crematorium. Nobody would dream of burning a body these days, any more than they'd dream of shovelling waste into a landfill or levelling a rainforest to graze cattle. No, there were far more ecologically friendly options now. Including the one being employed today:

Human composting.

Essentially, the body is placed in a warm, slowly rotating container and then bacteria does the rest, reliably turning a loved one into a couple of sacks of soil in the space of six weeks. *A gentler way to return to nature.* Or so the website says. Personally, Ben doesn't think being devoured by a bunch of bloodthirsty microorganisms sounds especially gentle. Still, Sophie had left detailed instructions in her will about exactly what she wanted. These instructions went further than just the funeral. Indeed, Ben had been surprised to open his door one day to find Amelia standing there with Sophie's fluffy Papatzu, Angel.

'What's this?' he asked when she handed him the lead.

'Mum wanted you to have him,' Amelia explained. 'She was very clear about it. She said you could do with the company.'

Ben shook his head. What was he going to do with a dog? Still, he took him all the same.

He never had been able to say no to Sophie.

Sophie.

God, how he wished she was here now. If only things had worked out differently with Johan. Nine months have passed since the disastrous annual meeting. He'd expected Johan's disappearance to make international news. For journalists to publish in-depth investigations. For traumatised guests to sell tell-all stories. For footage and photos to leak on social media. But there's been nothing. Complete silence. He can only assume that the powerful figures who hold shares in Evergreens Limited have flexed their influence to kill the story.

When he got back to London, he'd thought about keeping the incident from Sophie. His failure to secure the treatment – to save her – was crushing. In the end though, he decided to tell her everything. Even though he'd failed, he wanted her to know he'd tried. He really had tried. And so, during one of their weekly video calls, he laid out the whole sorry story. How he'd gone to Cornwall and begged for Johan's help. How the treatment had gone wrong and Johan had vanished. How there was no longer any hope of her getting better.

'I was so close, Soph,' he said. 'I really thought I could do it. I just wish things could have worked out differently...'

As he spoke, he found himself crying. Sophie was pretty far gone by this point. He wasn't even sure she was following what he was saying.

But then she made a noise. A small grunt of effort. And Ben saw that she was trying to move, her fingers quivering slightly, stretching out towards the keys of the deck. A single letter appeared in the chat box to the side of the picture:

S

Ben stared at the screen. In the entire year that had passed since she'd had her stroke, she'd never once communicated in this way. Slowly, she added more letters. It took maybe five minutes in total. When she'd finished, two words sat on the screen.

Silly boy

Ben laughed. He couldn't stop laughing. Because in those two words, he saw the truth. That even if Johan had agreed to treat her, she would never have accepted it. Never.

Silly boy.

It was the last thing she ever said to him. Though he kept up his regular calls, she never spoke or typed again. And then, a few weeks ago, Amelia's name flashed up on his deck.

'Oh, Ben,' was all she said.

Oh, Ben.

Standing on Sophie's doorstep now, he has a sudden urge to flee. He shouldn't be here. He's not family. Amelia had probably only invited him out of some misguided sense of loyalty to her mother. But Sophie isn't here. Even if she was, he would have found some excuse to avoid a gathering like this. All these young people. All the endless small talk. He feels a flutter in his chest. A prickle of perspiration across his back.

He can't do this.

He turns to walk away.

But before he can leave, their door groans open.

'Ben! You made it. Come in, come in!'

36

In the decade since Sophie and Ben first reconnected, he'd never once visited her house. Of course, he'd caught glimpses of it during their endless video calls. A shelf full of books here. A vase of flowers there. But nothing that really gave him a true sense of the place.

As Amelia leads him through to the living room now, he finds himself overwhelmed by how much it reminds him of her. There is something about the design, minimalist but still somehow cosy, that is intrinsically hers. Even with her gone, he imagines he can catch a hint of her scent in here. A faint trace of something sweet and peppery, the same Miss Dior perfume she'd worn ever since they'd first met.

While Amelia excuses herself to talk to someone else, Ben takes the opportunity to retreat to the back of the room, where a large selection of framed photos dominate the wall. Looking more closely, he sees a selection of fleeting moments from the period of Sophie's life he knows least about. There are lots of her children, pictured at various stages. In one photo they are toddlers on a beach, the next they are teens posing awkwardly in school uniforms. There are graduation photos, wedding days. And then eventually, her children are holding children of their own. And then those children are holding children.

There are plenty of pictures of Matthew, too. *Matt.* She never did like to talk about him much. Not that he got the impression she was sparing his feelings. But he noticed she would flinch slightly whenever his name came up, as if his absence was still too sore for her to discuss in any detail. In these photographs, he sees just how much of a central role he clearly played in the story of her life. The earliest photo shows the two of them sitting together in a restaurant. Sophie looks mid-thirties here, and with a jolt, he realises this can't have been long after they'd broken up. Whoever had taken the picture appears to have caught them unawares, their heads turned not to the camera, but bent towards each other, a secret smile on each of their lips, lost in the midst of some private moment.

Elsewhere, Matthew grins with Orson sitting on his shoulders, and then a few years on, with Amelia cradled in his arms. He is there between the three of them at the Parthenon in Athens, and then later in Italy, clowning around, pretending to hold up the Leaning Tower of Pisa with his index finger. He's there at Orson's wedding to Asheni, dressed in a creased linen suit and smiling proudly. And again later on, with an ice cream in each hand, his grandchildren Zayden and Ellery perched on his knees. In the most recent picture, it is just him and Sophie. The two of them holding hands at an industry event somewhere. He looks old in this one. His face lined, his hair completely white. But he looks happy, too. They all look happy, every photograph a moment of frozen joy.

Standing here, examining these souvenirs from Sophie's life without him, Ben feels a pang of jealousy. Or is it simply sadness? He can't help thinking that if things had worked out just a little differently, it could have been him eating ice cream in these photos, or larking around in Italy. It could have been him with a small boy sitting on his shoulders. Him holding on to Sophie's hand, smiling defiantly as the cameras fizzed and flashed around them.

Only then he wouldn't still be here, he reminds himself.

Sophie, Matthew, they're both gone now. Their journey completed. Whereas his goes on and on and on.

Amelia arrives at his shoulder, breaking his reverie. 'Here, let me introduce you to someone.'

Reluctantly, Ben allows himself to be led through to the kitchen, where a man in his early fifties is trying to guard the buffet from two young toddlers who are circling the table like sharks around a bleeding diver.

'Hey, bro,' Amelia says, greeting him with a kiss. 'This is Ben. Ben, this is my big brother, Orson.'

Ben's stomach drops. Though Amelia has always treated him warmly, he's wary about the rest of Sophie's family. What must they think of him? The asshole ex from their mum's hazy past who came back to gloat the moment their father was in the ground? He's not too sure how welcoming he'd be in their position. Yet at the mention of his name, Orson seizes up Ben's limp hand and pumps it enthusiastically. 'Ben! Holy shit, dude. I've heard so much about you.'

Ben forces a smile, somehow resisting the urge to tear his hand away. 'Likewise,' he says. 'Good to meet you.'

There's an awkward pause while the men size each other up. Orson is tall and barrel-chested, with a full beard that's turning white at the tips. Though he doesn't say it outright, something about Ben's appearance seems to amuse him.

'You know, Amelia told me how much you did for Mum when she got sick. Calling her every day? It made a huge difference to her quality of life at the end. We can't thank you enough.'

Ben shrugs. Orson seems like a nice guy, but there's something in his tone that reminds him of the way the teachers used to talk to him at school. His words slow and deliberate, as if he were speaking to a child, despite the fact that Ben is more than thirty years his senior. Before he can reply, one of the boys reaches up and knocks over a bowl of crisps on the table.

'Easy, Gary,' Orson says, scooping up the kicking child with one arm and dumping the crisps back into the bowl with the other. 'I'm getting too old for this.' He laughs. 'I thought I was done clearing up after children years ago. Turns out that was just round one. Still, at least with grandkids you get to hand them back. Speaking of which... Look, boys, here's Mummy.'

Ben follows Orson's gaze to find a young woman standing in the doorway behind him.

At the sight of her, he almost jumps out of his skin.

It's Sophie.

'Oh hey, Ell, I'd like you to meet Ben. You know, Nana's friend? Ben, this is my daughter, Ellery.'

The girl waves. 'Nice to meet you.'

As she moves, the illusion is broken, and Ben sees there are in fact subtle differences between Ellery and Sophie. Her skin a little darker, her lips a little thinner. Still, the similarity is startling. 'Has anyone ever told you how much you look like your grandmother?' he manages to ask. 'When she was younger, I mean.'

Ellery looks confused for a moment. 'Oh, right! You're the guy who knew her back then. Yeah, people say I look like her. I can't see it, myself. Don't get me wrong. I *wish* I looked like her. I've seen those old pictures of Nana. She was like a movie star or something. Utterly gorgeous.'

Ben nods. He's suddenly finding it difficult to speak. 'Oh, she was,' he manages to whisper. 'She really was.'

Just then, Amelia returns to the kitchen and takes Orson by the arm. 'Hey, bro, I think it's time. Everyone's here.'

Orson nods and they head back through to the living room, followed by Ellery and the boys. Ben, meanwhile, takes the opportunity to talk to Amelia. 'Hey, thanks so much for having me today. But actually, I need to head off now, so...'

'Oh no,' she pleads. 'Not yet. Orson's just about to raise a toast to Mum in the other room. It would be so nice if you could be there for it. Can you hang on for just two more minutes? It won't take long, I promise.'

Ben smiles. Swallows his reluctance.

'Sure. I suppose I can stay a little longer.'

37

There are thirteen of them altogether, standing in a loose circle in the living room. All of them family, apart from Ben. There's Orson and his wife Asheni. Zayden and his boyfriend Thomas. Ellery and her partner Ambrose, with little Gary and Nigel running in circles around their feet. And then there's Amelia, with her husband Jeremy, their son Xeno and his girlfriend Anya standing beside them. All of the adults are holding a glass of gin and tonic in Sophie's memory, while Orson gives a brief eulogy, rattling through the biographical details of his mum's life. All of it, Ben notices, covering the period after they'd split up.

As Orson talks, Ben glances around at the people who are crammed into the living room. Again, he is struck by how cheerful everyone looks. There are no silent tears streaking cheeks. No bitten lips or blotted mascara. People are smiling. Laughing, even. As for Orson, he's treating his speech like an open mic at a comedy gig. Cracking jokes. Playing to the crowd. Ben doesn't get it. All he's heard since he's been here is how much everyone loved Sophie. She was brilliant. They adored her. She was the apple of everyone's eye.

Well, if that's the case, why does everyone look so fucking delighted at the fact she's dead?

Everyone except him. He doesn't feel like joking around. No. He feels like climbing into bed and never getting up again. He feels like falling to the floor and wailing. Or punching someone, anyone, as hard as he can in their face, in the hope that maybe they'll punch him back. And then he'll have something else to think about for a while, other than this unbearable emptiness in his chest.

'And so, before we raise a glass to Mum,' Orson continues, 'I want to say a couple of words about legacy. It's a funny idea, isn't it? What we leave behind after we're gone. Now I'm sure we all saw the papers last weekend, didn't we?'

There are a few knowing chuckles around the room.

'I'm not sure what Mum would have made of it all. All those critics gushing about her *body of work*. Not that they're wrong, necessarily.' He pauses to gesture towards the various awards and statuettes that line the mantelpiece. 'The work that Mum left behind does matter. I suspect people will be watching it and talking about it and enjoying it even long after all of us are gone. The work will last. Not that Mum would believe *that* for a second.'

More laughter.

'You know I actually talked to her about it once. About her legacy. I was helping her clear out some stuff after Dad died. She had these boxes from the office. Old scripts. First drafts. Character notes. The collectors would have had a field day. It would have fetched a fortune at auction. And here was Mum, ready to just dump it all in the recycling. I nearly had a heart attack. "But don't you want to keep this stuff?" I said. "You know, for your archive? You could donate it to a university or a museum or something." Well, you can imagine what she said to that! Still, I tried to reason with her. "But Mum. What about your *legacy*?" Well, she almost died laughing. "Legacy?" she said. "This stuff? Orson baby, this is just some scribbles on old paper. It's not worth a bloody thing. The only thing I'm leaving behind that's worth anything is you guys. You. Amelia. The kids. That's all that matters. That's all that's ever mattered. You were the greatest stories I ever wrote. Everything else is just words."'

And then, finally, the tears do come. Not great shuddering

sobs of grief. But fat, happy tears, sliding down the cheeks of her smiling children.

Orson clears his throat. 'And I guess that's where I want to leave it today. With a toast not just to Mum, but to all of us who are here today because she put us here. To this wonderful, crazy, loud, messy legacy she's left behind. To Mum's stories.'

He raises his glass into the air and the others follow suit.

'To Mum's stories.'

Before Ben can take a sip, another voice speaks up from the circle.

'Wait. I've got something I'd like to say.'

Ben turns to see it's Xeno, Amelia's son, who's spoken. In his face, too, Ben catches a trace of Sophie.

'I was going to wait until later to tell you this. But I think Nana would prefer it this way. You know how she always liked a dramatic reveal.'

He grins.

And Sophie is grinning with him. Through him.

'Anyway, I have some news. Or rather, me and Anya have some news.'

He reaches out his hand and pulls the girl who's standing beside him closer to him, wrapping his arms around her.

'There's going to be a new addition to the clan. It's early days yet, but if all goes well, she'll be here next April.'

The announcement is met with a rapture of congratulations, everyone collapsing in on the couple to hug them and shake their hands and slap their backs and kiss their cheeks. Glasses are raised again. Another toast is given.

And everyone drinks.

And everyone smiles.

And everyone laughs.

Everyone apart from Ben, who has stepped back from the circle. And who, for the first time since Sophie died, finds that he is crying.

38

Later on, once he has said a quiet goodbye to Amelia and ghosted away in a taxi, Ben sits in his living room. It's late, a little after midnight, and the lights are low. On the sofa beside him, Angel is asleep, his back leg twitching slightly, as he dreams whatever it is that old dogs dream about. In his hand is a tumbler, filled with a thick finger of whisky. He hardly drinks these days, but tonight, he is making an exception. Tonight, he knows he won't be able to sleep.

When he'd said goodbye to Amelia, she'd thrown her arms around him. She thanked him again for coming and made him promise that he'd stay in touch. Maybe he would even call round some time?

'Definitely,' he'd said. 'Absolutely.'

Of course, he already knew this was a lie. He wouldn't see her again.

He wouldn't see any of them.

He feels the rumble of a message notification in his pocket. He takes out his phone and scans his messages. It's from Navsegda, a Russian start-up which has been trying to contact him for the last few months. Their premise is the same as Evergreens's. Life extension, age reversal. While it might not have been reported in the mainstream media, news of Johan's 'unfortunate accident' had evidently reached Evergreens's competitors. They'd written to offer him an all-expenses-paid trip to Moscow for a 'complimentary consultancy', with a view to making him a brand ambassador. Apparently, they've already signed up two of the other remaining Evergreens. He deletes the message and blocks them. Although something tells him it won't be the last he hears from them. Or if not them, somebody similar. Just the other day, he'd read about another company in China offering an almost identical service to the Russians. And there are others out there, he's sure. Even without Johan, it seems the billionaires will get to live forever, after all.

He throws down his phone and takes a sip of whisky, the amber liquid burning his throat. The house is so quiet it almost hurts, the silence roaring like the ocean in his ears. He thinks about putting on some music to drown it out. Something old and sad from the last century. Stream a show. Watch a film. Scroll through something mindless.

But he doesn't do any of those things.

Instead, he knocks back the last of his whisky, places the glass on the table, and slumps on the sofa, his head settling into the arm. His eyes flicker shut.

To his surprise, he finds he is tired, after all. His breathing slows. His thoughts spiral away from him. The day unpacks itself in fractured snapshots.

He sees Amelia standing on Sophie's doorstep. He sees the wall of photos. He sees Orson and Ellery and Xeno and Anya and all the others. All of them laughing and joking and smiling. All of them surging with the life that Sophie gave them.

Next to him, Angel lets out a little sleep-bark, half growling at some imaginary foe. Ben hardly hears it. He's almost asleep himself now. His mind on its final descent towards oblivion.

But just before he drops off, he sees one final image. It's a memory of a young girl standing at the edge of a pier. She leans out over the black, choppy water. And then, with a final glance back at him, she lets go.

And now Ben is dreaming. The memory bending and warping. Deviating from the truth and becoming its own story, the way all memories ultimately do. And in this dream, Ben is running to the edge of the pier. He is chasing after her. When he reaches the railing, he hauls himself over and peers down into the darkness below.

But it's no good. He can't see anything. And the wind is howling all around him now. The sea thundering below. And he is scared. My God, he is scared. Terrified of what's waiting down there for him. And yet, he knows he doesn't have a choice. He knows what he has to do. And so he kicks off his shoes. Unbuttons his shirt.

And then he leaps forward. After her. Forever after her.

Tumbling and turning through the dark.

ACKNOWLEDGEMENTS

Thanks to all at Legend Press for their continued faith in my writing. In particular, thanks to Cari Rosen for her tireless work beating this book into the best possible shape.

Thanks to Jonathan Davidson and all at Writing West Midlands for their ongoing support of me and other writers in our often-overlooked corner of the world.

Being a writer is difficult at the best of times, and the last few years have not been the best of times. Thanks to The Society of Authors and the Authors' Foundation for their financial support, without which this book might not have happened.

Thanks to Mum for your endless love and grammatical advice.

Thanks to Dad for the wise words and encouragement.

Thanks to Elliot and Felix for the bottomless laughter and never-ending adventures. Elliot: tidy your bedroom.

Thanks to you, for buying this book and reading it all the way to the acknowledgements.

Finally, thanks to Simone. You are the most patient person I know.

One last thing: As well as writing books, I also write songs. You can find my band **Absent Fathers** and my solo project **Dead Slow Horses** on Spotify, Apple Music, YouTube and maybe even playing on a small, dark stage in the corner of a dive bar near you. Come say hello. Mine's a Guinness.